SURRENDER

BRENDA JACKSON
SURRENDER

ARABESQUE®

Recycling programs
for this product may
not exist in your area.

SURRENDER

An Arabesque novel published by Kimani Press April 2009

First published by BET Books, LLC in 2001.

ISBN-13: 978-0-373-83136-4
ISBN-10:   0-373-83136-6

www.kimanipress.com

Printed in U.S.A.

Acknowledgments

To my husband, Gerald Jackson, Sr.,
with all my love.

To my goddaughters: Chimeka Jeanae Hodge
and Ty'ra Jere Malloy.

To my family and friends for their continued
support: You are loved and appreciated.

To Felicia Laverne Edwards:
You are truly one in a million.

To all my readers who asked for Aston Sinclair's
story: This one is especially for you.

To fellow authors Carla Fredd and Carmen Green:
I appreciate the friendship, the bond
and most of all the support.

To my best friend, Syneda Walker:
Thanks for such a special friendship.

To my Heavenly Father, who makes
everything possible.

THE MADARIS FAMILY AND FRIENDS SERIES

Dear Reader,

I love writing family sagas, and I am so happy that Harlequin is reissuing my very first family series, the Madaris family. It's been twelve years and fifty books since I first introduced the Madaris family. During that time, this special family and their friends have won their way into readers' hearts. I am ecstatic to be able to share these award-winning stories with everyone all over again—especially those who have never met this family up close and personal—in this special-edition reissue.

I never dreamed when I penned my first novel, *Tonight and Forever,* and introduced the Madaris family, that I was taking readers on a journey where heartfelt romance, sizzling passion and true love awaited them at every turn. I had no idea that the Madarises and their friends would become characters that readers would come to know and care so much about. I invite you to relax, unwind and see what all the hoopla is about. Let Justin, Dex, Clayton, Uncle Jake and their many friends transport you with love stories that are so passionate and sizzling they will take your breath away. There is nothing better than falling in love with these Madaris men and their many friends.

For a complete list of all the books in this series, as well as the dates they will be available in a bookstore near you, please visit my Web site at www.brendajackson.net.

If you would like to receive my monthly newsletter, please visit and sign up at www.brendajackson.net/page/newsletter.htm.

I also invite you to drop me an e-mail at WriterBJackson@aol.com. I love hearing from my readers.

All the best,

Brenda Jackson

THE MADARIS FAMILY

Milton Madaris, Sr. and Felicia Laverne Lee Madaris

Milton Jr. (Dora)
— Milton III (Fran)
— Blade and Slade (Skye)⑭, Quantum, Jantzen

Lee (Pearl)
— Lee Jr. (Alfie)
— Lee, Kane, Jarod

Nolan (Bessie)
— Nolan Jr. (Marie)
— Nolan, Corbin, Adam, Victoria, Lindsay

Lucas (Carrie)
— Lucas Jr. (Sarah)
— Lucas, Reese, Emerson, Chance

Robert (Diana)
— Felicia (Trask)⑦

Jonathan (Marilyn)
— Justin (Lorren)①, Dex (Caitlin)②, Clayton (Syneda)④, Tracie (Daniel), Kattie (Raymond), Christy (Alex)⑬

Jake (Diamond)⑧

KEY:
( ) — denotes a spouse
◯ and number —denotes title of book for that couple's story

① Tonight and Forever
② Whispered Promises
③ Cupid's Bow
④ Eternally Yours
⑤ One Special Moment
⑥ Fire and Desire
⑦ Truly Everlasting
⑧ Secret Love
⑨ True Love
⑩ Surrender
⑪ The Best Man
⑫ The Midnight Hour
⑬ Unfinished Business
⑭ Slow Burn

THE MADARIS FRIENDS

Maurice and Stella Grant   Angelique Hamilton Chenault   Kyle Garwood (Kimara)③

Trevor (Corinthians)⑥,
Regina (Mitch)⑪

Sterling Hamilton (Colby)⑤,
Nicholas Chenault (Shayla)⑨

Nedwyn Lansing
(Diana)⑭

Ashton Sinclair
(Netherland)⑩   Drake Warren
(Tori)⑫   Trent Jordache
(Brenna)⑨

KEY:

( ) — denotes a spouse
◯ and number —denotes title of book for that couple's story

① Tonight and Forever	④ Eternally Yours	⑦ Truly Everlasting	⑩ Surrender	⑬ Unfinished Business
② Whispered Promises	⑤ One Special Moment	⑧ Secret Love	⑪ The Best Man	⑭ Slow Burn
③ Cupid's Bow	⑥ Fire and Desire	⑨ True Love	⑫ The Midnight Hour	

A prudent man foresees the difficulties ahead
and prepares for them; the simpleton goes
blindly on and suffers the consequences.
—*Proverbs* 22:3

Prologue

There was just something about a good-looking woman, Marine Colonel Ashton Sinclair thought as he sat alone at a table in the back of the restaurant called Sisters. The owner of the establishment, a beautiful and breathtaking woman by the name of Netherland Brooms, had captured his gaze and was holding it with an intensity that he did not find unnerving. In fact he found it to be an enjoyable experience, especially since he intended to marry her.

The woman, however, had other ideas about that.

He shrugged. There was nothing wrong with her having other ideas except when those ideas placed limitations on the future he intended to have with her no matter what obstacles she placed in his way.

He leaned back in his chair as he continued to watch his wife-to-be. Even from across the room he saw her soft skin that he knew would feel like silk. Her hair, a dark black, had a gloss to it as it cascaded around her shoulders. He could even imagine her scent, a warm, musky fragrance that was exclusively hers. Fantasizing about how she would taste when he kissed her, as well as how good she would fit in his arms, sent everything male about him into overdrive. Then there was the way she walked and talked as she moved around the room, greeting the customers who frequented this restaurant of hers. She had nice rounded hips with even nicer curves, and her breasts, which lifted high and pushed against the fabric of the blouse she was wearing, were a total turn-on.

A male smile touched Ashton's lips. He had known, from the first time he had seen her a few years ago, that she would be his one and only love. Thanks to his African-American heritage, which included ancestors that had been fierce tribal medicine men with mystical powers, and his Cherokee Indian heritage that had included a great-great-grandfather who'd been a shaman, he had been delivered a vision. In fact there had been two visions, and both indicated it was a foregone conclusion that he would marry Netherland Brooms sooner or later.

He preferred sooner.

She preferred never.

She was a stubborn woman, but then he was a stubborn man.

She thought her mind was made up about him, absolutely closed. But on that same note, he knew he was going to enjoy every single minute it took to make her change her mind, open it.

This assignment would be difficult. He had to convince her to accept the love he wanted to offer her. He would have to show her how the two of them could be good together. He would have to prove to her that she was indeed the woman for him and that he was the man for her. She couldn't see what he already knew, what the visions had shown him—their destinies were entwined. She would be the one person to give him an all-consuming love, a meaningful life and three sons, triplets. One who would grow up to be a doctor, one a lawyer and the other, he thought smiling, an Indian chief. That had been one of the visions that he could not repute. One of his sons would do what he himself had not done and that was to rightfully take his place among his father's people in the Cherokee tribe.

But there could be no babies until he was able to bind the woman to him that would one day be his sons' mother. He knew he had a challenge on his hands, but a smart man prepared himself for the difficulties ahead.

And there was no doubt in his mind that Netherland Brooms would be difficult. She was acting the part already.

The first step was to get rid of her negativity concerning military men. It wouldn't be easy but then nothing worth having was, and as far as he was concerned, Netherland Brooms was definitely worth having. He wanted her complete surrender.

And he intended to get it.

Chapter 1

He's here again tonight.

Netherland Brooms inhaled deeply as she watched the man enter her restaurant. Not waiting to be escorted to a table by a hostess, he moved across the polished floor and took a seat at one of the vacant tables in the rear. His overwhelming presence demanded attention. And he was getting it.

Sheer panic made Netherland take another breath, an even deeper one. Ashton Sinclair was intent on breaking her resolve and making her do the very thing she had never done in all her twenty-eight years, which was to lust after a man. But then, after glancing around the room, she concluded that lusting after Ashton Sinclair wasn't such a hard thing to do when she noticed she wasn't the only female suffering from that same dilemma. She could tell by the way the other women were licking their lips that, unlike her, they didn't think lusting after him a serious problem. After all, he was the epitome of everything male and then some.

Half African-American and half Native American, the man was jaw-dropping, stomach-churning, eye-crossing handsome. And to top that off, he exuded strong male animal sexuality that was seductively dangerous. He was tall, almost six-four, and beautifully proportioned. His hair, which flowed freely down his back and around his shoulders, was coal-black and framed dark eyes, high chiseled cheekbones, a strong nose and full lips. At the moment, it was his dark eyes that were giving her the most worry because they were focused dead on her. They were piercing, compelling and challenging. The last of which was what she resented the most since the challenge in them was always directed at her. Whenever he looked at her, it was as if he saw something he intended to have.

Netherland felt her breasts tingle against her blouse. She took another deep breath, refusing to let Ashton Sinclair get next to her again tonight. After all, he was totally wrong for her, and she had told him that on several occasions. As handsome and alluring as he was, in her eyesight he had one tiny flaw she couldn't discount or overlook.

He was military.

She was what one would consider a military brat. Her father had made a career in the army, which meant her family was never able to put down roots anywhere. She couldn't recall ever living in the same place for more than two years at a time. The constant moving had never bothered her mother or her four brothers. But with Netherland things had been different. She had grown up feeling like a gypsy, never having a place to really call home. And she had never stayed in one place long enough to develop lasting friendships with anyone. She envied women whose friendships had spanned years. She had never been that fortunate, which was one of the reasons she had established Sisters. Sisters was an exclusive restaurant located in the heart of Houston's downtown district for women to meet, be entertained and establish lasting friendships with other women. Not surprisingly, anywhere sisters assembled in huge numbers, the brothers were sure to congregate, as well. So, on any given day, it wasn't unusual to find just as many men patronizing her establishment as there were women.

Netherland sighed. Although Ashton Sinclair had to be the most tempting man she had ever met, she would not get involved with a man who didn't have roots, and a man who was a replica of her father and brothers. All four of her brothers had followed in their father's footsteps and entered military life. Paris, the oldest at thirty-two, was in the army; Belgium, at thirty, was in the navy; Rome, at twenty-seven, was in the marines and Dakota, the youngest at twenty-three, was in the air force. All of Ernest and Nadine Kalloren's five children had been named after the places where they had been born.

"I see your admirer is here again tonight, Nettie."

Netherland broke eye contact with Ashton to glance over at Rainey Gilford, head hostess for the restaurant as well as her good friend. Rainey was always observant, which usually was a good thing. However, tonight, to Netherland's way of thinking, it was not. "Yes, he's back."

Rainey smiled. "Evidently he doesn't take no for an answer."

Netherland couldn't help but return her friend's smile. "Evidently he doesn't. I don't know what else to do."

"You could bend a little and give the brother a break," Rainey said between chuckles, knowing Netherland was too stubborn to do such a thing. Netherland saw Ashton Sinclair's presence in the restaurant each night as a nuisance, but Rainey and most of the other women considered it sheer pleasure. Men couldn't get much finer than Ashton Sinclair. Unless, however, you considered the three Madaris brothers and their childhood friend Trevor Grant. But since the four of them were now married, they no longer counted. And she didn't want to even think about the good-looking Trask "The Max" Maxwell, ex-football star who broke a lot of hearts when he got married on New Year's Day. Now whenever the Madaris brothers, Trevor Grant and Trask Maxwell patronized Sisters, they came with their wives. Fortunately, Ashton Sinclair was single, but unfortunately, he only had eyes for Netherland.

"Oh, Nettie, I wish I was in your shoes right now," Rainey whispered. "Do you know what I would do if I were?"

Netherland shook her head. She really did have an idea but wanted to hear it from Rainey's lips anyway, just in case she was mistaken. "No, what?"

"I would waltz right over to Ashton Sinclair and tell him that I've changed my mind and that I will go out with him."

Netherland smiled. She had figured as much. "Rainey, going out with him won't serve any purpose. You know how I feel about military men."

"Yeah, but take a look, Nettie, there is never anything military about him whenever he comes in here. Every time I see him I want to submit his picture for the cover of one of those romance novels. Can you imagine taking a book with his picture on the cover to bed every night? Talk about pleasant dreams."

Netherland smiled. "He is kind of handsome, isn't he?"

"Kind of? Nettie, no man has caused such a stir in this place since that time a few years back when Dex Madaris walked in. You have to admit Mr. Sinclair has been good for business. Just look around. This place is packed and has been every night since word got out about him. You're the envy of every woman here. Do you know that some are taking bets?"

Netherland lifted a dark brow. "Taking bets on what?"

"On how much longer you'll be able to resist his sexual pull, his magnetic draw, his sensual smile."

"I'm immune."

"If you believe that, then you're in deeper waters than I thought."

"What's that supposed to mean?"

"It means that I can't help noticing you're starting to return his hot looks."

"I am not!"

"You are, too. And if you don't realize it or acknowledge it, you're in real trouble." Rainey heard Netherland's soft grunt and allowed her smile to deepen. "If you are immune to him, then prove it."

"Prove it how?"

"Take his dinner order. It's obvious that whenever he comes in here he prefers for you to wait on his table. But he's too much of a gentleman to hurt our feelings and specifically ask for you."

"That's nonsense."

Rainey smiled. "No. That's a man who's patient yet determined."

Netherland looked at Rainey. As the owner of Sisters, her duties were administrative. She seldom had the time to serve the customers unless there was some special event. "Take his order, huh? You don't think I can handle it, do you?"

"Oh, you'll handle it on wobbly knees, with bated breath and a luscious pool of heat between your legs like the rest of us. If his smile doesn't get to you, then his voice certainly will. It's so sexy."

Netherland had to agree. He did have a sexy voice. But she had to believe she could be strong and resist everything about Ashton Sinclair. Hadn't she done a good job of resisting his charm at Trevor Grant's wedding last year? Ashton and Trevor were good friends from Trevor's military days. At the reception Ashton had cornered her and had again asked her to go out with him. She had almost been overcome with weakness since he had looked so darn good in a tux. But luckily, she had gotten a firm grip on her senses before agreeing to date him.

"Taking his order isn't a big deal," Netherland said, pulling a menu out of the rack.

"So you say."

"I can do it."

"So you claim."

"And nothing will happen."

"So you think. Good luck."

Netherland glared at Rainey. She then took a deep breath before moving across the room. She didn't need good luck. What she needed was a good prayer.

Ashton Sinclair watched Netherland as she walked toward him, all formal and businesslike, with a menu securely in her hand. From her intense expression, he could tell she felt she was at her wits' end with him. Well, as far as he was concerned, she hadn't seen anything yet. He was getting ready to turn up the heat. He had only six weeks of leave time before he had to report to Washington. He intended to spend every chance he got pursuing his future wife. Soon she would discover that denying what was between them would be pointless, a definite waste of time.

He leaned back in his chair. *What a woman.* She was beautiful, sexy and intensely stubborn. His smile widened. He could handle her stubbornness. He rubbed his jaw thinking he could handle just about anything Ms. Brooms dished his way. The result would be well worth it.

Tension gripped Netherland's entire body as she continued walking toward Ashton on wobbly knees with each bated breath she took. The pool of luscious heat between her legs that Rainey had warned her about got almost unbearable when she saw his gaze roam over her from head to toe. His gaze was blazing with intensity as if burning to ashes every barrier she had erected between them. She knew a lot of other gazes were on her, wanting to see if she could or would resist his sexual charm. She sighed, hoping she would not make a fool of herself. Talk was cheap and when she had taken Rainey up on this dare, she had felt confident she could handle things. But now, the closer she got to where Ashton was sitting, the more she wanted to turn around and hightail it the other way.

She fought to control the intense desire that was running rampant in her midsection and the increased tingling of her breasts against her blouse. No man should have this much of an effect on a woman. No man.

Angry with herself as well as with him for placing her in such a predicament, she took a deep, calming breath when she reached his table. She met his gaze with exasperated eyes. "Ashton."

"Netherland."

She took another deep breath upon hearing her name spoken in a satin-smooth tone from his lips. "Welcome to Sisters tonight."

"Thank you."

She placed an opened menu in front of him. Before she could recite that night's dinner special, he said, "I don't need that. I know exactly what I want." He closed the menu.

She nodded, thinking he probably did since he had patronized her restaurant every single night this week. "All right. What is it that you want?"

Ashton's eyes darkened even more, exuding strong sensuality, virility and masculinity. When he spoke, his words were husky, sexy and unerringly clear.

"I want *you,* Netherland."

Chapter 2

The look in Ashton's eyes told Netherland he was as serious as a heart attack and just as lethal. The four words he had spoken suddenly changed the rhythm of her heartbeat when their impact sent a jolt of desire through her. It wasn't what he had said. It was how he had said it and how he'd looked at her while saying it. Then to top things off, without warning, the most devastating smile caught the corners of his mouth and extended deep into his dark eyes.

Netherland cleared her throat. She noticed that a hush had spread across the restaurant and wondered if Ashton's words had been loud enough to be heard by others. Taking a quick glance at the table next to his, it was quite obvious that the three women sitting there had gotten an earful. One of the women's jaw was dropped open in shock. Another was fanning herself with the menu as if the room had suddenly become overheated, and the third was gulping down the contents from her wineglass as if it were destined to be her last drink.

Netherland frowned. Ashton Sinclair's foolishness had gone on long enough, and it was time she told him so. And what she had to say would best be said in private.

She returned her attention to him and said as calmly as she could, "May I speak with you privately?"

He nodded smoothly as he stood. "Sure. Just lead the way."

Netherland's first inclination was to take Ashton into her office but then she immediately dished the idea. There was no need to have her customers speculate as to what they would be doing behind those closed doors. So instead she led him to a section of the bar that was vacant and not quite visible to prying eyes. She took a seat on one of the bar stools and Ashton slid next to her on another.

"Nothing for me, Kit," Netherland said to the bartender who walked up to take their order. She gave Ashton a quick look. "What about you? Do you want anything?"

Ashton's devastating smile returned. "I told you what I wanted, Netherland."

Netherland sighed deeply before returning her gaze to Kit. "There won't be anything for either of us."

When Kit walked away Netherland turned her attention to Ashton once more. "Ashton," she began slowly. "You take pleasure in stirring me up, don't you?"

He turned up the wattage on his smile even more. "Yeah, but not the way I'd like," he responded in a husky voice, full of hidden promises.

Netherland shook her head, wondering what on earth she was going to do with this man. "It's time we had a long talk to straighten out a few misconceptions, don't you think?"

"What sort of misconceptions?"

"Evidently you think that if you keep showing up here each night, you'll finally wear down my resistance, and I'll consent to go out with you. It won't work."

Ashton lifted a brow. "It won't?"

"No. So stop wasting your time. Any of the women here would jump at the chance to go out with you."

"But not you?"

"No, not me. I thought I had made myself clear about the reasons I won't get involved with you. It's nothing against you personally, but I have this hangup about military men. I thought I had explained that."

He nodded. She had but what she didn't know was that her hang-up didn't matter. Their destinies were entwined. He shifted around on the bar stool to face her. "How you feel about us getting involved doesn't matter anymore," he said softly.

Netherland lifted her dark brow in surprise. "It doesn't?"

"No. Because it will happen."

Netherland's forehead bunched in a frown. She couldn't believe anyone could be this stubborn. "No, it won't happen, Ashton, because I won't let it."

"You won't be able to stop it, Netherland."

Netherland's stomach made a sudden flutter of dread that she quickly dismissed. Although Ashton was proving to be quite difficult, she didn't for one minute believe that he would physically harm her in any way. He was a marine colonel, for heaven's sake! Having been surrounded all of her life by military men, she knew they—and marines in particular—believed in a strict code of honor.

The silence between them lengthened, and the look in his eyes was remarkably determined. "And why won't I be able to stop it?" she finally asked him.

Ashton hesitated for a long moment before answering. "I had a vision."

"A vision?" Netherland chuckled, thinking he meant it as a joke. The look on his face indicated he hadn't. She sobered quickly. After a brief awkward silence she asked, "This vision...was about me?"

Ashton ran a slow, assessing gaze over her before answering. "Yes."

His gaze was like an intimate caress. Netherland was glad she was sitting down because her knees began to feel like rubber. "And what was this vision about?" She somehow managed a smile. She wanted to make light of their conversation but Ashton was too serious.

Ashton stared at Netherland. He sighed before taking a deep breath, needing to reorder his thoughts and answer her question. He'd decided to only tell her about the first one of his visions about her. He didn't think she was ready to know about the triplets just yet. "The vision I had indicated that our spirits and souls would be joined as one. In other words, you will be my wife and I, your husband. For always."

Netherland looked at Ashton as if he'd spoken a foreign language. She then stiffened her back and gave him a look that would have fried a lesser man's soul. "Your vision was wrong. I'm not marrying anyone ever again. And I definitely wouldn't think about marrying someone in the military."

Ashton watched her, frowning. Evidently she didn't get it. It no longer mattered what she wanted. Their futures together were set. "We will marry, Netherland." Upon seeing her anger increase he sighed deeply once again, thinking it was time to give her the facts. "According to my family's history, Netherland, my great-great-grandfathers from both my African-American side and my Native American side had tribal mystical powers to see into the future. These powers were passed down to various members of the family."

The seriousness in both Ashton's tone and his eyes made Netherland uncomfortable. "Are you saying you can foresee the future?"

"No, but I have, on occasion, had visions that have turned out to be true." He didn't want to tell her that with his first vision he hadn't acted quick enough and because of it he'd lost a good friend. It had been during one of his special military assignments as part of the marines' Force Recon Unit.

Ashton watched as Netherland shook her head and her manicured fingertips tapped slowly on the bar's countertop. He couldn't help but notice that the red of her nails matched the succulent coloring of her lips, and he immediately realized it was a definite turn-on. Not that he wasn't turned on by her already. As far as he was concerned, Netherland Brooms was in a class all by herself.

As he continued to watch her, getting even more turned on by the way she was nervously gnawing on her bottom lip, he knew that she was thinking about what he'd just said and trying to come up with a rebuttal. She finally met his gaze once again.

"Ashton?" Netherland said with what little patience she had left.

"Yes?"

She paused and took a deep breath. "I hear what you're saying but I'm not buying it. I can't. I don't discount that you may believe what you're saying, but I have to assure you that what you're proposing won't happen."

Ashton nodded. "I understand," he said sympathetically. He knew the understanding of mystical powers was hard for most people to understand and accept. He'd had a problem believing so himself until he'd been shown otherwise.

"And what do you understand, Ashton?"

"I understand how it would be hard to believe. But everything I've told you is true, Netherland. You and I will get married. You can't continue to fight what will be."

"No."

"Yes. I didn't want to break things to you this way. I wanted to court you properly, take you out and give us a chance to get to know each other. But you've made those plans difficult, near impossible. So the matter has now been taken out of your hands." Ashton heard Netherland's sharply indrawn breath and saw her body tense.

"What do you mean?" she asked softly.

He leaned toward her. Twin dimples indented his bronze-colored features as a slow smile spread across his lips. "It means you should start planning a wedding. And I'll make plans for the wedding night," he said softly.

Unexpected warmth rode up Netherland's legs, beginning at her toes, and settled in her center. She inhaled deeply. She had to pull herself together. Ashton Sinclair was almost too much for her to handle. The soft huskiness of his voice and the determined intensity in his eyes stirred something to life deep within her.

"You're wrong. There won't be a wedding," Netherland finally said firmly, looking at Ashton with a deep frown on her face.

He stood. His gaze was intent. He reminded her

of her brother Dakota when he was hell-bent on having his way. "Yes, there will. You can bet Sisters on it. Good night, Netherland."

Netherland watched, barely breathing, as Ashton turned and walked out of the restaurant.

"Some people have all the luck. I wish some good-looking man would ask me to marry him."

Netherland blew out an exasperated sigh. "Have you heard anything I've said, Rainey? Ashton Sinclair didn't ask me to marry him. He told me in no uncertain terms that we were getting married."

"How romantic."

"How ludicrous. Just who does he think he is anyway?"

Rainey smiled. "Evidently he thinks he's the man who will become your husband." Rainey leaned closer to Netherland. She had quickly slid into the seat Ashton had vacated, dying to get the scoop. "Did he actually say he was going to plan the wedding night?" she whispered.

Netherland nodded. "Yes, can you imagine his nerve?"

Rainey giggled. "Umm, right now I'm too busy imagining other things."

"Rainey!"

"Okay, okay, I'm back in check. I'll behave." After a moment she said, "So, Nettie, what are you going to do? Go to the police?"

Netherland raised a brow. "The police?"

"Yes, if you think he's harassing you."

Netherland shook her head. That thought was too ridiculous to think about. Ashton wasn't harassing her. He was just being a pain in the rear end. "He's not harassing me."

"So you kind of like having him here checking you out every night," Rainey quickly concluded. Too quickly for Netherland.

"I wouldn't say that. It's just that so far he's been harmless enough. Like you said earlier, he's been good for business. And now that I know where his mind is, I'll know how to handle him."

Rainey lifted a brow and crossed her arms over her chest. "And how do you plan on handling him?"

Netherland shrugged. "I'm sure a good night's sleep will give me some answers."

Chapter 3

Netherland didn't get a good night's sleep. Neither did she have any answers upon awakening the next morning. If it hadn't been for the fact that she had a ten o'clock appointment at the restaurant, she would have been tempted to stay in bed a while longer.

The wind tossed the dark curls around her face when she got out of her car. She recognized the Mercedes sports car parked in the space next to hers as belonging to Syneda Madaris. Netherland couldn't help but admire the gorgeous car the woman drove. It was real class—just like the woman herself. Although Syneda and her husband Clayton were prominent attorneys in Houston, Netherland had heard the car had been a gift to Syneda on her thirtieth birthday from her father, oil magnate Syntel Remington.

Netherland pushed the curls out of her face once more as she walked up the sidewalk to her restaurant. There was once a time when Clayton Madaris had been Houston's most eligible bachelor and a frequent customer of Sisters. Now Clayton was a happily married man and a father-in-waiting. Netherland smiled. Miracles never ceased to amaze her.

Rainey looked up from what she was doing the moment Netherland entered the building. "Syneda Madaris is here."

Netherland nodded. "Has she been waiting long?"

"No, she just arrived. I told her it was okay to wait in your office."

"Thanks, Rainey. Our meeting shouldn't last for more than an hour or so."

Rainey nodded. "I'm dying to know if any answers came your way last night," she said before Netherland could walk off.

Netherland shook her head, frowning. "No, not a one." She quickly moved toward her office before Rainey could question her further. She hadn't missed her friend's smirky grin. Okay, so she hadn't come up with any answers yet. That didn't mean anything. It certainly didn't mean she was headed for the altar as Ashton Sinclair had claimed.

She found Syneda sitting in her office busy scribbling notes on a legal pad. Evidently Syneda had a court date sometime that day and was getting prepared.

As usual, Netherland noted, the woman was dressed to the bone. Her melon-colored shoes were the exact shade of her two-piece business suit. Amazing, Netherland thought, coming into the room. Not everyone could wear a color that vibrant and get away with it. Syneda, with her light complexion and hair the color of golden bronze, was the epitome of style and sophistication in the outfit. "Sorry I'm late, Syneda."

The other woman waved off her words. "Don't apologize. I was early. I let Clayton talk me into having breakfast with him at Barneys. He knows I have a weakness for their bagels." She laughed. "He also knows I'm not a morning person—unless I'm tempted with a bagel from Barneys, or," she said, curving her lips in a sheepish grin, "I'm tempted with one other thing..."

Netherland smiled as she sat behind her desk. It was evident that even after almost a year of marriage, Syneda and Clayton were very much in love. Anytime she saw them together, they were all into each other, probably even more so now that Syneda was expecting the couple's first child. "And how is Clayton doing these days?" she asked.

Syneda leaned back in her chair smiling. "Clayton is Clayton, what can I say? He's being difficult as usual."

Netherland shook her head. "And what are you two disagreeing about now?" It was a long-standing joke with everyone that Syneda and Clayton rarely agreed on anything.

Syneda's smile widened. "The baby."

"The baby's name?"

"No, we're in full agreement there, believe it or not. Boy or girl, our child will be named Remington."

Netherland nodded. Since that was Syneda's father's last name, she could only assume the child was being named after him. Remington was a name Syneda never got to claim as her own while growing up, thanks to her grandfather's deceitful plan to keep her from her father. "What is it about the baby the two of you can't agree on?"

"Where he or she will be born. I want a home birth with a midwife. Clayton is adamant about me going to the hospital. This is an argument I intend to win even if I have to lock myself in the bathroom when the labor pain starts coming."

Netherland chuckled. She'd really like to see that one. Clayton would be a basket case by the time that was over. She shook her head as she opened the file on her desk.

"You said in your phone call Tuesday that you had someone else for me."

Syneda smiled excitedly. "Yes. Are you sure you can use the help?"

"Yes. Business is good and so far everyone you've recommended has worked out well for us." Netherland thought about the increase in business lately. Although in part Rainey had been right, it was due to Ashton Sinclair's presence, she believed those people who were patronizing Sisters for the first time would enjoy themselves and return.

"That's good," Syneda replied. Her expression indicated she was glad to hear that. She occasionally handled cases where the woman was an abused victim trying to get out of a hellish marriage. She worked closely with the local women's shelter by working behind the scenes whenever she could to find the women some sort of steady employment until they could get on their feet and become stable. The last thing an abused woman needed was to be made to feel that she was dependent on anyone for anything. The quicker they became productive and self-sufficient, and built up self-esteem about themselves, the better. Syneda had already recommended two others who were working out wonderfully. Both women had divorced their abusive husbands and were now in control of their lives. One of them had begun taking night classes at Texas Southern University.

"This one is a little touchier than the other two, Nettie. Not only am I representing her in a divorce case but charges were filed against her soon-to-be ex-husband for kidnapping. After she left him, he kidnapped her and took her to Louisiana. Luckily the authorities found out where he'd taken her. He had held her against her will, threatening to kill her for at least three days."

"Oh, how awful that must have been for her."

"Yes, it was."

"How is she handling things now?"

"She's gotten some good counseling and is doing fine. She'll be better once the trial is over."

"What's her name?"

"Jada Roberts."

Netherland smiled. "How soon can she start working here?"

Syneda returned Netherland's smile as she placed one folder back in her briefcase and pulled out another. "Now that we've gotten that matter with Jada Roberts taken care of, we can move on to the issue of the Brothers Auction. I need to give you an update."

Netherland nodded. Last year Syneda had come up with the idea of holding a Brothers Auction. The proceeds benefited the Children Home Society, which was badly in need of additional funds for a number of worthy causes to aid the children who lived there. The auction would be held at Sisters and was only two weeks away. Some predicted the event would again be one of the biggest highlights of the year. Single women would get the chance to bid on single, eligible men and all for a good cause. "Don't tell me you're still having men back out."

"A number of them did when word got out that Angela Meadows plans to bid again this year."

Netherland chuckled. Angela was a thirty-year-old man-hater of the third degree, after having been dumped by two fiancés just days before the weddings. She'd been the highest bidder last year. No man wanted to get bidden on by Angela for fear of what she might have in store for them. Going out on a date with her could very well be their last supper. The guy she'd bidden for last year had called it the date from hell. "Do you really think she plans to bid high again this year?"

Syneda giggled. "Word's out on the street that she's been saving half of her paychecks each week just for this event. She also plans to take out a loan with her bank."

Netherland shook her head. "All for the sake of making some man's life miserable for an evening?"

"Yes. To her it would be well worth it, and that's what has Clayton's cousins and Alex Maxwell worried." Syneda smiled. The cousins she was referring to were the grandsons of Clayton's uncles Milton and Luke. The twins, Blade and Slade Madaris, were twenty-seven, and Luke Madaris was only a few months behind at twenty-six. "I told them to relax since they were probably too young for Angela's taste anyway." Syneda then frowned as she thought about twenty-nine-year-old Alexander Maxwell. "I can't seem to convince Alex of that though. He wants to withdraw his name."

"Did you stress to him that all this is for fun, and the money is going to charity?"

"Yes, but Alex said it stopped being fun when Angela voiced her intentions, and that there's only so far a person should go to help charity. The possibility of putting your life on the line by going out on a date with Angela was going too far."

Netherland tried to cover a laugh behind a cough and failed. She cleared her throat. "What about Sterling Hamilton coming that night?" Clayton's Uncle Jake's wife, movie actress Diamond Swain Madaris, was going to use her connections and get her friend, movie actor Sterling Hamilton, to make an appearance. He would definitely be a big draw.

Syneda shook her head. "I spoke to Diamond a few days ago and Sterling will be here, which is good news. The bad news is that our headliner, neurosurgeon Dr. Lloyd James, just got engaged, and his fiancée doesn't want him to participate. The Lord answered my prayers, and I was able to find someone at the last minute, thanks to a tip I received this week. It seems this man is hot in demand. I bet the bids for him will bring in a lot of money," she said excitedly. "Women think he's sexy as all outdoors. I spoke with him last night, and he consented to do it. Some lucky sister will be spending a weekend with him in New Orleans."

Netherland's interest was piqued. "Now you have me curious. Just who is this man who's so hot in demand?"

Syneda smiled. "Trevor's friend who's visiting him. Colonel Ashton Sinclair."

Ashton inhaled deeply and silently counted to ten. A quick glance across the room indicated that his good friend Trevor Grant was doing likewise. They both watched the very pregnant woman in the center of the room tilt her head way back and look up at the ceiling.

"Are you sure there's no way the ceiling can get wallpapered today?" she asked, glancing first at her husband and then at Ashton.

As if on cue, Ashton and Trevor answered simultaneously, "Yes, we're sure."

Corinthians Avery Grant lifted one dark brow as she stared at each man again. "I hope I didn't work you too hard today, but I don't have long before the baby gets here, and I want to make sure everything is perfect."

"And things will be, honey." Trevor walked over to his wife and pulled her into his arms. "But don't you think wallpapering the ceiling is a bit much?"

"I want Baby Grant to look up and see pretty things instead of a dull white ceiling."

Trevor nodded, trying to understand her reasoning but failing miserably. "Then how about if Ashton and I paint it another color—a sunny yellow or something?"

She nodded as if considering his idea. "That might work."

"But not today, sweetheart. Ashton and I are beat. You've already gotten your money's worth out of us. Is there any way we can take a break, relax and watch the basketball game?"

Corinthians nodded. "Yes, that's fine. I feel tired anyway." Kissing her husband on the cheek and smiling gratefully at Ashton, she turned and waddled out of the room.

"Why is she tired, Trev? All she's been doing all day is standing in one spot giving orders."

Trevor chuckled, knowing his friend was telling the truth. "Yeah, but she looked so beautiful while giving them, don't you think?"

Ashton shook his head, grinning. "I'll cut on the TV. You can grab the beer out of the fridge." Both men quickly left the room before Corinthians had a change of heart and found something else for them to do.

A while later during a commercial break Trevor asked Ashton how he was doing with Nettie. "I finally had to level with her, man, and let her know that we're getting married."

A grin covered Trevor's face. "I'm sure that went over well."

Ashton chuckled. "I didn't stick around too long after that to find out just how well it did go." He cast Trevor a determined look. "I thought seriously about kidnapping her. What do you think about that?"

"I'd rethink that plan if I were you. Last I heard kidnapping was still a federal offense. You'd be faced with a dishonorable discharge for sure."

Ashton nodded. "I could seduce her into submission."

Trevor grinned again. "That might work. There's nothing illegal about that. By the way, I heard you volunteered for the Brothers Auction. I wonder how Nettie is going to feel about that when she finds out."

"I plan to make sure she's the one I take with me to New Orleans."

"Then I strongly suggest that you have a very good plan in place. Rumor has it that Angela Meadows is going to be the one with all the money that night. No one will be able to outbid her."

"Who's Angela Meadows?"

"Although she's a good-looking woman, she's every man's nightmare. A real man-hater."

Ashton raised a brow. "If she hates men, then why go out with them?"

"To give them one night of pure hell. Two men dumped her at the altar so she's out for revenge. You should ask Clayton about her. He dated her once, and once was enough. The woman's crazy, man."

The two men fell silent when the basketball game resumed.

Netherland angrily paced the floor of her office. "Can you believe him? I can't believe he would do such a thing!"

Rainey leaned back in her chair smiling. To say her friend was upset would be an understatement. "I still don't understand why you're in such a tiff, Nettie. It's a charity function, and the money is being raised for a good cause."

Netherland waved off her words. "I'm well aware of that, Rainey. It's just that Ashton Sinclair agreed to do it on the same night he claimed he wanted me. He even had the nerve to mention a vision he had of marrying me."

Rainey raised her eyes to the ceiling. "Correct me if I'm wrong but I thought you had no intentions of getting involved with him."

"I don't."

"Then why are you so upset?"

Netherland stopped pacing and gave Rainey her full attention. "It's the principle of the thing. No man claims he wants one woman then volunteers to be placed on an auction block to spend a weekend with another."

Rainey smiled. "Maybe he's hoping that you'll be the highest bidder."

"I don't know why he'd hope that. I've told him countless times that I won't go out with him."

"Then what's the big deal, Nettie? Why are you wearing a hole in your carpet about it? Ashton must mean something to you for you to have gotten so upset about it."

Netherland took a deep calming breath and perched her rear end on the edge of her desk, crossed her arms over her chest and shook her head. "I can't let him mean anything to me, Rainey, he's military," she said softly.

Rainey heard the lack of conviction in Netherland's voice and decided to use another approach. "If Ashton wasn't military, would you go out with him?"

Netherland thought long and hard on the question before answering. "Yes."

"Would you even go so far to think he's possibly husband material?"

Netherland thought about the dreams she'd had of him lately. "Yes, possibly. I wouldn't know the answer to that until I got to know him better. There are a few things I do like about him. Although he's

persistent, he's never pushy, he's confident but never
cocky, and he's assured but never arrogant." She
sighed deeply. "But none of that matters because he
is military, Rainey."

"Your ex-husband wasn't in the military, yet your
marriage to him didn't work out, either, Nettie."

Netherland met Rainey's gaze. She was one of the
few people, other than her family, who knew the
reason for her divorce. "No, he wasn't military, but
Erik and I married young, and for all the wrong reasons. Then, there was the fact that I couldn't give him
the very thing he wanted."

"A child?"

"Yes, a child." Netherland lowered her head and
studied her left hand, specifically the finger where
she'd worn a wedding band for all of ten months. She
and Erik had begun dating at the beginning of their
last year of high school. When her father's military
orders had come for them to leave Camp Bullis,
Texas, for some godforsaken country in the Middle
East six months before graduation, she and Erik,
both seventeen, had eloped one night and had gotten
married. After that, her parents had had no choice but
to leave her behind with her new husband when they
left the country. She and Erik lived with his parents
for the remainder of the school year. Her parents and
brothers had returned for her high-school graduation, and it seemed everything was going great until
she'd had a long talk with her mother. Her mother
had told her something she should have been told

years ago. A severe case of childhood mumps had left Netherland sterile. After telling Erik about it, he had begun acting as if her inability to conceive were some sort of disease. Soon after that, their storybook marriage began falling apart and eventually ended in a divorce. That had been nearly eleven years ago. Over the years she'd heard that Erik had remarried and had four kids, which hadn't surprised her. He'd always talked about having a large family someday.

Netherland was happy for him. Since then she had accepted the fact that she would never be anyone's mom unless she adopted a child. She was okay with that and hoped whatever man she eventually married would be okay with it, as well.

"Are you going to warn Ashton about Angela, Nettie?"

Netherland lifted a chin. "Why should I?"

"Because once she hears he's in the auction she'll save every penny she can get her hands on for him. What woman wouldn't?"

"I won't."

"Only because of your hang-up about military men."

Netherland looked at her friend. "What about you, Rainey? Are you going to bid for him?"

Rainey gave Netherland a smirky smile. "It would serve you right if I did. But at the moment, I have my sight on someone else."

"Who?"

"The elusive Alexander Maxwell."

Chapter 4

Ashton's gaze drifted around the restaurant for the umpteenth time since arriving more than an hour ago. He had yet to see Netherland. He had eaten his meal with his senses on full alert, but she hadn't made an appearance. He couldn't help wondering if perhaps she was avoiding him.

"Is there anything else I can get you, sir?" asked a hostess who came up to the table.

He smiled and leaned back in his chair studying her name tag. "What you can do, Rainey, is tell me where Netherland is tonight."

The woman glanced around the room before bringing her gaze back to his face. "She must be in her office working."

Ashton nodded. "And where's her office?"

The woman seemed reluctant to tell him at first, then studied him intently before finally inclining her head toward an archway. "At the very end of that hall."

"Thanks."

"Don't mention it."

Smiling, Ashton grabbed the wine bottle off the table in front of him, along with two wineglasses. Standing, he headed in the direction the hostess had given him. He knocked when he came to the closed door.

"Yes, come in."

And there she was, sitting behind her desk looking so beautiful it nearly took his breath away. He could tell from her expression that he was the last person she had expected to see. Her surprise quickly transformed into a frown.

"Ashton? What are you doing here?"

He came into the room and closed the door behind him, locking it. He leaned against it for a moment before slowly walking over to her desk, his gaze not once leaving hers. Her brow lifted when he placed the bottle of wine and the two wineglasses in front of her.

"Since you won't go out with me, Netherland, I've decided to stay in with you."

Netherland pulled in a long, slow breath. The room had become silent. For some reason she could no longer hear the music that had been playing moments ago. Nor could she hear the clinking of the dishes and silverware from the kitchen that was located on the other side of the wall.

She took another deep breath, telling herself firmly that she would not let Ashton get to her. *Too late,* her body silently chanted. *He's already gotten next to you.* Raw, primitive heat coursed through her body as he continued to look at her, making her heart pound and her blood race. And then, as if on cue, there was that heat settling between her legs again, this time making her thighs tremble.

To gain some semblance of control, she forced her gaze from his to focus on the wine bottle and wineglasses in front of her. "I have too much work to do, Ashton."

"Do you?"

"Yes."

He leaned against the edge of the desk facing her. "I can wait until you're through."

Netherland frowned. "It may be a while."

"I have nothing else to do. Go ahead and finish what you're doing and pretend I'm not here."

Fat chance! Netherland thought as she tried to refocus on the documents in front of her. Out of the corner of her eye she saw him move away from her desk to settle in the love seat on the other side of the room. As hard as she tried, she could not gather her train of thought to complete the task she'd been working on before he had arrived. Considering that he had been on her mind constantly all day, she had hoped that staying in her office and catching up on some paperwork would be the perfect solution to not having to see him tonight. It appeared that he had no intentions of letting her avoid him.

After wasting a good ten minutes trying to un-scramble her brain and feeling his presence too close for comfort, she finally had enough. "That's it," she said, standing up. "I'm through with what I was doing. We may as well go back and join the others."

Ashton didn't stand. Instead he leaned forward and rested his forearms on his thighs and looked up at her. "Are you afraid to be alone with me, Netherland?"

Netherland looked at him, astonished. He didn't know how close to home he'd hit. Yes, she was afraid to be alone with him, but not for fear of what he might do to her. She was afraid of what she might let him do. Her attraction to him was too strong. There was no way she could deny that. If she stayed around him too much longer she would forget about the very reason they could not become involved. "I'm not afraid of being alone with you, Ashton."

"Then let's share a drink together. One drink is all I ask. Is that too much to ask?"

You don't know the half of it, Netherland thought. But if sharing one drink with him would get them out of her office that much quicker, then she would go along with it. "Okay, I'll share one drink with you. Just one and not much."

He stood and walked over to her desk and re-trieved the wine bottle and glasses. He came back to her and handed her a wineglass. "Most people would envy you, Netherland," he said, pouring her a small amount of wine.

She lifted a brow. "In what way?"

"The one thing you hated about the military most people would find rewarding."

Netherland took a sip of her wine before asking, "What could be rewarding about being uprooted every two to three years?"

Ashton took a sip of his own wine before replying. "In your travels you've probably seen places that most people only dream about seeing."

"I would gladly have let them trade places with me. Although I do admit it was nice seeing most of those places, I'd rather have had stability. You don't know how devastating it was for me whenever my father received new orders. That meant leaving the house behind that I had just started to consider home, and leaving friends behind that I had just gotten to know. There was never anything constant in my life."

Ashton nodded. "Didn't your parents try to make the moves easier for you?"

"They did what they could but it's not easy being the only girl with two older brothers and two younger brothers. Things might have been different if I'd had a sister who could have been my best friend, but that wasn't the case. As close as I was to my brothers while growing up, I couldn't always get them to do girly stuff with me. They were boys, who were their father's sons with aspirations of a life in the military."

Ashton nodded as he leaned against the edge of her desk. "Did all four of them go into the military?"

"Yes." She then told him about her brothers and what branch of service each belonged to. "So as you can see I've been surrounded by military men practically all my life. That's another reason I don't want to become involved with one." She smiled. "Military men are some of the bossiest men I know."

Ashton quirked a brow. "I'm not bossy."

"You think you're not?"

"Yes."

Netherland shrugged as she sat down on the love seat, feeling relaxed. "Well, that's your opinion of yourself."

"Do you think I'm bossy?"

A smile touched Netherland's lips. "Although I have to admit that I've never seen you in action, I would think being a marine colonel would demand a certain degree of bossiness, wouldn't it?"

Ashton chuckled. "Yes, a certain degree." He took another sip of his wine. "Earlier you mentioned how often you had to move. I have one up on you. I had to move about every six months instead of every two to three years."

Netherland sat up. "Every six months? Were you a military brat, too?"

"Kind of. I was what you would call a custody brat. After my parents' divorce I had to spend half the year with my father on the Cherokee reservation and the other half with my mother and her family wherever they happened to be. My maternal grandfather was a high-ranking officer in the army, and every year he was reassigned. Since my mother chose to live with her parents after the divorce, that meant I had to live with them when I was with her."

Netherland nodded, finding the story of his childhood fascinating but sad. He was right. He'd had it worse than she had. "If you spent half the year on the reservation and the other half with your mother and grandparents, how were you educated?"

"Luckily I was able to keep up with the two different educations as well as the two vastly different cultures, but it wasn't easy. Like you, whenever I had to make another move I left not only friends but family and cultures behind, as well." One day he would tell her how his grandparents had tried, during the six months he spent with them, to make him forget he was part Indian. He couldn't speak the language around them or do anything to remind them that their grandson had two heritages.

"Then why, Ashton? Why did you choose a life in the military? Knowing how unstable your childhood had been, why didn't you seek stability in your life when you got the chance?"

Ashton walked away from the desk and came and sat next to Netherland on the love seat. She was so absorbed in hearing his response she didn't notice at first. When she did, it was too late. He was sitting so close to her that his thigh was touching hers. So close that she could see the irises of his eyes.

"My main reason, which I'm sure was the same for your father and brothers, was a sense of doing something for my country. I'm a product of two heritages but foremost, I consider myself an American. I love this country and will defend it until the end. And believe it or not, the military gave me all those things I missed out on having while growing up. My stable home was being part of the marines. In that home I obtained a family that included every other marine. In my early days there, during boot camp, I met two men who today are closer to me than any blood brothers could be."

"Trevor?"

Ashton nodded. "Yes, Trevor is one, and the other is a man by the name of Drake Warren, whom we fondly call Sir Drake." He smiled. "Hopefully, you'll get a chance to meet Sir Drake when he arrives for the christening of Trevor and Corinthians's baby. He's one of the godfathers."

Netherland lifted an arched brow. "Just how many godfathers will this baby have?"

"Three."

"Three?"

"Yes. Sir Drake, Dex Madaris and myself."

Netherland nodded. She wasn't surprised to hear Dex Madaris's name among them. Everyone knew that Clayton's brother Dex and Trevor had been friends since childhood.

"Who's the godmother? Or should I say godmothers?"

"As far as I know there's only one godmother. Corinthians's best friend Brenna St. Johns, or Brenna Jordache since I understand she recently got married."

Netherland nodded. Although she didn't know Corinthians's best friend Brenna personally, she had heard from Syneda how the woman had gone on a three-week cruise and met the man of her dreams on the ship and married him.

Netherland was about to take another sip and noticed her glass was empty.

"Want some more?"

She looked at Ashton, again noticing how close they were sitting on the love seat. "No, I think I've had enough." Netherland looked down at her empty glass before raising curious eyes to Ashton. There was something she wanted to ask him, something that had been bugging her all day.

"Why did you volunteer to be a part of the Brothers Auction?"

Ashton studied her, remembering something Trevor had said. "Does it bother you that I did?"

Inhaling deeply, she blew out her breath in a rush. How could she explain to him that yes, it did bother her and make him understand why it did, when she didn't fully understand it herself? She had no dibs on him, and he was free to do as he pleased with whomever he pleased. "It shouldn't."

He looked at her, met her gaze intently. "Does it?"

Netherland hated that he was making her admit to something she didn't want to admit to. A part of her wanted to lie to him and say, "No, it doesn't matter." But another part, the part that had asked the question earlier of why he had volunteered to do it, still wanted an answer. "Yes, it matters."

He was silent for a moment as he continued to hold her gaze. "And why does it matter, Netherland?"

Netherland bristled slightly. She had answered several of his questions and he had yet to answer one of hers. "It just does, okay," she said curtly. "Now will you tell me why you volunteered to do it?"

He reached out and traced a finger along her cheek. "The reason I did it was that I thought the money was being raised for a good cause and that my participation would be my contribution. You contributed by volunteering the use of your restaurant."

Netherland nodded. "So your volunteering had nothing to do with…"

When she didn't complete her question, he raised a dark brow. "Had nothing to do with what?"

She looked at him. "Knowing all those women would want you and that one of them will get the chance to spend a weekend with you in New Orleans."

Ashton wanted to pull her closer. He wanted to tell her that the only woman who would be spending that weekend with him would be she. What Netherland didn't know was that he had devised a plan and had given someone strict orders to top the highest bid, no matter what it was. In essence, that person would be bidding on his behalf. There was no rule that said a contestant could not bid on himself and present the winning bid to the woman of his choice. He had no intention of letting any woman choose him. He would be the one doing the choosing.

"The notion of spending time with a woman had nothing to do with it, Netherland," he said finally. "Because no matter what those other women may want, you are the only woman that I want." Instinctively he pulled her closer to him. "You are the only woman who matters."

Netherland wanted to tell him that although she'd wanted to hear those words, she shouldn't be the only one who mattered because there would never be a future for them as long as he was in the military. But she couldn't force herself to say the words. The only thing she could do was to continue to look into the darkness of his eyes and see how the lighting from a nearby lamp shone on his features making them more profound, more handsome. As he continued to look at her she felt that same jolt of awareness she had felt the first time she had met him, nearly three years ago, and the same jolt she felt upon seeing him every time since then. Around her he generated heat, electricity, desire.

Without a word she tilted her head up when she saw his mouth move closer to claim her lips. She knew she should stop it now because once they had crossed over the line, there would be no going back. She had waited almost three years for this kiss.

He took her breath away the moment his mouth came down on hers, and the jolt of awareness exploded through all parts of her body. When he parted her lips with the tip of his tongue she was ready and opened completely for him.

Netherland felt him cup the back of her head to bring their mouths closer, tighter, to mate in hungry passion. As if they had a mind of their own, her hands reached up, wrapped her arms around his neck as she moaned gently to the feelings he was evoking within her. She felt herself being picked up, lifted and placed in his lap as he continued to kiss her, absorb her mouth with his, as her heart continued to beat out of control.

She couldn't help but recall the many nights since first meeting him that she had yearned for this moment to find out what his taste was like, to share such an intimate experience with him. His mouth was pleasuring her beyond anything she had known. He was demanding stirring and explosive sensations from within her. He was unfolding a need she hadn't known existed, and his kiss was beckoning her to taste, to feel and to feast on everything about the man who so gently held her in his arms as he gave her the experience women only dreamed about.

Netherland's hands tightened around his neck, urging the intoxicating intimacy to continue forever. She took his tongue into her mouth, savored it, exulted in it and connected with it. No man had ever kissed her this way before, and she knew that no man would ever kiss her this way again. Ashton Sinclair had his own brand of style and was meticulously stamping it all over her mouth with kiss after kiss after kiss.

The kiss eventually came to an end when the need to breathe overrode everything else. Ashton released a ragged breath and touched his forehead to hers. "Netherland, do you want to know something?" he asked, barely able to catch his breath.

She inhaled deeply, trying to catch a breath of her own, almost failing in the process. "What?"

"You don't ever have to agree to go out with me as long as you let me stay in with you doing this." He then kissed her again, more thorough and hotter than before.

There was no telling how long they would have continued to kiss if the knock on the door had not interrupted them. Netherland drew in a deep breath and released it with a sigh before pulling herself out of Ashton's arms and lap, making it to the door. Without opening it she answered, "Yes?"

"It's Rainey, Nettie. I just wanted to make sure you're okay."

Netherland turned slightly and looked at Ashton. He was sitting on the love seat watching her. The dark sensual look in his eyes was making her consider things she shouldn't. Already she had gone beyond a point of where she should have with him. He knew it, too. They also knew there was no way to go back to where they had been before tonight. They had done more than acknowledge the attraction between them. In that short space of time, they had tasted the passion, and she had gotten addicted to it. A part of her wished that nothing stood in the way of indulging in the desires he stirred within her.

"Nettie? You're okay?"

The worried tone of Rainey's voice drew Netherland's attention back to her friend. There was no way she could tell Rainey that she was okay when deep in her heart she knew she would never be okay again. Drawing in a deep breath, she unlocked the door and cracked it open slightly. "I'm fine, Rainey."

Rainey looked at her with those ever-observant eyes. After a brief moment she said, "Yes, Nettie, I see that you are." She placed a smirky grin on her face, turned around and headed back down the hall.

Netherland closed the door and turned back around to Ashton. He was now standing in the middle of the room. His eyes were simmering with promises of pleasures that went beyond kissing. He was tempting her mindless with the very thought. Tension gripped her entire body as she watched him slowly walk over to her. He must have felt her anxiety and reached out and bracketed her face in the palms of his hands. He probed her eyes for a moment before saying, "We'll work through whatever is keeping us apart, Netherland," he said simply, easily.

Netherland shook her head. "There isn't a middle ground, Ashton. I refuse to become involved with someone who's in the military."

His smile was slow, endearing, determined. "You are involved, Netherland. And now that I've tasted you, you're a craving I can't do without, so don't ask me to. There *is* a middle ground and we will find it. Together." He took her back into his arms and placed a gentle yet possessive kiss on her lips. Once again her body automatically responded to his.

He then brought his lips to her ear and whispered, "Surrender, Netherland. Surrender your fears about us to me, and I promise to make things right for us."

Netherland wanted to believe it would be that easy but knew he was promising the impossible. "I can't, Ashton. I've got to have stability and that's something you can't give me as long as you are in the military."

Without waiting for his response, she opened the door and walked out of her office.

Later that night after Netherland had gotten into bed, she lay there and remembered the kiss—or should she say kisses?—that she and Ashton had shared in her office. A part of her wanted to regret what they had done, but another part of her continued to rejoice and forbid her to worry about the consequences of her actions.

She tossed around in the bed a few times before finally finding a comfortable spot. As much as she tried not to, her mind reflected to that day almost three years ago when she and Ashton had first met. Maybe if she had known from the first that he was military, her attraction to him would not have been so great, so overpowering, so downright unnatural. But it had been. The first sight of him had been like a magnet, pulling her in, and it was a day she would never forget.

As Netherland watched the blades of the ceiling fan

swirling overhead, cooling off her overheated body, her mind became occupied with memories of that day...

"Nettie?"

Nettie lifted her head from the document she was reading. "Yes?"

"I hate to disturb you but Trevor Grant and Clayton Madaris are here," Rainey said, smiling. "They brought some other gentlemen with them and would like to introduce you to them."

Netherland smiled. Trevor and Clayton were two of her biggest clients, and as single men they patronized her establishment at least three to four times a week, claiming the restaurant's good food was the big draw. She knew their interest in her place also went beyond food. Their frequent visits were designed to check out the single women there, as well. "Do you know who these other men are?"

Rainey smiled dreamily. "One I recognize as Clayton's brother Dex Madaris. I remember him from the last time he came in and had all the women drooling. The other one I think is Clayton's other brother. He favors Clayton and is handsome as sin. The other man I believe is a friend of Trevor's—and he's a total knockout. His hair is longer than mine. He seems to be part Indian or something. All I know is that the man is to die for, three times over."

Netherland chuckled as she placed the papers she'd been reading aside. "He's *that* good-looking?"

"Judge for yourself, Nettie."

And she did.

While only a few feet away from the table she had to agree with Rainey. The man who sat next to Trevor at the table was to die for. He'd had his head bent, chuckling at something Clayton had said, and suddenly it seemed he had heard her approach and turned his head sharply toward her.

Their eyes met, and there was instant sexual awareness.

Immediately, spontaneously, Netherland's heart began hammering deep within her chest, and her pulse began racing. Her knees weakened, which made her slow her pace somewhat. The palms of her hands felt damp. She blinked as if the action would will him away. It didn't. He was still sitting there looking at her as intently as she was looking at him. There was something overpowering and aggressive about him and instead of backing away from it, she found herself drawn closer, so she kept on walking until she had reached their table. All five men stood.

She barely heard Trevor telling the others how wonderful the food served at her restaurant was. She barely recalled the introductions of the other men, Clayton's two brothers—Justin and Dex. Her mind, body, soul and spirit were on the man who stood next to Trevor. She knew his eyes had not left her since he had seen her from across the room. She breathed in deeply when she presented her hand to him. "Nice meeting you, Ashton."

She found her hand folded gently in the warmth

of his as he looked deep within her eyes and said softly, "The pleasure, Netherland, is all mine. Please sit down and join us for a minute."

She knew she shouldn't. She had a million things to do. A wedding reception was being planned for the next day in one of her banquet rooms. But his request sent her entire body into overdrive, and she found herself sitting in the chair he pulled out for her—next to his.

It was only later, after enjoying herself immensely as she listened to Justin and Dex Madaris try and convince Trevor, Clayton and Ashton about the benefits of marriage that she discovered the explosive attraction between her and Ashton had been a complete waste of good energy. The discovery had come when Trevor jokingly called Ashton "Colonel."

She had turned to Ashton and saw his eyes were still on her. "Why did Trevor just call you Colonel? Were you once a colonel?"

He smiled at her with the sexiest grin she thought she would ever see on a man. "Yes, ma'am, still am. I'm a colonel in the marines."

She blinked as she felt a heavy hand clamp itself around her heart. "You're in the marines *now?*" she asked softly, hoping he would say no and that he had recently retired or something. Instead he met her inquisitive eyes. Something in her tone must have alerted him to the fact that she was asking for a reason—a very important reason—a reason he didn't quite understand.

"Yes, I'm in the marines now, and I'll probably stay in the marines until the day I die."

She shook her head, confused. He didn't resemble a military man, especially by the head. "But your hair?" she asked, making sure she understood him correctly. "Isn't it too long?" She had been around enough military men to know the low crew cut was Uncle Sam's standard.

"No, my hair isn't too long. Since I'm legally part Indian, the right to wear my hair this length is protected by federal law."

Netherland nodded. She knew then and there that any thoughts of ever becoming involved with him were over. The last thing she would let happen was to allow a man in her life who didn't have roots. She had been through that with her father, and had promised herself never to go through it again. She had worked too hard for independence and stability in her life to toss them aside for overactive hormones.

Netherland brought her thoughts back to the present. She had promised herself that day that she would not start anything with Ashton she couldn't finish.

Yet, tonight in his arms, she had broken that promise.

Chapter 5

Netherland swiveled around in the chair at her desk. "What do you mean he left town?"

Rainey shrugged. "That's the rumor on the floor tonight. Carolyn Taylor claims she saw Ashton getting on a plane for D.C. yesterday while she was at the airport. She says he was wearing his military uniform and was giving all the women at the airport heart failure because he looked so good." Rainey looked pointedly at Netherland. "Everyone wants to know when he's coming back."

Netherland picked up the papers she'd been reading and tossed them in the tray on her desk. She hated admitting it but she had missed seeing Ashton underfoot for the past two nights. "And how would I know?"

Rainey smiled sweetly. "After Tuesday night, I'd think you'd know everything about him. The two of you stayed in your office close to an hour."

Netherland frowned. She didn't need Rainey reminding her of that. "So? That doesn't make me privy to all his business."

"Considering you're the woman he plans to marry, I'd think that—"

"He is not marrying me, Rainey. Regardless of how long we stayed locked in my office, nothing has changed. My position is still the same. We're not involved."

"Yeah, if you say so. And I guess there was a pretty good reason why your lips were all swollen the other night. Looked to me like someone had done a job on them. A very delicious job."

As she scowled furiously at Rainey, a logical voice in Netherland's head told her to quickly change the subject. So she did. "How's Jada working out?"

The glimmer of amusement in Rainey's eyes indicated she'd caught on to Netherland's ploy and decided to go along with it...for now. "Jada's working out fine, and pretty much keeps to herself. She seems to be a real nice person who looks more like she's eighteen than twenty-three. She's too young to have had so much sadness in her life, and she continues to look sad."

Netherland nodded, agreeing. Jada Roberts was going out of her way to be a good employee but on several occasions Netherland had noted the sadness in the young woman's eyes.

At that moment the phone rang, and Netherland picked it up. "Sisters." She smiled at the voice on the other end. "Yes, Syneda, I do cater occasionally."

Netherland nodded. "Yes, this is short notice but I think I can handle it. What time did you have in mind?"

Netherland gave another nod. "All right. I can drop the food off on my way home." She smiled. "That's fine, don't mention it. I'll see you in a little while."

"Oh, Nettie, you're a lifesaver," Syneda exclaimed as she opened the door and took a couple of the boxes from Netherland's hands. "There's no way I could have prepared this much food after a late day in court. I don't know what possessed me to volunteer to be the hostess for tonight's poker game."

"Don't mention it," Netherland replied, smiling as she followed Syneda, carrying the food Sisters had prepared. "I hope I didn't bring too much."

Syneda grinned. "Too much food for a bunch of hungry, gambling men? Is there such a thing?"

Netherland chuckled. "No, I guess not." When they reached the kitchen she was surprised to find a group of women assembled around the table.

"You know everyone, don't you, Nettie?" Syneda asked as she took the rest of the boxes out of Netherland's hands.

"Yes." Netherland had met all of them at a bridal shower given for Syneda at Sisters last year. There was Trevor's very pregnant wife, Corinthians; Dex's wife, Caitlin; Justin's wife, Lorren; the Madaris brothers' two sisters, Kattie and Traci; and the Madaris's cousin, Felicia. "Hi, everyone."

"Hi, Nettie," they said returning the greeting in unison.

"We're glad you were able to deliver. For a minute we thought Syneda was going to have to cook for us," Felicia Madaris Maxwell said, grinning. "I have too much to do tomorrow to be out sick."

"Okay, knock it off," Syneda said, trying to hide her smile behind a frown. "A good attorney I am, but a good cook I'm not. Clayton didn't marry me for my cooking skills."

Felicia chuckled. "Not for one minute did any of us think that's what he married you for."

Syneda tried glaring but was unable to keep a straight face when she said, "And stop insinuating that your cousin only married me for my body."

Netherland smiled. Not for the first time, she envied the six women and their close friendship. They felt comfortable enough to say just about anything to one another. "I'll be going now," she said, turning to leave.

Syneda grabbed her arm. "Why don't you stay and join us, Nettie? You were on your way home, right?"

"Yes, but I don't want to intrude."

"You won't be intruding," Caitlin Madaris said, grinning. "We were discussing the best way to make sure Corinthians gets to the hospital when she goes into labor without Trevor falling apart."

"Trevor won't fall apart," Traci Madaris Green

was saying. "For Pete's sake, give him credit for something. He used to be a captain in the marines."

"And what's that supposed to mean?" Kattie Madaris Barnes chimed in. "When it comes to their wives having babies, all men fall apart and act downright silly." She laughed. "Remember when the ever cool, calm and collected Raymond jumped into the car and took off and forgot I was still sitting in the living room? He'd driven an entire block before he noticed."

Netherland laughed when the story was retold. Then Caitlin shared how Dex had gone off on the doctor when he thought the man wasn't moving fast enough when her labor pains had begun hitting her fast and furious. The women then began talking about the gory details of giving birth.

"Please change the subject. Nettie might think twice about ever getting pregnant," Lorren Madaris said, smiling.

Netherland smiled. "No, I'm fine listening to it. Besides, I can't get pregnant anyway. A childhood illness made that impossible."

Syneda came up to her. "Oh, Nettie, we're sorry. We didn't know and—"

"Trust me, it's okay. I've had a long time to come to terms with it, and I'm comfortable with it. There are too many kids out there who need adopting, so whenever I decide to become a mom, I'll go that route," she said, smiling and assuring the women she hadn't gotten offended.

"Do I smell food?"

The women turned around when Clayton stuck his head around the corner.

Syneda grinned. "That man can sniff the aroma of fried chicken a mile away," she whispered to the other women. To her husband she gave an exuberant smile. "Yes, sweetheart, it's food. Are you guys at a stopping point where you can come out for air and for food?"

Clayton smiled. "If they aren't, I am. I'm starving."

It didn't take long for the other men to detect food and start filing into the kitchen. Netherland was talking to Syneda about something when she felt someone watching her. She turned to see Ashton leaning against a counter. Her breath caught in her throat. She hadn't known he was there. She tried to downplay the feeling of sheer exhilaration when he smiled at her. Again she wondered what there was about him that could make her so attracted to him. It was more than his physical features that attracted her. There was also something else. There was the passion he stirred within her that she couldn't deny. She still had thoughts of the kisses they shared in her office and that had been more than three days ago.

As if he read her thoughts, Ashton continued to hold her gaze. And then it happened like always. A sharp electrical jolt raced through her, sensitizing her entire body to his gaze, and blocking out all sights and sounds around her. A voice inside her head warned her to put up her defenses, but she wasn't quick enough. Already Ashton was slowly walking over to her. A part of her wanted to turn around and run but couldn't. It was as if her feet were cemented to the floor.

"Seeing you here is a pleasant surprise, Netherland," Ashton said silkily when he reached her.

Netherland's lashes lifted. "I'm surprised to see you here, too. I heard you had left town."

"Yes, for a couple of days. Government business."

She nodded as she met his dark gaze. Sexual tension surrounded them. She wondered if any of the others in the room could feel it. Could anyone detect the fierce attraction she had for him? "Did you have a nice trip?"

He smiled. "It was okay."

"Hey, Ashton, aren't you going to eat?" Trevor called from the other side of the room.

"I'm not really hungry," was Ashton's response. He looked back at Netherland. "What about you? Are you going to eat anything?"

"No, in fact I was about to leave. I only stopped by to drop off the food."

He looked at her. "I think I'll call it an early night myself since Dex won most of my money anyway," he said, grinning. "Would you drop me off at my hotel? I rode over with Trevor instead of driving the rental car."

Netherland lifted a brow. "Hotel? I thought you were staying with Trevor and Corinthians."

"I was until I got back. I decided to give the parents-to-be space. They need the rest of the time before the baby gets here to be by themselves." He smiled. "In a few more weeks there won't ever be just the two of them again. There will be a third person who will be dominating their lives." He looked at her for a long, slow minute before asking again, "So, will you give me a lift to my hotel?"

Warning bells went off in Netherland's head. "I suppose I could."

The wry resignation in her tone stirred Ashton deeply. "I don't bite, Netherland."

Her mind instantly recalled how during their kiss he'd relentlessly nibbled away at her mouth as he plowed it with kiss after kiss. Yes, he did bite. He'd certainly taken more than a bite-size chunk out of her sensibilities that night.

"Netherland?"

"Yes?"

"You still won't go out with me?"

For several moments an air of sadness hovered over her, as she remembered why she wouldn't. "No, I still won't go out with you."

His gaze was intense, determined. "When we get to the hotel, will you 'stay in' with me…for a little while?"

Netherland's body stirred all the way down to her toes when she remembered what happened the last time they had stayed in. And as much as she wanted to deny it, her body wanted to experience his kisses again.

She focused her attention on his lips. Doing so shortened her breathing. It became difficult to get air past her lungs. It seemed her own lips suddenly felt sensitive. Convincing herself that a few kisses wouldn't hurt as long as she didn't let it go any further, she finally gave herself up to the inevitable. "Yes, I'll stay in with you for a little while."

When Ashton curled his fingers around hers she tried to steady her nerves. But nothing could bring calmness to her body that was tense with wanting him.

Chapter 6

Holding Netherland's hand firmly in his, Ashton walked her to her car.

"Would you like to drive, Ashton?" Netherland asked him, after inhaling deeply and blowing out a rush of air. She didn't think her hands were steady enough to handle the steering wheel.

"Sure."

Moments later with the windows down and the crisp feel of May air rushing at them, Ashton steered Netherland's Pathfinder onto the highway.

"Where are you staying?"

"In one of those extended-stay facilities owned by Marriott."

Netherland nodded. "I heard those type of places are nice."

"Yes, they are. And this is a nice vehicle."

"Thanks."

"How long have you had it?"

"About six months."

After several moments of tense silence Netherland said, "You were a hero last year when you rescued Trevor and Corinthians from the jungles in South America."

Ashton shrugged massive shoulders. "The media got carried away as usual. Trevor had the skill and know-how to survive in that habitat for another couple of months or so had I not found them."

"Because of his military background?"

"Yes. Trevor, Sir Drake and I used to be part of the marines' Special Forces—the Force Recon Unit. We were trained how to survive in difficult situations. Each of us had a specialty. Trevor's specialty is the ability to survive in the jungle or any other unusual or dangerous environment or domain. Sir Drake's a whiz at ammunition and explosives." Ashton smiled. "He likes blowing up things." Ashton's smile faded when he thought about the fact that right now Sir Drake was living his life pretty much like the explosives he enjoyed handling—dangerously. He liked living close to the edge by taking chances he shouldn't. Ashton didn't want to think about the things that Sir Drake was possibly doing working for the CIA.

"And what's your specialty, Ashton?"

He looked at her when he brought the car to a stop at a traffic light. "Like this vehicle, I'm a Pathfinder, which is another name for a tracker. Being able to locate anything and anyone in thick woods, jungles, forest and any type of uncivilized or impenetrable territory is my special skill."

Netherland nodded, deciding not to tell him that tracking wasn't his only special skill. He was doing a pretty good job in the seduction area. The man was seducing her with the ease of someone who was an ace at it. Even now incredible sensations were skittering inside her. She had known from the moment Ashton had smiled at her at Clayton and Syneda's house that she would be spending time with him tonight. She would have to approach what was happening to her logically and intelligently. Although there could never, ever be a future between them, there was no reason they couldn't enjoy each other during the time he was in Houston on military leave. She was sure once she presented the idea to him that he would go for it. Something was better than nothing. She would get him out of her system, and he would get her out of his; then they would go their separate ways. He would travel around the world playing soldier, and she would remain in Houston contented.

She had gotten into this thing with Ashton, and she might as well finish it.

Ashton tightened his hands on the steering wheel. Dealing with Netherland was just as bad as dealing with any band of terrorists. The woman was giving him the battle of his life.

He wondered what she was thinking. He could tell she had gotten relaxed. Out of the corner of his eye he could see she had undone the top button of her blouse. Was she deliberately trying to get next to him? He doubted it. Like him, she was probably beginning to feel hot.

"Ashton?"

"Hmm?" He had come to another traffic light. He looked at her, then wished he hadn't. Her eyes were dark, desirously dark. And all that desire was focused on him.

"How much longer until we get to the hotel?"

He continued to look at her for a moment more before saying, "Not much longer."

"Good."

They rode the rest of the way to the hotel in companionable silence.

Netherland began questioning her actions when they walked into Ashton's hotel room, and he closed the door behind them. Especially when she saw his marine uniform in a dry cleaner's bag neatly placed diagonally across his bed.

She started to turn around and leave, then decided to take another approach. Without saying anything to him she walked over to his bed, picked up the dry cleaner's bag and walked over to the closet and hung it up. She closed the closet door behind her.

"That won't eliminate who and what I am, Netherland," Ashton said, leaning against the closed hotel door.

"I know, but tonight I don't want it to matter." She walked back over to him and placed her arms around his neck. "And for the rest of the time you're here in Houston, it won't matter."

"Why won't it?"

She leaned up and brushed her lips gently across his, once. Twice. Then she answered, "Because we're looking at this like two sensible adults who want to be together. Let's enjoy today and not concern ourselves with tomorrow."

"Are you suggesting we share a bed tonight and go our separate ways in the morning?"

She brushed another kiss across his lips before saying, "No, I'm looking at something a little longer than a one-night stand. I'm suggesting we share a bed while you're in Houston and when you leave for parts unknown you won't look back and I won't have any regrets. The time we'll spend together will be a memory we'll have forever. What do you think of that?" She brushed another kiss across his lips.

Ashton knew it was time he showed his future wife just what he thought.

This time when her mouth touched his, he cupped the back of her head with his hand. Parting her lips with his tongue he swept inside her mouth, stealing her next words—whatever they may have been. And when she moaned in a shuddering breath, he stole that, too. He continued kissing her with more fire and more passion than he'd kissed her that night in her office.

That was only the beginning.

He broke off the kiss and took a step back from her and began tugging the tails of his shirt out of his jeans. He then began unbuttoning his shirt while she watched him.

The rate of Netherland's breathing increased when he removed his shirt and tossed it aside. His chest and shoulders looked firm, muscled, strong, and she wanted to feel the naked strength of them beneath her fingertips. Her skin began to feel heated when she watched him slowly unzip his pants. Her eyes widened. She blinked when he tugged down his jeans and revealed…a loincloth?

Netherland blinked again. Her jaw dropped. Ashton's underwear was styled as a loincloth. She inhaled deeply. She had seen men in boxers. Her father and brothers still preferred those kinds. Erik had preferred wearing briefs. But she had never seen a pair of loincloth underwear and hadn't known such a thing existed. Standing before her, he could have been either primitive Indian or primitive African. The loincloth could have served either purpose.

"Now your turn, Netherland." The deep hoarseness in his voice filled the room.

She blinked again. "You want me to undress?" She could barely get the words out. She could barely swallow. The man had the best-looking body she had ever seen. All hard and firm.

She inhaled deeply and continued to look at him. He looked magnificent.

"Yes, I want you to undress. But keep your panties and bra on."

She inhaled deeply once more. Then she did as he had instructed and began removing her clothes. He watched her every move.

First she unhooked her skirt and let it drop to the floor. Then came her blouse, which left her in her bra and halfslip. His eyes never left hers when she tugged her slip down past her hips, grateful that she'd had the mind that morning to wear a matching bra and panty set with—of all things—a tiger print.

If that didn't beat all.

Here he stood before her looking like something straight from some African jungle or some American wildlands, and she was dressed like prey. A willing prey at that. Whatever fight or resistance would have been in her had left the moment he'd dropped his pants.

Their gazes locked and held as he walked slowly over to her. "You are about to be captured, Netherland. Totally and completely. You may as well surrender," he said softly. "But make no mistake about it. If you surrender, you have to surrender all. I won't take anything less than that. Do you understand what I'm saying?"

Not really, but Netherland nodded anyway.

"Do you know how much I want you, Netherland? Do you have any idea?"

She swallowed, then heard herself say, "It can't be

any more than I want you, Ashton. This attraction between us is unnatural."

"No, it's not," he whispered, reaching out and sliding his fingertips down her abdomen and beneath the band of her panties. Gently, soothingly, he touched her damp heat with his fingertips. "There's nothing unnatural about it. You are my soul mate. Our spirits are entwined. I knew it the very first time I laid eyes on you. It was confirmed in my visions."

At the moment, Netherland didn't want to hear anything about visions. She could barely think about anything at all. Ashton's fingers were driving her out of her mind. She was very close to the breaking point.

"Do you surrender, Netherland? Do you surrender all?"

Before she could respond he captured her mouth in a kiss. Instinctively, she closed her eyes and stood on tiptoe to lift her hips to press herself against the heat and hardness of him. The kiss became hotter, more demanding, more fulfilling. She felt herself being lifted into his arms and carried across the room. Moments later he placed her on the bed. Her mouth protested when he pulled back and looked down at her.

"Sit up, Netherland," he instructed gently. "Indian style."

She blinked, wondering if she had heard him correctly. He evidently saw the look of confusion in her eyes because he repeated himself. She still couldn't comprehend what he was telling her. He wanted her to sit up in an Indian-style position? Was this some unusual way to make love or something?

Not knowing what to expect, she did what she was told. She then watched as he joined her on the king-size bed and did likewise. "Ashton, what—"

"Shhh. I'll give you the rules." He sat in an Indian-style position facing her.

Netherland lifted a brow. There were rules?

"Now, before you surrender all, I want you to know just what you're getting yourself in to, Netherland. We talk."

Talk? She didn't want to talk. She wanted him to make love to her. And here they were sitting in the middle of the bed like two Indians getting ready to smoke a peace pipe or something.

"This bed, Netherland, is sacred ground. It's our reservation, our jungle. Our home. The floor surrounding this bed represents misunderstanding, mistrust and doubt. For now, neither you nor I can leave the safety of our reservation, our jungle and our home alone. We must make the journey together. Understand?"

The only thing she understood was that he was not going to make love to her. He wanted them to play some type of pretend game instead. "And what's the purpose of all of this, Ashton?" she asked quietly. Her body still hummed with wanting him. Sitting in front of her half-naked wasn't making things easy.

"The purpose of all of this, Netherland, is for the

two of us to have a meeting of the minds, to be in sync and on one accord. It's important that we're a united front about certain things."

"What things?"

"What part we will play in each other's lives. Not just for tonight but for forever."

"But there isn't a forever for us, Ashton," she said in frustration. "Why can't you understand that? Why can't you see that?"

He smiled tenderly. "Because I have the gift to see things that you don't see, sweetheart. I've told you about my vision but you refuse to accept it."

"I can't."

"Then you can't fully surrender until you can accept it. Look at me, Netherland. Look hard and tell me what you see. I want your complete honesty."

She looked at him while he looked back at her. After a few moments she said, "I see a very stubborn man." She then took a deep breath. "But I also see the most beautiful man I've ever seen in my life. Your features are strong, profound. And I want you."

"I want you, too," he said gently, truthfully. "But one thing you didn't mention that you see is love. Surely you can see all my love for you, Netherland."

Netherland gasped. Love? Surely he was mistaken. This man couldn't love her. He didn't even know her. He didn't know everything about her. "You can't possibly love me, Ashton."

"Why can't I?"

"It's just not possible. You don't know me."

He smiled. "I know you a lot better than you think."

She frowned. "Then you should know how I feel about military men."

"I do. And I know your reasons for them are groundless."

"Groundless!" Netherland sat up on her haunches. "How dare you tell me that something I feel so strongly about is groundless?"

He sat up on his haunches and met her glare, face-to-face, nearly nose to nose. "I can dare and I will dare, Netherland, because I am your soul mate. You don't have to concern yourself with instability because my love will be the most stable thing you will have in your life. You won't have to worry about not having a home because your home will always be with me, wherever I am. Home is where the heart is, and your home will always reside in my heart, like my home will always be in yours. You love me."

Netherland sat back down, Indian-style, and looked up at him. "No, I don't love you," she said quietly, wondering how he could assume such a thing. How could he make such a claim as if he were privy to her innermost feelings and emotions? "There are things you don't even know about me, Ashton. Do you know why my first husband left me?"

"It doesn't matter."

"To some men it might. The reason he left me was that—"

"It doesn't matter, Netherland," he interrupted.

"What matters to me is that you understand my position. We will not make love until you surrender all to me."

"What you want I'm unable to give, Ashton," she said softly, as tears glistened in her eyes. Why was he determined to make things difficult? Why couldn't he take what she was offering and be satisfied with that? "You don't know how hard it was on me for my father to be gone off somewhere when I had my birthdays, on Christmases, and important events at school. I was named homecoming queen at the beginning of my senior year, and because he was away, he didn't see me get crowned."

"Don't you think he probably wanted to be there, Netherland? Instead he thought he was somewhere doing something equally as important, like protecting and safeguarding your freedom. Not only yours but the freedom of all the kids in your school, their parents and a whole lot of others. Even the person who placed that crown on your head at that coronation."

Netherland sniffed and wiped a tear from her eye. She hadn't ever thought of her father's numerous absences in that light before. "Mrs. Jones."

Ashton lifted a dark brow. "Mrs. Jones? Who's Mrs. Jones?"

Netherland shrugged slightly. "She was the home economics teacher who placed the crown on my head."

Ashton nodded. A slight smile touched his lips. "Very well. Your father was protecting and safeguarding Mrs. Jones's freedom, as well." He reached out and pulled her into his arms. "Come on, let's go to bed."

She pulled back. "Bed? But you just said we wouldn't make love until I believe in the vision."

"We won't. We're going to bed to go to sleep."

Netherland stared at him. "Can you do that? Sleep with me and not touch me?"

"Oh, I plan to touch you, I just don't plan to make love to you. I have a strong constitution when it comes to you, Netherland. I haven't slept with a woman since the day I laid eyes on you."

Netherland blinked. That was almost three years ago. She couldn't imagine a man as virile as Ashton going without that long. Her brothers would have thrown up their hands in frustration long ago. Whenever they came home from a long-term deployment, they would quickly pull out their little black books and look up old girlfriends. "Why?"

"Because you're the only woman I want. Come on, let's get under the covers and go to sleep." He pushed the covers back and looked at her, waiting for her decision.

Netherland glanced down at the floor. He'd said the floor represented misunderstanding, mistrust and doubt. That was stuff she didn't want to deal with at the moment. More than anything she wanted to spend the night in his arms, sharing his bed. But she had no intentions of surrendering to him by committing to what he wanted her to commit to.

She watched as he slipped under the covers, lay back and held out his arms for her. Taking a deep breath, she joined him under the covers and went willingly into his embrace.

Ashton pulled Netherland to him, satisfied. For the time being, he had her just where he wanted her. In his arms, in his bed. Now if he could only get her to accept his place in her life.

There would be more difficult days ahead with her, but he was prepared for them.

Chapter 7

Netherland stood at the window in her office and pulled in one long, shuddering breath as memories of last night assailed her. Even now she couldn't believe that she had actually slept in Ashton's bed practically half-naked while he held her in his arms, with her back pressed against the solid, muscular wall of his chest, and his knees tucked behind hers.

She remembered waking to find him sitting at the foot of the bed, Indian-style, with his eyes on her. She'd watched as his gaze had drifted over her features slowly, like a loving caress. Then with measured movements, he had covered the distance between them and, drawing her up close, he had taken her into his arms, kissing her fully awake.

Her body had quickly responded to him as his mouth
claimed her and branded her as his. She had wrapped
her arms around him, and for brief moments she had
claimed him as hers, as well. However, when the kiss
had ended, reality for her had set in. When he'd left to
go get them something for breakfast, she had dressed
quickly and had made her escape. She wondered what
he'd thought when he returned and found her gone.

Netherland's pondering of Ashton's reaction to
her disappearance came to an end when she heard the
soft knock on her door. "Come in."

Her office door opened slowly. "You wanted to see
me, Ms. Brooms?"

Netherland smiled. "Yes, come in, Jada, and have
a seat." She watched Jada Roberts's face carefully.
Rainey was right. She looked a lot younger than
twenty-three. She could pass for an eighteen-year-old
easily. And not for the first time Netherland thought
that Jada was indeed a beautiful young woman,
although it seemed she went to great lengths to hide
that fact. However, even without trying, her natural
beauty shone through. Jada didn't need any type of
makeup to enhance her features.

From the information Netherland had gotten from
Syneda, she knew that Jada's mother had died when
Jada was fourteen, and she had been raised by her al-
coholic father. She had gotten mixed up with
Anthony Roberts and had eventually married him. It
wasn't until after she had married him that she had
found out what a control freak he was. He'd taken joy

in beating his wife each and every time he thought she'd been messing around on him, threatening the life of her father if she ever left him. After her father had died of a liver disease Jada decided to get out of the two-year abusive marriage.

After Jada had taken the chair in front of her desk, Netherland walked over from the window and took the chair behind her desk, as well. "We haven't had a chance to really talk since you started working here, and I was wondering how things are working out for you, Jada?"

"Everything's fine, Ms. Brooms. Everyone here has been really nice to me."

Netherland nodded. "I'm happy to hear that, and I'd be happier when you feel comfortable enough to call me by my first name. 'Ms. Brooms' makes me feel so old, and I'm only about five years older than you."

Jada smiled. "I'll try, but it isn't easy. I think of you as my boss so I automatically feel I should call you by your last name."

"Well, we're not all that formal here. Calling me Netherland or Nettie is fine."

"Which do you prefer?"

Netherland thought about that question. Everyone, including her parents and brothers, called her Nettie. Ashton, however, called her Netherland. And as far as she was concerned, no one could say her name the way he did. When he said it there was always this sensuous sound to it.

"Nettie will do."

Jada nodded. "I appreciate your giving me those two days off last week to attend the trial."

"And how did that go?"

Jada inhaled what appeared to be a deep cleansing breath. "It's over and that's what matters. I'm no longer married to Anthony Roberts, and he's no longer free to hurt me, although he did make those threats while they were taking him away."

Netherland raised her brow. "What threats?"

"He threatened to hurt both me and Mrs. Madaris if he ever got out. He blames me for everything that has gone wrong in his life, and he blames her for our divorce and for him going to jail."

"How long did he get?"

"Seven years with no chance of parole until he makes at least five."

"Well, hopefully he'll have a lot to think about over the next five years and will get out of prison a different person."

Jada shook her head sagely. "He can do whatever he likes when he gets out as long as he leaves me alone. I hate the day I ever got mixed up with him."

"Well, that part of your life is over now, Jada. You have an opportunity for any kind of future you want."

Jada smiled. "Yes, Nettie, I do. I've had so many blessings in my life lately, and I thank God every night for them."

Later that evening Netherland's heartbeat skittered, increased, then slammed against her rib cage when Ashton walked into Sisters. He looked around briefly before his gaze locked with hers. She swallowed heavily as she watched him walk over toward her. Memories invaded her brain of how she had seen him last night, and also of how he had seen her, had touched her.

She saw the lack of emotions on his face and would have given anything to know what he was thinking. Had he gotten upset when he'd returned to his hotel room to find her gone? She took a deep breath. It lodged in her throat when she saw the darkness of his eyes and the intensity in them.

She met his gaze directly when he came to a stop in front of her. "Ashton," she said softly, hesitantly.

"Netherland. Is there someplace we can go and talk? Privately."

She swallowed. The last thing she thought she could handle right now was being someplace alone with him. "Does it have to be private?"

He shrugged. "Not unless you want everyone here tonight to know our business."

Netherland definitely didn't want that. She didn't have to glance around to know that the two of them were the recipients of curious stares. "Let's go into my office."

Once they reached her office and closed the door behind them there was a long pause. "What did you want to talk to me about, Ashton?"

He was quiet for several long moments more before he spoke. "Why did you leave like that this morning, Netherland?"

"Because it was for the best," she said, although she would be the first to admit to the pang of regret she felt at having done so. At the time she had been confused and had done the only thing she could think of doing, and that was to run.

"Best for whom?" he asked, staring down into her eyes.

"It was best for the both of us, Ashton. I lost my head and played with fire last night. Too many more times doing that, and I'm liable to get burned."

Ashton gave her a long, thoughtful look. "Do you think I would hurt you?"

"Not intentionally, no. But there is a possibility. You said some things last night that I can't let go to my head."

Ashton reached up and smoothed a curl from her face. "Then let them go to your heart instead. I meant what I said, Netherland. I love you."

"You might think that you do," she responded quietly.

Ashton smiled tenderly. "I'm not a man who does not know his mind or his heart. I know love when I feel it, Netherland."

"Do you?"

"Yes."

"Have you ever been in love before?"

"No."

Netherland frowned at how quickly he had answered. "Never?"

"No."

"But you have been involved in affairs?"

Ashton nodded. "What I did in the past does not concern you, just like what you've done doesn't concern me. What matters is here. Now. Us."

Feeling distinctively uncomfortable with where the conversation was headed, Netherland drew in a deep breath. "If we're through talking, I suggest we go back and rejoin the others."

"Will you come to my hotel room when you leave here tonight and sleep with me again? I enjoyed the feel of your body cuddled against mine."

The mental picture his words, spoken in a deep, husky voice, evoked was simply too much to think of or to remember. But she did. He had held her tenderly in his arms, and had kissed her passionately during all hours of the night. He had touched her intimately whenever he'd felt good and ready. But that was as far as he had gone. He had stuck to his word and not made love to her, although she'd known that his body had been in a hard state during most of the night.

"I can't, Ashton."

He reached out and took her hand in his and placed his hotel-room key in it. "Keep this in case you change your mind."

She stiffened slightly. "I won't."

He looked at her, his eyes delving deep into hers. "I hope you will."

He leaned forward and placed a kiss on Netherland's lips before turning and walking out of her office.

* * *

For the remainder of the night Netherland tried keeping busy and ignoring Ashton's presence, which wasn't an easy thing to do. She even tried pretending nonchalance when she noted some woman had boldly decided to join him at his table. She refused to believe that the emotion that was rearing its ugly head inside of her was jealousy. She had no reason to get jealous of any woman who made a pass at Ashton.

"Don't worry about Tasha. It's obvious that Ashton is bored stiff."

Netherland quirked a brow at Rainey. "I beg your pardon."

Rainey smiled. "And I beg yours. Don't pretend you haven't noticed Tasha McQuire sitting at Ashton's table or the way she's trying to come on to him. She's wasting her time."

Although Netherland didn't want to admit it, she hoped the woman was indeed wasting her time. "It doesn't matter to me."

"Doesn't it, Nettie? When are you going to come out of your hard shell and admit that you feel something for Ashton Sinclair?"

Rainey's question had bugged her most of the night, long after she had closed the restaurant and driven home. She refused to take the highway that led to the place where Ashton was staying. Instead she kept her mind and attention focused on the route that went directly to her house.

Once there she undressed and took a leisurely shower. After getting dressed for bed she took the time to enjoy a cup of herbal tea while reading the latest issue of *People* magazine.

Later when she got into bed, images of Ashton flooded her mind. They were images of how he had looked last night wearing just a loincloth and how he had looked that day wearing a pullover shirt and a pair of jeans. Then there were images of them sitting across from each other in the middle of his bed, Indian-style, in their underwear, while he told her he loved her.

As she adjusted the pillow beneath her head, she couldn't help but close her eyes and dream of last night and how he had held her close.

Netherland opened her eyes out of a deep sleep. Her bedroom had somehow gotten warm. It didn't take long for her to realize that it wasn't the room that had gotten warm but her body. She had awakened from amidst a dream she'd been having of Ashton.

Kicking her bedcovers aside she flipped to her side to find another comfortable position and suddenly, unerringly, became joltingly aware that someone else was in the room with her. She took a deep breath, telling herself that couldn't be possible. She had an alarm system. Her alarm would have sounded had anyone entered her home uninvited. But she still pulled herself up in the bed, and fighting against the darkness surrounding her, glanced around the room as fear coursed through her.

She then detected movement and moments later a figure moved into the dim lighting that came through the bedroom window from one of the streetlights.

Ashton!

He stood at the foot of her bed, looking at her and wearing nothing but a loincloth. The look in his eyes was dark and sensual. She blinked, wondering how he'd known where she lived and how he had gotten inside past her alarm system, but at the moment not caring about either of those things as he continued to watch her without saying anything.

Netherland's breath lodged in her throat. Her breathing became irregular, and the heat in the center of her began to flame. He wore a band around his head and his hair, which had been pulled back in a ponytail the last few times she had seen him, was now undone and flowing wildly about his shoulders.

He looked savage. Untamed. Primitive.

Then slowly, he climbed onto the bed with her. When they came close, almost face-to-face, he paused and met her gaze. "I came to you, Netherland."

She reached out, and his body felt hot to her touch. She made a sound of a moan deep within her throat just moments before he captured her lips with his. Her body melted, any resistance dissolved as their mouths mated and at the same time aroused every part of her body. She didn't understand why he had come to her tonight but he was here, holding her in his arms and kissing her as if there would be no tomorrow.

And then he began touching her, letting his hands roam all over her body, eliciting a moan from deep within her throat. His hands were working their magic on her, touching her everywhere.

"Ashton!"

"Shhh, it's okay, baby, I'm right here. Please let me love you this way."

And she did.

He made love to her with his fingers and mouth, touching her gently, tasting her and driving her over the edge. Netherland's breathing came faster as tension and sensations built within her. When she came apart in his arms—when the waves of fulfillment raced through her body, he continued to kiss her, tasting each one of her moans, tremors.

Afterward, he held her tight in his arms and, pulling her down beside him, he held her tenderly as they slept.

The next morning, Netherland came awake and glanced around the room. She blinked once, twice, wondering if perhaps she had dreamed the entire thing. But then she glanced at the nightstand next to the bed, which provided proof of Ashton's midnight visit.

He had left his headband so that she wouldn't have any doubt that what she shared last night with him had been real. He hadn't made love to her, at least not in the traditional sense, but love her he had. Her body was still tingling from the aftereffects.

She took a deep inhaling breath. She had no defenses against Ashton. He was determined to breech through any wall she erected. She wasn't safe from him even in her own home. But then, last night, she hadn't wanted to be safe from him. She had wanted everything he had given her and then some.

Netherland knew he would not give up until he had her just where he wanted her, and she couldn't help wondering what his next move would be.

"Did you get the information I asked you to get, Billy?"

Billy Roberts looked at his cousin through the glass partition. Anthony Roberts, known to family and friends as Tony, was not in a good mood. "Tony, why don't you just let it go?" he said, trying to keep his voice low. There were prison guards all around them. "Jada doesn't want you anymore. She divorced you, man."

Tony Roberts's hands tightened to fists at his side. His face got hard as stone. "She's going to pay for doing that, right along with that hotshot attorney of hers. Now tell me what you found out."

Billy shook his head. He hated spying on Jada as Tony had instructed him to do but everyone in the family knew that Tony had a mean streak. The last thing Billy wanted was to make his cousin angry and give him a reason to come looking for him, just as Tony intended to go looking for Jada, once he got out of the slammer.

"Jada's working at this restaurant, man. It's a real nice place. She's been working there for over two weeks."

Tony frowned. "Who owns the place?"

Billy raised eyes to the ceiling. "How would I know and what difference does it make, Tony?"

"It makes a lot of difference to me. No one should have given her a job. I take care of what's mine. No one takes care of Jada but me."

"And just how were you supposed to take care of her locked up in here?"

Tony's features darkened. "I wouldn't be in here if it wasn't for that hotshot attorney getting into my and Jada's business, but her day is coming." His eyes became chilling. "I plan to take care of her when I get out of this stinking place." The look in his eyes was as cold as ice. "I want to know where Jada's living, and I expect you to let me know if she begins messing around with anybody. She's mine and will always be mine. And as soon as I get out of here I'm going to make sure she never forgets that fact again."

Chapter 8

The baby shower for Corinthians Avery Grant, given by Caitlin Madaris and Corinthians's best friend, Brenna Jordache, was a lot of fun. Netherland watched Corinthians open one gift after another. According to Corinthians this was her fourth and final shower. The pressure she'd been feeling in the lower part of her stomach indicated it wouldn't be too much longer before she and Trevor became parents.

"So, Nettie…" Syneda Madaris, who was sitting next to her on a love seat, leaned in close and whispered beneath the hum of "oooohs" and "ahhhhhs" going around the room with each gift Corinthians opened. "What's going on with you and Ashton Sinclair?"

Netherland took a slow sip of her wine and met

Syneda's curious gaze. Syneda was known to be direct and straight to the point. "What makes you think something is going on?"

A smile twitched at Syneda's lips. "I have eyes, Nettie. Even a blind person would be able to detect there's something going on between the two of you. It's so obvious."

Netherland frowned. "In what way?"

Syneda gave a rueful smile. "In the way he looks at you. I couldn't help noticing the way Ashton's face lit up when you arrived here today. And the way he hesitated to leave when the guys suggested they become scarce and go to my place for drinks. The man acted like he didn't want you out of his sight."

Muffling a sigh, Netherland said softly, "I don't know what I'm going to do with him."

Syneda chuckled. "Do you actually need some ideas?"

Netherland couldn't help but find amusement in what she'd just said, too. "I know that any woman would be gloating if they were the center of Ashton Sinclair's attention."

"But not you?"

"No, not me."

Syneda's smile faded. "This sounds serious." She reached for her cup of milk. "Come with me for a minute. We need to talk."

Moments later Netherland found herself alone with Syneda in Caitlin's kitchen and opening up and telling the other woman why she and Ashton could never have a future together. Syneda hadn't said anything but had attentively listened to her every word.

"Did you know I almost lost Clayton because of something similar?" Syneda said, her voice dropping as she remembered that time. "Because of my childhood I didn't want to fall in love and get close to a man. In fact I had broken things off with Clayton."

"But the two of you got back together."

"Yes, because a very wise woman, who ended up being my mother-in-law, had a long talk with me and made me aware of one important thing."

"And what was that?"

Syneda smiled. "That when you love someone, truly love someone, nothing else matters because together the two of you can work out anything."

Netherland sighed deeply. "I'd never ask Ashton to give up military life for me."

"Then there has to be another way, Nettie. It has to be a way that the both of you are comfortable with. But first you have to decide if what you feel for him is worth it."

"And what makes you think I feel anything for him?"

Syneda tilted her glass of milk to her lips and took a leisurely sip before saying, "Woman's intuition along with what I'm seeing with my own eyes. I noticed Ashton's reaction to you but I noticed your reaction to him, as well."

"What you saw was sexual attraction."

Syneda chuckled. "Yeah, I know all about that,

too. Trust me. That's something Clayton and I still have plenty of. I didn't get pregnant because we didn't have anything better to do at the time." Her smile widened. "The biggest question in our minds is not when I got pregnant but where I got pregnant. We think it was the time in the elevator."

Netherland placed her hand over her mouth to keep from laughing. "You and Clayton are simply scandalous."

Syneda shared Netherland's amusement. "No, we're in love first and scandalous second. Clayton is the type of man who needs a woman who keeps him on his toes…and his back. He needs excitement in his life, and I make it a point to give him all the excitement he can handle and then some. I can see us still making out in an elevator when we're in our eighties."

Netherland shook her head as she pinched tears of laughter from her eyes. Knowing Clayton and Syneda, she could see it, too. They were perfect for each other in every way.

A few moments of silence passed before Syneda said, "I'm curious, Nettie, on just how you plan to handle next week."

Netherland raised a brow. "Next week?"

"Yes. The Brothers Auction. Ashton is the headliner, and you know women will be bidding on him right and left. Do you plan to bid on him?"

"Why would I?"

"Because if you don't, some other woman will be

spending a weekend in New Orleans with your man. Do you want that?"

Netherland didn't say anything for the longest time before she finally admitted, "No." The thought of another woman spending time with Ashton didn't sit well with her. Although she knew the two of them didn't necessarily have to become intimate, a weekend was a weekend. A lot could happen in two days.

"Then I think you should come up with a plan to do something about it," Syneda whispered. "If that was Clayton being bidden on, the only woman he would be spending a weekend with is me. I'd make sure of it," Syneda said, smiling tenderly. "And maybe that's just what you and Ashton need."

"What?"

"Time alone somewhere. To talk and come up with some solution to your problems."

Netherland looked at Syneda thoughtfully. Maybe she was right.

The men sat around Clayton's living room talking. Trent Jordache, the man who recently married Corinthians's best friend, Brenna, was telling them how he had met and fallen in love with Brenna when she had taken a three-week cruise to Africa aboard the cruise ship he owned.

Ashton sat listening attentively as all the other men then recalled how they had met their wives and subsequently gotten them to the altar. He was glad to know that none of them had had it easy. All of them had faced some kind of challenge from their spouses during the courtship. He sighed with relief, knowing that at least he wasn't the Lone Ranger. Netherland wasn't the only stubborn woman in the world.

"Excuse me, but can we change the subject? All this talk about love and happiness is boring me to tears," Alex Maxwell said, frowning before he took another swallow of beer. At twenty-nine he was the youngest among them and evidently the least likely to be hauled to the altar anytime soon.

"Don't mind him," Trask Maxwell said in defense of his brother. "He's pissed because there's a good chance Angela Meadows is going to snatch him up the night of the Brothers Auction. Rumor has it that she has enough money to bid on two men this year."

Alex glared at his brother. He then turned his glare on Clayton. "I can't believe I let your wife talk me into doing it."

"Chill, man," Clayton said, grinning. "Don't get mad at me. You can't turn Syneda down any more than I can, especially after she turns those beguiling sea-green eyes on you. Admit it."

Alex reluctantly smiled. "Yeah, okay, I admit it. But I don't have to like it." He then turned his attention to Ashton. "You're pretty calm about all of this, and you're being billed as top dog. Why aren't you sweating at the possibility of spending a weekend in New Orleans with Angela the Man Hater?"

Ashton took a swig of his beer, then said, "It won't happen. I've got a backup plan."

Alex raised a dark curious brow. "What sort of backup plan?"

Ashton smiled. "I'm going to plant someone in the audience who will be given instructions to top the highest bid no matter what it is, using my money, of course. Then I will present the winning bid to the woman I want. Netherland."

Dex Madaris chuckled. "I hope the person you're planting in the audience is a woman. It would definitely raise a few brows if another man came forward and bid on you."

Ashton grinned. "I've taken that under consideration."

"Hey, what about me?" Alex said to the other men. "Maybe I should come up with some sort of plan just in case."

Trask Maxwell smiled at his brother. "That may not be a bad idea. Is there any particular woman that you want to bid on you and win?"

Alex thought of all the single women he knew. Like most men he appreciated women. However, he also knew his priorities. His busy schedule as a private investigator did not allow a lot of free time, which didn't bother him in the least. Maxwell Security and Investigators was the most important thing to him right now. An involvement with a woman was low on his totem pole. "No, not really. And although it's dinner for just one night, I'm leery as to whom I may end up with. Any of you got any bright ideas? I prefer not suffering through any meal with a woman I don't know."

Trevor shrugged. "You know Gina, and she would do it in a heartbeat to help you out. Unfortunately, she'll be out of town that night." Gina was Trevor's twenty-eight-year-old sister.

Alex nodded. He would have felt comfortable with Gina since they were friends and had been for years.

"What about Christy?" Justin Madaris asked, smiling. "She'll be there that night. Why not let her bid on you?"

Alex raised a brow. Christy was the Madaris brothers' twenty-year-old sister who would be cele-brating her twenty-first birthday in a few months. He saw her rather infrequently these days since she was away attending college at Howard University in D.C. But he had seen a recent picture of her a few months ago in her uncle Jake's office. She was no longer the gangly kid he remembered. "Do you think she would do it?"

Dex Madaris grinned. "I don't see why not. She'll be getting a free meal out of it. Besides, she won't be spending her money to do the bidding but yours."

Alex nodded. "I would feel a lot better if I was taking a person out to dinner that I knew."

Clayton chuckled. "Well, you do know Christy. You've known her since the day she was born. She'll do it if we were to ask her."

Alex looked at the three Madaris brothers. He knew how overprotective they were of their kid sister. "And my taking her out won't bother the three of you?"

Dex shrugged. "Why should it? It's not like you'll be taking her out on a real date."

Alex nodded. "You're right. It won't be like a real date."

Ashton, who'd been following the conversation, leaned back in his chair and covered his jaw with the palm of his hand. He wondered if he'd imagined things or if he had seen a flicker of apprehension in Alex Maxwell's eyes just now. Or was it interest?

"And that, ladies, is how I met Trent and fell in love," Brenna Jordache said, winding up her conversation. The baby shower had officially ended half an hour ago and everyone who'd remained had gathered in Caitlin's kitchen to eat more cake and sip more wine.

"Trent was living in Chicago, and you were living in Austin. Weren't you concerned about where the two of you would be staying?" Netherland couldn't help but ask. To her that would have made a monumental difference in whether or not things would have worked out.

Brenna smiled. "No, not really. I travel around a lot with my job, so technically I can live anywhere, which in a way is exactly what we'll be doing. Trent has a number of business interests in Chicago, Jacksonville, Florida, and Atlanta. He even takes periodic cruises on his ship to make sure things are running smoothly. When I'm not traveling on business, I plan to travel with him. I love traveling and now I look forward to doing so with my husband. I'll make whatever sacrifices I need to make to be with him." Her smile widened. "It will be worth it."

"I agree with Brenna," Caitlin Madaris piped in as she walked around the kitchen, returning things to their proper places. She smiled when she turned and looked at the women sitting at her kitchen table. "When I first met Dex I was only twenty-one, and had just finished college and was looking forward to going back to school in the fall to work on my master's degree. He was thirty-two, and on his way to spend two years at work in the oil fields of Australia. But when I fell for him, I fell so hard it didn't matter to me where he was headed. I had decided to give up everything to go wherever he went. I loved him just that much."

Netherland took another sip of her wine, thinking that evidently her mother had felt the same way about her father. During the thirty-five years her father was in the army, her mother had traveled wherever he went and not once had Netherland heard her complain. She couldn't help but wonder how her mother had handled it during the times her father was away, sometimes as long as six months at a time. Her father, now retired from the military, had moved his wife to his birthplace, Columbus, Ohio, and they were living the easy life of retirees.

"More fruit punch, Netherland?" Syneda asked, bringing Netherland out of her thoughts.

"No, I've had enough. In fact I think I'll call it a night. I want to go home and get to bed early so I can attend early-morning service at church tomorrow."

Syneda nodded. "I hope you don't feel I was getting all into your business earlier tonight when we had our little talk."

Netherland shook her head. "No. I enjoyed our conversation. It gives me a lot to think about. A whole lot."

The eleven o'clock news was just coming on by the time Netherland got into bed. She had called the restaurant to make sure things were going okay. Since it was Saturday night, Sisters didn't close until two in the morning.

She had just turned the television off when her doorbell rang. As she was putting on her robe, her pulse increased at the thought it might be Ashton. Had he decided to use the door instead of entering her home as he had done the night before, like a thief in the night? She still couldn't figure out how he had gotten past the alarm system. The technician she had called to check it that day had indicated it was working fine.

Netherland smiled after looking through her peephole. She snatched her door open immediately.

"Rome!"

She immediately went into her brother's outstretched arms. It had been almost a year since she had seen him last. His last deployment for the marines had taken him to Iran. "When did you get back to the States? You weren't expected home until the summer. Do Mom and Dad know you're back?"

Rome Kalloren smiled at his sister as he continued to hold her. "Yeah, the folks know I'm back. I just spent a week with them. Now it's your turn to put up with me for a while."

Netherland looked up at her brother, smiling. Because of his size and height he looked older than she did, when in fact he was a year younger. He stood tall and was proudly wearing his Marine Corps uniform. "I'd gladly put up with you anytime. We have so much to catch up on and I—"

"There better be a good reason why you're holding my woman in your arms, Sergeant."

The low, lethal voice penetrated the night air. Netherland felt her brother's body stiffen. With his arms still around her waist, Rome slowly turned around.

And so did she.

The man walking toward them was not smiling. In fact he looked as if he was ready to kill somebody, and the stare he was giving her brother indicated he was the intended victim.

Chapter 9

Netherland hardly recognized Ashton. The anger pulsing out of him made him appear like a different person. Something deep tugged at her insides with the knowledge that the anger was because of her. She'd never known a man to show any possessiveness toward her.

But she immediately told herself to get a grip. Ashton's anger may be on her behalf but at the moment it was directed at her brother. She took a step forward. "Ashton, this is my brother Rome Kalloren," she said softly, quickly. "Rome, this is Ashton Sinclair."

"Colonel Sinclair, sir!"

Netherland watched as her brother immediately

snapped to attention and focused his gaze on the man now standing in front of him.

"At ease, Kalloren," Ashton said.

Netherland frowned. "Of course he can be at ease," she said curtly, looking at the two men. "He's on his own time, not the military's."

Rome drew in a long, deep breath as he relaxed somewhat. But his gaze still remained on Ashton. He wondered if Netherland knew just whom she was talking to. Colonel Ashton Sinclair was a legend in his own right among the marines. He had earned every stripe he wore as well as the deep respect from other marines. The man used to be part of the Force Recon Unit, for heaven's sake! There weren't too many marines who hadn't heard, at one time or another, about the "Fearless Four," which consisted of then Captain Ashton Sinclair, Captain Trevor Grant, Captain Drake Warren and the only female that had come close to becoming a Recon, Captain Sandy Carroll. Although Captain Carroll had been killed in the mission, the team had managed to successfully rescue a group of United States dignitaries held hostage in Haiti. That had been around four years ago.

Rome studied Ashton intently and wondered what the colonel's relationship was to his sister. Had he heard the man correctly when he had referred to her as "my woman"? Rome cleared his throat. "Nettie, I'm a marine, twenty-four-seven, in uniform or out."

Netherland crossed her arms over her chest. "Not tonight you're not. You're my brother who I haven't seen in more than a year." She then gazed at Ashton. "I don't appreciate your pulling rank on Rome."

Rome raised his eyes heavenward. Was Netherland trying to get him court-martialed or something? The man had every right to pull rank if he wanted to. "Nettie, please, I—"

"No, Kalloren," Ashton said, interrupting whatever Rome was about to say. "Let me handle your sister." He then turned his complete attention to Netherland, who stood glaring at him. "I was not pulling rank, Netherland. What your brother did when he recognized who and what I was, is a matter of respect. And he's right. A marine is a marine at all times."

Rome looked at Ashton. He then looked at Netherland. Something was definitely going on between them, and he found that hard to believe. Everyone in the family knew of Netherland's aversion to any man in the military. And Colonel Sinclair was definitely military. He cleared his throat again. "Is there something going on here that I should know about?"

"Yes."

"No!"

Both Ashton and Netherland said the words simultaneously.

Rome nodded. "I see." But he didn't see really. There was evidently some lack of communication between the two, and he decided to get to the bottom of it right away. Ashton may be a colonel but Netherland was his sister. His only sister. He reached his hand out to Ashton. "It's nice seeing you again, sir.

The last time was around three years ago when I was stationed in South Carolina."

Ashton nodded as he returned the firm handshake. "Same here, Kalloren."

"Ashton, why are you here?" Netherland decided to ask. It seemed both men had forgotten her presence.

Ashton smiled at her. "I came to see you."

She frowned and tried to ignore the deep fluttering in her stomach with his words and megawatt smile. "As you can see, I have company. Rome just arrived."

Ashton's smile widened. "Yes, I'm aware of that now." He then glanced back at Rome and saw the zillion questions lodged in the younger man's eyes and decided he may as well set the matter straight since he doubted Netherland would. "How would you like to go to Sisters and join me in a drink, Kalloren?"

Rome met Ashton's gaze. "That sounds like a winner."

"But you just got here, Rome. You haven't taken your bags out of the car. You can talk to Ashton some other time," Netherland said, glaring at the two men.

Rome glanced at Ashton, then back at his sister. He needed to have a talk with the colonel tonight. He was determined to find out what the man's intentions were since he seemed so possessive of Netherland, and she appeared not to want to be possessed. "No, I think Sinclair and I should talk tonight." He leaned over and kissed her cheek. "Don't wait up, sis. I'll use my spare key."

* * *

Rome pulled in a long, deep breath as he watched the man sitting across from him take a leisurely sip of his drink. All the while Ashton's gaze was on him. He would rather face a firing squad than draw Colonel Sinclair's anger, but he needed answers to all the questions buzzing around in his head.

"It might be better if you just go ahead and ask me what you want to know, Kalloren."

Rome took a sip of his own drink before he said, "Yeah, it might be better at that." He leaned back in his chair. "Is something going on between you and Nettie? Earlier you hinted there was, and she hinted there wasn't."

A long minute passed in tense silence before Ashton finally answered. "Yes, there is something going on between me and Netherland, although she wishes otherwise."

Rome nodded. "Because you're in the military." It was a statement, not a question.

"I see you know your sister fairly well."

"The entire family does. We know that of all of us, she had the hardest time dealing with moving around. And because of it she swore up and down that she would never get involved with someone in the military."

"Yeah, I've heard the story but I'm not buying it."

Rome studied the colonel. He'd heard the man could be a stubborn cuss when he wanted to be. "I hate to be the one to tell you this but I always figured she meant it."

"And I'm sure she probably thinks the same thing."

"But you don't?"

"No."

"I'm curious to know why."

Ashton took another sip before responding. "My and Netherland's destinies are to be joined as one, entwined. It was shown to me in a vision."

Rome released a slow smile. "Did you tell Netherland that?"

"Yes."

"Did she believe you about the vision?"

"No."

Rome wasn't surprised.

"Would either of you like anything else to drink?"

Rome's breath became lodged in his throat when he glanced up into the most beautiful pair of brown eyes he had ever seen, and the features that went along with those eyes made him exhale a soft breath. He quickly looked at the name tag the woman wore, which read *Jada*. He swallowed before saying, "No thanks, ma'am, that's all for me."

She nodded before glancing at Ashton.

"That's all for me, too. Thanks."

Jada nodded and quickly walked off. Rome couldn't take his eyes off her and watched until she had disappeared around a corner.

"Do you have any suggestions on the best way to handle Netherland?"

Rome had been so attentive watching Jada that he jumped when Ashton's deep voice rumbled across the table. He tried to laugh it off by saying, "Sorry about that. My mind must have drifted elsewhere."

"Evidently."

"What were you asking me about Nettie?"

"I asked if you had any suggestions on the best way to handle her."

Rome looked at Ashton intently. "To be honest with you, I'm wondering why you want to. Nettie can be a pain in the rear end when she gets a bee in her bonnet about something, and that bee has been in her bonnet about military men for a long time."

"Then it's about time that I get rid of that bee, don't you think?"

Rome figured if any man could, it would be the colonel. He was one tough marine. However, knowing Nettie, the assignment wouldn't be an easy one.

At that moment Jada walked past their table again and immediately captured Rome's attention. Ashton shook his head, smiling as he watched the younger man's mind drift off again.

Chapter 10

The next morning Netherland sat across from Rome, eating breakfast, refusing to give in to the urge to ask what went on with him and Ashton last night. It had been late when he had gotten back but she had refused to rush out of her bedroom for details.

"You've made a number of changes at Sisters and all of them I like," Rome said, breaking the silence.

Netherland took a sip of her coffee before saying, "Thanks. Business has increased over the past year so I decided to stay on top of things. If you're good to your business, then it will be good to you."

Rome nodded and cleared his throat before saying, "I also note you have a lot of new people working for you."

Netherland lifted her gaze from her coffee cup when she heard the tightness in her brother's voice. She could always tell when something was on his mind by the tone of his voice. "Yes, I've got a number of new people working for me. Any one of them in particular you noticed right off?"

"Now that you mention it, there was one person," he said, casting one quick look at Netherland to see if he had her attention. "It's one of your hostesses, a woman by the name of Jada."

Netherland frowned, nodding. "What about Jada?"

Rome shrugged and to Netherland's way of thinking her huge hunk of a brother suddenly became somewhat shy. "She's beautiful."

"Yes, she's certainly that." Netherland studied her brother and slightly curved her lips in a smile. Of her four brothers Rome was the most easygoing. He was also the only one of them who didn't make it a point to constantly be in and out of relationships. This was the first time she had known him to show any interest in a woman since Kimmy's death. Rome's fiancée, Kimberly Albright, who'd also been a marine, had died when the military aircraft she'd been a passenger on had gone down somewhere over the Pacific Ocean due to mechanical failure. That had been nearly five years ago, and Rome had taken her death extremely hard.

Netherland then thought of Jada and all the things that had gone wrong in her young life. If Rome was interested in Jada, he had her full blessings. Both

Jada and Rome were individuals who should experience happiness. But still she felt she needed to inform Rome of some things. "Jada just got out of a bad marriage, Rome. If you're interested in her, she may not easily reciprocate."

Rome smiled. "In other words she may be difficult with me the same way you're being difficult with Sinclair?"

Netherland slowly fingered the design on her coffee cup, for the moment refusing to meet her brother's gaze. "I'm not trying to be difficult with anyone. Ashton just doesn't want to accept what is not to be."

"He's a good man, Nettie."

Netherland lifted her gaze. "He's military."

"And because of it you're condemning him?"

Netherland's gaze narrowed. "I am not condemning him. I made it clear to him when we first met nearly three years ago that I had no interest in anyone in the military."

"It didn't look that way to me."

Netherland lifted a brow. "What?"

"That you aren't interested."

Netherland pushed away from the table and stood. "So we can turn each other on. Big deal."

"Yes, I think for Sinclair it's a big deal. And the sooner you realize that, the better. I don't think he's going to give up until he has you just where he wants you. You're one battle he's determined to win."

"Then he'll continue to have one hell of a fight on his hands."

A slow smile touched Rome's lips. "I believe he knows that and has gotten prepared for it."

Netherland glared at her brother. "Then he's in for the fight of his life."

"Or you're in for the fight of yours."

Netherland sighed. Over the past week or so she'd been wavering on her feelings about Ashton. Having spent two nights sleeping in his arms hadn't helped matters. Now her common sense was returning. He couldn't be an unexpected midnight visitor as long as Rome was staying with her. Then after Saturday night he would be someone else's concern for a weekend. His time and attention would be given to whatever woman bid the highest for him.

"I'll see you after I get back from church." She made her way out of the kitchen, then turned around. "Better yet, why don't you meet me later at Sisters for lunch?" She smiled. "I know for a fact that Jada is working today."

He nodded briefly, then smiled and said, "I'll be there."

Netherland knew she could always depend on the after-church crowd on Sunday to keep things busy at Sisters, and today was no exception.

While at church, the pastor had held her attention while he'd preached a good sermon about the essence of giving. But now at Sisters something else was holding her mind captive, she thought as she watched Ashton enter her establishment.

Her heart thundered in her chest when their gazes locked. Her heartbeat accelerated and she began wavering about how she felt at seeing him. For some reason she couldn't help but think how lonely her bed had felt the previous night without him holding her through the night in his warm embrace.

She inhaled deeply and tried shaking off those thoughts. She had to stand firm. She couldn't let Ashton break down her resolve. She'd felt so confident when she had given Rome her spiel that morning at breakfast because she had meant what she'd said. She would give Ashton the fight of his life or die trying.

"Hey, there's the colonel," Rome said, smiling. Before she could stop him he had motioned Ashton over to their table. Netherland glared at her brother. He hadn't been much company since all of his attention had been on Jada since arriving; however, it seemed that he was able to snap out of it long enough to notice Ashton's entrance. And without asking if it was okay, he had invited him to eat with them.

Ooh-rah, just what I need. The last thing I want is for him to be sitting with me at the table, Netherland thought. "Thanks for asking if I mind Ashton sitting with us, Rome," she said in a bitter tone.

Rome glanced back at her. He studied her surly expression. "It won't kill you to be hospitable, Nettie. Did you want him to eat by himself?"

"It wouldn't bother me in the least if he did. He's been doing it for the past two weeks or so. Anytime he comes in here he eats alone." *He eats alone and stares at me,* she wanted to expound and decided not to. Taking a deep breath she braced herself for Ashton's arrival.

"Netherland. Rome. How are things going?" he murmured, and the rumble of his voice, deep and sexy, rolled up her spine.

Netherland watched as Ashton took the chair across from her. When he had gotten seated, she glanced into his eyes, and the flicker of desire that suddenly quickened her insides made the hand holding her fork tremble slightly. She placed the eating utensil down. "Things are going well, Ashton," she managed to get out.

Rome chuckled. "Personally, I'd be doing a whole lot better if I could get one of Nettie's hostesses to notice me."

Ashton laughed gently as he glanced around the room and looked at the woman that he knew was the object of Rome's interest. He then returned his full gaze to Netherland although his words were directed at Rome. "Sometimes you can't wait for a woman to notice you, Kalloren. Every once in a while you have to take matters into your own hands and do whatever has to be done to make sure she knows that you're interested. I believe you should always let a woman know when she's wanted."

Netherland inhaled sharply as Ashton's gaze became a heated caress. She tried to think of something to say and couldn't. So she picked up her fork again and began eating the rest of her meal as she tried to ignore him as well as the comment he'd made.

"So you don't believe in the subtle approach, Colonel?"

"No. I believe in going after what you want when you think the time is right."

Rome nodded. "And how do you know when the time is right?"

Netherland couldn't help but glance back at Ashton. His gaze held hers, and as she watched, his eyes seemed to go darker, deeper. A flush of heat spread up her legs and worked its way to her center. Then the curl of something hot and delicious settled there and stayed. Even shifting in her chair couldn't get rid of it. Ashton's gaze was doing things to her insides.

"Trust me, you'll know when the time is right," he responded to Rome.

"Some women don't want to know they are wanted," she decided to add to break whatever exchange was passing between her and Ashton.

"And some don't think they want to know but actually they do. I would think any woman would want to know they were loved and wanted."

Netherland had a difficult time swallowing her food when she thought of the two times Ashton had held her in his arms while she'd slept. Most times when she had awakened during the night to find his body tucked close to hers, he had instantly become awake and had whispered words to her that had made her feel wanted and loved. And they hadn't made love either of those times. But yet, their minds and bodies had somehow connected in another way. It was in a way she didn't want. It was in a way she hadn't realized until now.

"I think being direct may not be a bad approach," Rome said to no one in particular as he stood. He saw Jada gather her purse and belongings. Evidently her shift had ended. "Will the two of you excuse me for a minute?" He threw a few bills on the table and without waiting to see if Ashton and Netherland would excuse him or not, walked off, leaving them alone.

Netherland watched her brother move across the room to Jada. "I hope he takes things slow with her," she said softly.

When she looked back around at Ashton he met her gaze directly. "Some things aren't meant to be taken slow, Netherland."

She stared into his eyes and felt her body melt. She forced herself to blink to rid her mind of thoughts that should not be there.

"I have to leave town for a while."

Netherland blinked again when Ashton's words registered. "You're leaving?"

He smiled. "Yes. Something has come up in D.C. that I have to handle."

Netherland nodded. She didn't want to feel the sense of loneliness his words had instilled within her, but she did so anyway. She missed him already. "Are you gone for good or will you be back?"

Ashton gave her a smile. "Oh, I'll be back. In fact

I'll be back in time for the Brothers Auction on Saturday night."

Netherland nodded. She knew there would be a number of women who would be glad to hear that. "I hope you have a safe trip, Ashton."

"Thanks."

Netherland chewed at her bottom lip. Suddenly she was no longer hungry for the food on her plate. At that moment a hostess came up to take Ashton's order. Netherland used that time to excuse herself and immediately went to her office. Closing the door behind her, she leaned against it. She wondered why the knowledge of Ashton's leaving was affecting her this way. She wondered why she felt such an extreme sense of loss. Ashton was a complication she didn't want or need in her life.

Images flashed in her mind, especially the image of the two times he'd stood before her wearing nothing but a loincloth. Netherland lifted her head upward, seeking strength from the madness that consumed her and her mind. Maybe with Ashton gone those few days, her life, as well as her mind, would get back to normal.

Netherland sighed as she wondered if anything about her would ever be normal again.

Jada tried not to glance over at the man who had offered to drive her home. At first when he had asked she had hesitated but then she had accepted his offer. She knew from the other hostesses that he was one of Nettie's brothers. She had noticed him right away when he'd come into Sisters the night before. There had been something about him that stood out, even when he'd stood next to Ashton Sinclair; and everyone knew that Mr. Sinclair at times seemed bigger than life. There had been something calm and trusting in Rome Kalloren's eyes that had drawn her to him last night and again today.

"Looks like rain."

Rome's observation on the weather pulled Jada from out of her thoughts. "Yes, it does, doesn't it."

Rome nodded as he brought his car to a stop at a traffic light. "Where are you from? Do I detect a northern accent?"

Jada smiled. There was also something about him that made her feel comfortable. "Yes, afraid you do. I'm a New Yorker, born and raised in the Bronx."

"What brought you to Texas?"

Pain settled on Jada as she remembered what had brought her to Texas. "My husband."

Rome nodded. "You mean your ex-husband, don't you?"

Jada glanced over at him. "Yes, my *ex*-husband. I just recently got divorced."

"How long ago?"

"Only a few weeks, but we had been separated for five months." Jada wondered if Netherland had told him about her particular situation.

"So things are over between the two of you?"

Jada had a reason to smile. For the first time in her

life she could answer yes to that question. "Yes, things are over between us."

"Are you currently involved with anyone?"

"No."

"Good."

Jada lifted a brow at Rome's response. "And why is it good?"

Rome glanced over at her, smiling. "Because I want to get to know you better while I'm here in town."

"You may not want to do that."

"Why?"

"There are reasons."

Rome shook his head when he brought his car to a stop in front of her apartment building. "There aren't any reasons that matter to me."

A part of Jada wanted to believe that. She wanted so much to believe what he'd just said was true. "Thanks for bringing me home, Rome."

"You're welcome." And in the next breath he asked, "Would you go to a movie with me tomorrow night?"

A part of Jada wanted to say no, but another part wanted to say yes. It was the part that wanted to put her ordeal with Tony behind her and to get on with her life. She didn't respond to Rome's question for a few brief moments before finally saying, "Yes. I'd love to go to the movies with you."

Chapter 11

It had been the longest week of her life, Netherland thought as she did a quick walk-through of Sisters to make sure everything was in place for tomorrow night's affair. All week she had battled the flare-up of memories that assailed her at different times. Ashton's nightly presence in her establishment had become such a norm that on numerous occasions during the week she had caught her gaze seeking him out, only to remember that he'd left for D.C. And then at night when she would close her eyes to sleep, images of him were there in her mind.

When Netherland heard a laugh she glanced across the room to where her brother and Jada were talking. It was unbelievable the difference Rome had made in Jada's persona in just a few days. The woman was now actually smiling most of the time. Netherland knew that Rome had taken Jada to a movie on Monday night and had taken her to the state fair on Wednesday. But according to Rome, things between him and Jada were moving slow. Although she had agreed to go to those two places with him, they had yet to get beyond just holding hands. Rome had mentioned that he noticed how skittish and nervous Jada was at times around him. Netherland had decided not to mention to him about Jada's ex-husband's abuse of her. Netherland felt that information was something Jada would have to share with Rome when and if she ever got comfortable enough to do so.

"They look good together, don't they?" Rainey observed when she noticed Netherland watching the couple. "That was the first time I've ever heard Jada laugh about anything. Rome's company seems to be good for her."

Netherland turned around and flashed Rainey a smile. "Yes, and I think he really likes her. She's all he's been talking about lately. It wouldn't surprise me in the least if he were to find a way to stay in contact with her after he leaves."

Rainey nodded. "Speaking of staying in contact, have you heard from Ashton any this week?"

Rainey's question made the pain of missing Ashton that much more profound within Netherland. She had tried to downplay her disappointment that he hadn't called her, but then she hadn't really given him any reason to. "No, but I would imagine he'll be here for tomorrow night's function. At least he said he would."

Rainey chuckled. "I'm so excited about tomorrow night I can't stand it. Just to think movie actors Sterling Hamilton and Diamond Swain Madaris are going to be here."

Netherland nodded. Sterling Hamilton and Diamond Swain Madaris would be serving as MCs for the charity event, which according to ticket sales would be a huge success. In fact it was already sold out. Sisters would definitely have a packed house tomorrow night. "You're still planning on bidding for Alex Maxwell?"

Rainey smiled. "Yes. He's the only one I would be interested in, but I don't intend to let my interest in him get me into the poorhouse. There's only so much of my money that I've set aside to use; after that he can go to the highest bidder with my blessings." She chuckled. "Now Ashton is another matter. I would gladly break the piggy bank for him if I thought it wouldn't test our friendship overly much."

"You can bid on Ashton if you want. This is a free country."

"Yeah, right. I'll pass. You're going to have enough trouble keeping Angela away from him."

Netherland lifted a dark brow. "I don't plan on keeping anyone away from Ashton. Any woman who wants him can bid for him."

"And you still don't plan to bid?"

"No."

"I think you'd be making a mistake. I'd love to see someone knock Angela off her high horse."

"What do you mean?"

"She's been going around bragging all week about the weekend she plans to have with Ashton after she wins. It appears she's no longer a man-hater where Ashton is concerned, but has turned into a number-one nymphomaniac. From what I hear she intends to get her money's worth out of him."

Netherland fought back the spark of jealousy that raced through her and said, "Then I'm happy for Angela."

Rainey shook her head and gazed thoughtfully at Netherland. "I hope you don't live to regret what you're saying, Nettie."

Netherland took a deep breath. She didn't want to tell Rainey but a part of her hoped so, too.

Rome stood just inside the door to Jada's apartment and stared at it in mute admiration. Although the furnishings were sparse, it was a neat, tidy place. They had known each other for almost a week. He had taken her out on two separate occasions, and this was the first time she had taken the initiative to invite him inside.

"Thanks again for bringing me home, Rome," Jada was saying as she walked nervously to the other side of the room. She cleared her throat. "You did say you wanted something to drink, right?"

Rome nodded as he came into the apartment and closed the door behind him. "Yes, I'd love a Coke or Pepsi if you have one."

"Yes, I do. I'll be right back."

Rome watched as she quickly left him to go into the kitchen. She shot one quick glance back at him before leaving the room. He pondered her actions for a minute. If he didn't know better, he would think she was afraid of him for some reason.

He studied her intently when she returned and handed him the ice-cold can of Pepsi. He found her even more beautiful than the first time he'd laid eyes on her. Her shoulder-length hair cascaded around her face like a halo, and her lips were firm and full. But it was her eyes that always managed to take his breath away. They were the most gorgeous set of brown eyes he had ever seen on a woman. "Thanks. Do you mind if I sit down?"

Jada's face tinted with embarrassment. "Oh, I'm sorry, I didn't think to ask you to have a seat. How stupid of me, and—"

"That's okay, Jada." Rome reached out to place a reassuring hand on her shoulders and immediately she recoiled from his touch and took a step away from him. He lifted a brow. "Jada? What is it? Why are you afraid of me?"

She dropped her gaze from his. "My inviting you here was a mistake, Rome. I think I shouldn't have begun seeing you in the first place."

"Why?"

She met his gaze again. "I have issues."

Rome chuckled. "Don't we all?"

"But mine are serious."

Rome studied her as his heart thundered deep within his chest, and a funny feeling settled in the pit of his stomach. "You're not sick or anything like that, are you?"

Jada lifted a surprised brow at the seriousness of his question. "No, it's not about an illness or anything like that."

Rome released a deep sigh. He had lost one woman he loved and he didn't want to lose another one. And a part of him knew that he loved Jada. He'd known that he'd fallen in love with her the first moment he had seen her less than a week ago. He wasn't amazed by that fact. The same thing had happened between him and Kimmy. He had known from the first, and hadn't been interested in another woman since Kimmy's death, until now.

Rome continued to study Jada and he saw her increased nervousness and tenseness as she shifted back and forth under his steady stare. He really didn't care about these issues she was talking about. They didn't matter to him. However, they seemed to matter a great deal to her. "Do you want to talk about these issues?"

She thought about it for a moment, then nodded. "Yes. Then you'll understand why I won't be seeing you again." She inhaled deeply. "You wouldn't want to see me again, anyway."

Rome's gaze slowly drifted over her, and he

wondered why she would think such a thing. There was nothing she could tell him that would keep him away. He took another chance and reached out and took her hand in his. He ignored the deep trembling he felt in it. He grasped it firmly but gently. "Come on, let's sit down and have that talk, all right?"

She nodded and let him lead her over to the sofa.

Netherland drove along the busy highway heading home. Traffic was bumper-to-bumper, which was unusual for this time on a Friday night. She then remembered a rock concert was being held in town.

She yawned, feeling sleepy. It was early yet but the day had been rather busy getting things prepared for tomorrow night. She needed to go home and get a good night's sleep. Things would be even busier the next day. She glanced at her watch. It was a little past eight. She couldn't help wondering if Ashton had arrived back in town. She hated admitting it but she had missed him something fierce. She had spent her nights tossing and turning in bed, waking up thinking, hoping that she would see him standing at the foot of her bed to turn her heated dreams into reality. The longer she went without seeing him, the more her mind and her body longed for him, his touch— every single thing about the man.

Making a quick decision and refusing to think about what it meant, she exited the highway and took the road that would take her to Ashton's hotel.

* * *

Like a dam bursting beneath the huge force of a tidal wave, words poured out of Jada's mouth, from deep within her soul as she told Rome about those days that she had been married to Tony, as well as his kidnapping of her. She lifted her head and met his gaze and said quietly, "So, as you can see I have some things I need to deal with before I jump into a relationship with anyone."

The anger that had consumed Rome while listening to Jada slid into oblivion when her words suddenly consumed him with something else. Compassion. He had compassion and respect for a woman who had gone through what she'd gone through and survived with her self-respect and dignity still intact. He would like to have some private time with Anthony Roberts for hurting her both physically and emotionally. No woman deserved that type of treatment, and no real man would have done that to her, especially the man who had vowed before God to love and protect her for the rest of her life.

"After listening to what you've just shared with me, Jada, I think you're one remarkable woman," he said, soft and low, sensing she needed to hear that but more importantly she needed to believe it.

She laughed shortly, harshly. "Remarkable? What's remarkable about being too afraid to stand up for yourself? I stayed with him for two years and let him use me like a punching bag because I was too weak to leave."

Rome shook his head. "No. The reason you didn't leave is because of the threat he made to your father. You didn't stay with him any longer than necessary after your father's death, did you?"

Jada took a deep breath. "No." In fact, she had left him right after the funeral, taking nothing more than the black dress she had worn and had gone into hiding at the women's shelter. After a month she'd felt it safe to reenter the real world. But it hadn't been. She hadn't known the extent Tony would go to in order to get her back. He kidnapped her, snatched her off the streets in broad daylight, less than a block from where she had begun working as a clerk in a library.

"And that ordeal you went through when he kidnapped you could not have been easy. Yes, Jada, I think you're someone who deserves some happiness in her life. But right now I think what you need is comforting from someone who cares. Can I hold you for a little while and comfort you, Jada?"

Jada nervously sank her teeth into her bottom lip weighing Rome's request. She believed him to be a good person, a strong person...but then she had thought the same thing about Tony in the beginning. She took a deep breath. She couldn't compare every man with Tony's mistreatment of her. And more than anything, she did want Rome to hold her. "Yes," she said quietly, swallowing hard. "You can hold me."

Slowly, Rome took her hands. Gently he pulled her closer to him on the sofa and when she was there, just a breath away, he pulled her into his arms. His grip on her tightened, and she clung to him, burying her face in the strength of his solid chest. Then he heard the sound of her crying and wondered if this was the first good cry she'd had.

"That's it, Jada. Get it all out," he said softly while his hands moved up and down her back in an attempt to aid in her cleansing process. His hold on her tightened when he felt the tremors course through her body. They affected him in a way he didn't know was possible.

A few moments later, her voice came soft, low and close to his ear. "Thanks, Rome, for holding me."

"Jada." His voice sounded hoarse, husky. "Can I kiss you?"

She pulled back and met his gaze. He then reached up and slowly slid the palm of his hand along the curve of her jaw. "Can I kiss you, Jada?" he asked again.

Robbed of any coherent thought, Jada could only nod. That was enough for Rome. He leaned in closer to her and gently took her mouth in his, invading her warmth, demanding her passion and eliciting her trust.

Moments later he groaned when he pulled his mouth from hers. He smiled, then kissed her again. And again.

Netherland used the key Ashton had given her to enter his hotel room. After closing the door behind her she glanced around. She could immediately tell that he had not returned.

She turned to leave and stopped before reaching the door. As much as she wished otherwise, she wanted to be here when he got back. Making another decision that she didn't want to think hard about, she walked back into the room and tossed her purse on a nearby chair. Not wanting to consider the implications of what she was doing, she began removing her clothes. When she had stripped down to her bra and panties and felt the slight chill in the room, she walked over to the closet.

Netherland inhaled deeply when she saw his military uniforms hanging there. She studied each one, imagining how Ashton looked wearing them. It then occurred to her that she had never seen him wearing his military attire. Was it a deliberate move on his part because he knew of her aversion to military men? She pulled a jacket off the hanger and slipped it on. The jacket carried his scent. At the moment she knew it was the closest thing of his that she had. That thought made her feel warm inside. A brief moment later she returned the jacket to the closet.

Still feeling the chill in the room she walked over to the dresser and pulled open a drawer to retrieve one of Ashton's T-shirts. She slipped the shirt over her head, liking the way it felt on her, big and loose. She then moved over to the window and looked out, wondering if he would be returning that evening. Tears stung the back of her eyes when she knew she could not fight what she felt for him any longer, no matter how hard she tried, and God knew she had. For three years she had fought anything developing between them and now she had to admit that she wanted him with a passion. He totally consumed her mind…and her heart. What Syneda, Brenna and Caitlin had said last week at Corinthians's baby shower was true. To sum it up in a nutshell, if you loved someone, really loved that person, then nothing else mattered, especially what he did for a living or where you lived. Somehow she believed in her heart that things between her and Ashton would work out. She had to believe that they would.

"I love him," she murmured, wrapping her arms around her middle. "I didn't want to love him but I do." She couldn't fight her feelings anymore, and she could no longer fight him. Each time she thought she had gotten stronger in her affirmation, then something would come along and contravene. Like this trip of his to Washington. She'd had no idea that not seeing him for five days would have this sort of an affect on her.

Thoughts then whirled around in Netherland's mind. What if Ashton was tired of pursuing her? What if he no longer wanted her? What if his vision had been wrong? There were too many "what ifs," and she didn't want to think about them tonight.

Deciding to save Rome from worrying when she didn't come home, she picked up the phone. When he didn't answer, she left a short message on the answering machine that simply said, "I won't be home tonight, Rome. Don't worry, I'm okay."

After hanging up the phone she went over to the bed, pushed back the covers and slipped between the sheets. She fell asleep instantly thinking about dark eyes, warm arms and the sexy smile that belonged to the man she loved.

"I'm sorry, sir," the airline receptionist was saying. "Your flight has been cancelled until morning due to the severe thunderstorms."

Ashton nodded, clearly upset. He had been in numerous meetings all week with top military officials and White House advisers regarding the recent uprising near the Jordan borders. Now he was ready to return to Texas. To Netherland.

He had avoided calling her all week hoping his absence would give her a chance to miss him but now he wanted to talk to her, hear her voice. Finding the most quiet spot he could in the busy and overcrowded airport, he pulled out his cell phone to call her. He frowned when he got her answering machine. Deciding not to leave a message, he hung up and glanced at his watch. Chances were she was still at Sisters.

He sighed. If things between the two sovereign nations occupying the land surrounding Jordan's banks continued, there would be more bloodshed, which meant there was a possibility that he would receive orders to depart on assignment immediately. The last thing he wanted was to leave Netherland with unfinished business between them.

Ashton inhaled deeply. Her time was up.

Chapter 12

Netherland gave Rome a half smile when she got home the next morning and found him sitting at her kitchen table drinking coffee and reading the morning's paper.

"Ashton's back?" he asked, setting the paper aside.

She shook her head as she joined him at the table. "No. I thought he would have gotten back last night but he didn't."

Rome nodded. "That's understandable."

Netherland lifted a brow. "Why is it understandable?"

"Because of the thunderstorms." When Netherland's features reflected her confusion, Rome said, "Surely you've heard about those severe thunderstorms that have rammed the East Coast over the past forty-eight hours?"

Netherland narrowed her eyes at her brother. "Rome, for the past one hundred and twenty hours I've been extremely busy getting things ready for tonight. I haven't had time to keep up with any weather reports."

"Well, from what I understand, all flights coming out of D.C. were canceled due to the severity of the storms. Chances are Ashton spent the night at some airport."

Netherland rubbed both hands across her face and took in a deep gulp of air. She had been disappointed upon waking that morning to find out that he hadn't returned to Texas. Her mind had begun thinking of all sorts of reasons he hadn't come back but now the thunderstorms explained everything. "So you think he'll get a flight out sometime today?"

"Yes. I heard on the news this morning that the flights are back to normal now. He should make it in about noon."

Netherland stood. "Well, I'm going to take a shower and—"

"Can we talk for a few minutes?"

Netherland studied her brother. She had heard the tightness in his voice again. Something was definitely on his mind, and she had a good idea it concerned Jada. "What do you want to talk to me about?"

"Why didn't you tell me about Jada?"

Netherland eased back into her chair. "Because it was private. You're my brother, but Jada is my employee, Rome. I decided if she wanted you to know, then she would tell you. It was not my place to tell you anything. Besides, it would not have changed a thing if you really cared about her. And you do care about her, don't you?"

Rome met his sister's gaze. "I'm in love with her, Nettie," he said simply, truthfully.

Netherland's surprise reflected in her face.

"You love her? Rome, you just met her a week ago."

"It doesn't matter." He smiled. "I'm my mother's son. She met and fell in love with Dad in the same night. And if you recall, I met and fell in love with Kimmy in a short period of time. I'm not like you, Nettie. I can recognize love when I see it."

Netherland folded her arms beneath her breasts, lifted her chin and glared at her brother. "For your information, I can recognize love, too. It just takes me a little longer, that's all."

Rome studied his sister. "Meaning?"

Netherland sighed deeply. "Meaning that I admitted to myself last night that I'm in love with Ashton."

"It's about time." He leaned back in his chair. "You do know that if there continue to be problems in Jordan, chances are Ashton will be going over there."

She stiffened slightly at what Rome had just said. Then suddenly a calm fell on her. She smiled at her brother. "That doesn't matter. I'll be here waiting for him to return."

Rome nodded. "And what if he asks you to move around the globe with him?"

"Then I'll do it, Rome. Ashton once said that home is where the heart is, and at the time I didn't understand what he meant. Now I do. It doesn't matter where I am as long as it's with him. I love him just that much."

Rome reached across the table and captured her hand in his. "I'm happy for you, Nettie. He's a good man who loves you."

Netherland smiled. "I hope he still does."

Rome lifted twin dark brows. "Why wouldn't he?"

She shrugged. "I've been rather difficult."

"But you won't be anymore?"

Netherland's smile widened. "No, not anymore. When I see Ashton again he won't have a reason to doubt ever again just how much I care."

As Jada walked the short distance from her apartment to Sisters she knew her first investment would be to get a car. The one she had owned with Tony had gotten repossessed, and she was working hard with the credit bureau to get her good credit rating restored.

Jada's thoughts then shifted to Rome. She still got goose bumps all over her whenever she thought about how he had held her in his arms and how he had kissed her tears away. They had kissed for a full twenty minutes with neither one of them getting enough. Then they had brought their rampant passions under control long enough for him to tell her about the sadness he'd once had in his life. She had sat beside him while he had told her about his fiancée's death and how hard he had taken it. And then, surprisingly, she had comforted him, which had led to more kisses. Not too long after that he had reluctantly left before things got too far out of hand.

Jada smiled. Rome had another two weeks to spend in Houston before leaving for Camp Pendleton in California. He had asked if they could spend the remaining time together, getting to know each other better. And he also wanted them to stay in contact after he left. Jada's smile widened. She definitely didn't have a problem with that. He was willing to take things slow with her and for that she was grateful.

When Jada stopped at the corner before crossing the street, she suddenly had the strangest feeling that she was being watched. She glanced around, then up and down the street. Other than people who, like her, were walking quickly to their destinations, she didn't see anyone who seemed interested in her presence.

Shrugging, thinking she must have been mistaken, she crossed the street and continued walking and thinking that today would definitely be a busy day at work.

It was nearly eleven in the morning when Ashton finally returned to his hotel room. He stopped as soon as he entered, immediately picking up Netherland's scent. His gaze flew to the unmade bed. As a child living on the Cherokee reservation he had been taught to recognize various scents, and he would know the scent of a woman anywhere. Especially the scent of *his* woman. Those two nights he had slept holding Netherland in his arms he had inhaled every delicious scent about her.

He walked over to the bed. Housekeeping had not been to his room, and Netherland's presence still lingered.

It appeared that she had come to his hotel room and had slept in his bed. He would have given anything to walk into his hotel room last night to find her there waiting on him.

Ashton pulled his sweater over his head and went to the closet to hang it up. He stopped short. Her scent was just as strong in his closet. Keen, observant eyes scanned every garment before zeroing in on his military jackets—one in particular. He reached out and pulled it off the hanger. He lifted the jacket to his nose before holding it tight against his chest. His jacket had come into contact with Netherland's body. There was no doubt in his mind that it had. Stunned, he shook his head and wondered what all this meant. When he saw her tonight he definitely was going to find out.

Chapter 13

The jazzy sound of Count Basie poured forth from the small orchestra as Netherland made her way around the room. She was pleased how Sisters had been decorated for this evening's affair. Even with a cost of three hundred dollars a ticket, the place was packed, and from the looks on everyone's faces they expected to have a good time and enjoy themselves. The sisters in attendance were decked out in striking evening gowns and glittering jewels, and the brothers looked utterly dashing in their tuxes. She had even encouraged her hostesses to come wearing after-five attire and all of them looked great. Dinner was to be served exactly at eight and once dinner was over, the bidding would begin. Afterward, everyone would celebrate and join in the dance that was planned from midnight until three. There was no doubt in Netherland's mind that the auction would be a huge success.

She slid her gaze across the room to the head table. Chicago businessman Nicholas Chenault and his wife Shayla had been the first to arrive with his in-laws, Paul Dunlap and Cassie Foster, and with their friends, Trent and Brenna Jordache. Jake and Diamond Swain Madaris had arrived a few minutes later along with their friends Sterling and Colby Hamilton and Kyle and Kimara Garwood. Also sitting at the table were Justin and Lorren Madaris; Dex and Caitlin Madaris; Trask and Felicia Maxwell; and Clayton and a young woman Netherland knew was the youngest Madaris sibling, twenty-year-old Christy. The young woman was simply gorgeous with her reddish-brown hair and a toasted-almond complexion. Netherland also noted Syneda's in-laws, Jonathan and Marilyn Madaris, were in attendance, as well as Syneda's father, Syntel Remington. Netherland glanced down at her list. According to the seating arrangements there would be close to twenty-five people sitting at the head table.

"Nettie, your gown is absolutely gorgeous, and you look totally fabulous in it," Syneda said, coming from behind. "It's so sleek, elegant and sophisticated-looking, and you have just the body, height and figure for it." She grinned. "It will be quite a while before I'll be able to wear anything that fits that well thanks to my thickening waistline."

Netherland chuckled. "But you have a very good reason for your thickening waistline."

Syneda's smile widened. "That's true." She glanced around the room. "Everything looks good, doesn't it?"

"Yes. You should be proud of yourself. Your hard work paid off."

Syneda pushed her hair back from her face. "I'm glad. Supporting the Children Home Society means a lot to me."

"You did a fantastic job at keeping the reporters in line."

Syneda nodded, thinking of all the local reporters who were in attendance, not to mention those who were camped outside the entrance. "Only because Sterling and Diamond have graciously agreed to interviews and will be posing for pictures after the auction."

Netherland glanced back over to the head table. "There seems to be a lot of celebrating going on at the head table."

Syneda chuckled. "Yes, Nicholas and Shayla Chenault announced earlier that Shayla's biological mother and biological father are getting married next weekend after being apart for nearly twenty-eight years. And then there were the announcements of the pregnancies."

Netherland lifted a brow. "What pregnancies?"

"You already know that Jake and Diamond are expecting. Well, Uncle Jake's friend Kyle Garwood and his wife, Kimara, shocked everyone when they announced they are expecting their seventh child in December. They claim it will be their last. And Caitlin is pregnant again. She'll be delivering in the middle of January."

"That's wonderful. Another grandchild for your in-laws to spoil, right?"

Syneda grinned in agreement. "Right."

Netherland then noticed the tall, distinguished, good-looking older man who had stood to make a toast. "Your father is a very handsome man, and the two of you favor a lot."

Syneda smiled knowing that was true. She and her father shared the same sea-green eyes as well as a number of other facial features. When standing next to each other, there was no doubt they were father and daughter. "Thanks, and I think he's handsome, too. I wished there were a special woman in his life but there isn't. Even after more than thirty years he can't let go of my mother's memory. He loved her very much."

Netherland sighed. "That's a lot of love."

Syneda chuckled. "Yes, but it's no different than the love I have for Clayton." She then studied Netherland intently when she said, "And what you have for Ashton."

Netherland met Syneda's gaze, no longer denying the truth. "Yes, you're probably right about that." She glanced around the room again. "Speaking of Ashton, did he get back from D.C.?"

Syneda lifted a brow. "Yes, he got back a little before noon, although I don't think he's arrived here yet; at least he hadn't the last time I checked fifteen minutes ago. You haven't spoken to him?"

Netherland shook her head. "Not since I last saw him last Sunday. But then he really had no reason to contact me. I didn't give him any encouragement to do so," she said, frowning thoughtfully. After a few seconds a smile tilted her lips and she said, "But all that will change."

Syneda smiled. "Sounds like you've made some important decisions about him."

Netherland shared the other woman's smile. "I have. I love him, Syneda, and I want to spend the rest of my life with him, no matter where that is. And when he has to leave on deployment, I'm prepared to be alone for a little while. I'm alone the majority of the time now anyway." Her smile widened. "But just think of all the fun we'll have whenever he returns." She sighed deeply, thinking about all the passion the two of them would generate after being apart for so long. Her mother had once told her that she had gotten pregnant with each of her five children after her father had returned home after a lengthy deployment.

Netherland had thought about her decision a lot since making it. Being a marine was not only what Ashton did, it was also who he was. And she was proud of the role he played in protecting their country. Spending time with Ashton and the conversations she'd had with him had made her realize just how proud her mother must be of her father and brothers for serving their country, too. Now, so was she. She had never fully understood, until now.

"I'm going to check on things in the back," Syneda said. "Ashton probably has arrived by now. The guys were instructed to come in through the kitchen so they wouldn't be seen. Do you want to go back there with me to see if he's there?"

Netherland shook her head. What she wanted to say to Ashton could hold till later when they were alone. "No, I'll stay out here and make sure things are running smoothly."

Syneda nodded before walking off.

More toasts were made to congratulate Brenna and Trent on their recent marriage as well as Nicholas and Shayla on theirs. Most people at the table already knew Nicholas Chenault as Sterling's half brother.

Everyone nervously shifted in their seats when Trevor and Corinthians Grant arrived. It looked as though she was going to have her baby any second.

"I'm a week late," she said to everyone after sensing their nervousness. She ran a hand across her overly large stomach. "But I doubt anything will happen tonight so all of you can relax."

Everyone's expressions indicated they were doubtful that nothing would happen that night.

"Her bags are in the car, packed and ready to go, just in case," Trevor said, grinning. "I tried talking her into staying home tonight but she wouldn't listen."

Corinthians smiled. "I couldn't miss out on seeing who's the lucky woman who'll get Ashton tonight. This is history in the making. From what I've heard, he's never let any woman choose him before for anything. Ashton prefers doing his own choosing."

Trevor started to tell his wife that tonight would be no different, then thought better of it. She would see soon enough. "Are you sure you're okay?" he asked her in a low, loving voice, leaning his head over close to hers.

She smiled up at him wondering how at one time she thought she couldn't stand the very ground he walked on. "Yes, sweetheart, I'm fine. It seems that Baby Grant has settled down for the night and isn't playing marines inside my tummy. Boy or girl, this has been one overactive child."

Trevor's smile widened. "Baby Grant takes after its parents. You and I are overactive in a number of things." His eyes darkened. "One in particular readily comes to mind."

The look Corinthians gave her husband was one of love and desire. "Yeah, I know just what you're talking about, and I can't wait for our baby to be born so I can get back into the swing of things."

Trevor gave his wife a sexy grin. "Neither can I, sweetheart. Neither can I."

Netherland and Rainey were standing at the door greeting the guests when Rainey leaned in close and whispered, "Ashton's here. I saw him a few minutes ago, and boy, does he look good. You'll be a fool to let Angela walk away with him tonight."

Netherland chuckled. "She won't."

Rainey raised a dark brow. After she studied Netherland for a few moments, a smile tilted the corners of her lips. "It's about time you come to your senses. I thought I was going to—"

"Excuse me. I'm to join the Chenault and Jordache party."

The deep, husky voice cut into Rainey's words, and she turned around, blinking once. Then twice. *Whoa!* Standing before them was what had to be at least six-foot-four inches of solid muscle. His dark eyes were sharp, assessing, and after a few seconds it occurred to Rainey that he'd been checking her out in her evening gown as she'd been checking him out in his tux. She cleared her throat. "Your name, sir?"

"Howard Reeves. And yours?"

Rainey blinked a third time before answering. "I'm Rainey Gilford, head hostess of Sisters, and this is Netherland Brooms, the owner."

Howard Reeves presented his hand to both women in a warm handshake. "Nice meeting the both of you."

Rainey let out a deep breath before lowering her head to look at the list in her hand, a hand still tingling from his touch. "The Chenaults and Jordaches are sitting at the head table, Mr. Reeves. If you would follow me I'll gladly escort you over."

"You lead and I'll definitely follow, Miss Gilford. And I do hope that it is *Miss*."

Rainey smiled up at the man. "Yes, it is." She glanced down at his hand and didn't see a wedding band there. She then met his gaze once more. "And I assume that you're single, too."

"Yes, that's right."

Netherland couldn't contain her chuckle as she watched Rainey walk away with Howard Reeves following behind. She couldn't quite decide who appeared to be more taken with whom—Rainey with Howard Reeves or Howard Reeves with Rainey.

A few minutes later Rainey returned. She was all smiles.

"If I were to cut all the lights out in here I'd bet any amount of money that you'd glow in the dark," Netherland whispered to her friend.

"I wouldn't doubt it. That man is something else. Wow!"

Netherland shook her head. "I take it he turns you on."

"And then some. I'd like to get to know that brother up close and personal."

Netherland lifted a brow. "Are you still planning to bid on Alex Maxwell tonight?"

Rainey smiled as she glanced over to the head table. Howard Reeves looked her way and their gazes locked. The rest of the room became a blur all around her. Her smile widened and when it did, one corner of Howard Reeves's mouth tilted likewise as his sharp, assessing eyes held her spellbound while he flirted with her using nothing more than his smile and his eyes in the process.

Rainey returned the soundless flirtation, letting him know she reciprocated his interest.

"Rainey? Rainey?" Netherland finally nudged her elbow into Rainey's ribs to get her attention. "Rainey?"

Rainey reluctantly broke eye contact with Howard Reeves. "What?"

"I asked if you're still planning to bid on Alex Maxwell tonight."

Rainey looked back over at the head table. Howard Reeves was still looking at her, and something electrical seemed to cross the room and pass between them. She reluctantly broke eye contact with him again to respond to Netherland's question. She smiled sweetly at her friend and asked, "Alex who?"

Promptly at eight, dinner was served. Excitement in the room began building an hour or so later when everyone's meal had been cleared away. It was time for the auction to begin.

Syneda went up on stage. Standing at the podium, she thanked everyone for coming and supporting the Children Home Society with their contributions. She then introduced the mistress and master of ceremonies for tonight's affair. Before Sterling and Diamond could make it to the stage, the audience became even more energized, and a furor of excitement surged through the room when the two movie stars were given a standing ovation. Their movie, *Black Butterfly,* was predicted to be the summer's blockbuster hit and was scheduled to be released at the theaters in a few months.

Sterling and Diamond spent a few minutes dazzling the audience before turning things over to the man who had agreed to serve as the night's auctioneer—three-time Heisman Trophy winner and the recipient of five Super Bowl rings; a man known worldwide as the greatest running back in the history of the NFL, legendary football great Trask "The Max" Maxwell. Trask, too, got a standing ovation.

After thanking everyone he rapped his gavel on the podium to silence the crowd and get things under way. "Ladies and gentlemen, but especially you lovely single sisters out there tonight, we've finally reached the moment all of you've been waiting for. As everyone who's come before me has stated, all proceeds, which includes the price you paid for your tickets, will go to the Children Home Society. If you will refer to your program booklet, you will find the names of all the brothers who are being auctioned tonight, along with their personal bios—which I'm sure you'll find impressive. As indicated the persons with the highest bids for the first nine brothers are entitled to dinner at various exclusive restaurants in the city. The person with the highest bid for Brother Number Ten gets to spend a weekend in New Orleans French Quarter. We will begin the bidding with Brother Number One, Blade Madaris."

At that moment Blade Madaris walked out on stage, dressed in a black tux. He gave everyone a dazzling smile, which made the sisters in the audience go wild. Trask smiled as he rapped his gavel on the podium to get the crowd under control. It seemed a new generation of Madaris men was up for viewing. "From Blade's bio you can see that he is a twenty-seven-year-old native of Houston, a graduate of Morehouse and a proud Alpha man. Presently he works as an engineer for Madaris Construction Company." Trask looked out over the room. "Who will open the bid for Mr. Madaris at one thousand dollars?" When a woman in the back held up her name card indicating that she would, Trask nodded with satisfaction. "Maureen Sullivan has offered one thousand. Do I have two?"

Less than five minutes later Blade Madaris was presented to Shawna Crews, who won Blade with the winning bid of six thousand dollars.

"For those ladies who lost out on Brother Number One, don't despair, just get ready for Brother Number Two, who happens to be Brother Number One's twin, Slade Madaris. Slade works as an architect for Madaris Construction Company and like his brother, he's a graduate of Morehouse and an Alpha man." Trask looked over the room. "Who will open the bid for the second Mr. Madaris at one thousand?"

Less than five minutes later Slade Madaris was presented to Pat Samuels, with a winning bid of six thousand five hundred dollars. Brothers Numbers Three and Four brought in eight thousand each; and Brother Number Five, twenty-six-year-old rodeo superstar Luke Madaris, brought in a whopping ten thousand. The auction was well under way with only five brothers left to bid on.

Everyone was given fifteen minutes of intermission. Netherland was tempted to use that time to seek out Ashton but decided against it. Instead she visited with various people who were present that night. At the end of intermission, Trask's voice rose and captured everyone's attention, encouraging them to return to their seats.

"The next brother is someone I know very well. He's my biological brother, Alexander Maxwell," Trask said once the auction was under way again.

Alexander walked out on stage and like the brothers who'd come before him, he was dressed in a black tux that fitted his body with unerring precision. He looked good, real good. And the expression he wore was serious, pensive and challenged any woman to be the one to put a smile on his face. There were a few in the audience who thought they could, which heightened the excitement in the room.

Trask hit the gavel on the podium to recapture everyone's attention. "From Alex's bio you can see that he's a graduate of Howard University and received his master's degree from MIT. After working a short period for the FBI, he's now CEO of Maxwell Security and Investigators." Trask looked out over the audience. "Who will open the bidding at one thousand dollars?"

A hand lifted somewhere in the back of the audience and a name card came up. "One thousand dollars," a woman called out.

Then the bidding began as several women who were intent on having that date with Alex and putting that smile on his face threw out their bids. The bidding became rapid, fierce and aggressive, as each woman forced the other to bid higher and higher, making Alex the hottest brother in demand thus far. In the end, surprising everyone, except for her brothers and a few others who knew of Alex's plan, Christy Madaris stood and topped the highest bid of thirteen thousand by offering fifteen thousand dollars.

"Miss Christy Madaris has offered fifteen thousand dollars. Do I have sixteen thousand?" Trask asked, looking around the room to see if anyone else would signal. When no one else bidded, he smiled and said, "Alex Maxwell is awarded to Christy Madaris."

Alex Maxwell released a deep sigh of relief. While the audience watched he left the stage and walked over to the head table to present Christy with a dozen red roses. He had seen her when he had first walked out on stage and had forced himself to keep his eyes off her. Christy Madaris had always been an awfully cute kid but now she had grown into a very beautiful young woman, something Alex tried real hard not to notice whenever he saw her. The last time had been at Trevor and Corinthians's wedding reception last summer and a couple of months before that, her brother Clayton's wedding. Both times he had found his gaze deliberately seeking her out. It was hard to believe she was the same person he had taught to ride her first bicycle, but then he would know her whiskey-colored eyes and reddish-brown mane of hair anywhere. She was wearing her hair down, and it rippled in soft curls around her shoulders. A part of him was glad she hadn't succumbed to fashion and dyed her hair blond or some other horrendous color, or chopped it off short as a number of young women her age were doing. She had opted to retain that natural beauty that had been so much a part of her from childhood. It was that natural beauty he was most attracted to.

Alex swallowed and tried to remember that Christy was the last person whose beauty he should be attracted to. She was like family. He forced himself to remember that Christy Madaris was still a kid, although she no longer looked the part. But he couldn't put the thought from his mind that even with the eight-year difference in their ages, there had always been a special closeness between them. They used to spend a lot of time together while growing up when she used to follow him around, something that had never bothered him.

He came to a stop when he reached Christy's side. She looked stunning. Too stunning. Her string-bean body now had luscious curves, and the flirty little gown she was wearing was definitely clinging to them. Her outfit was most assuredly a sexy number that ended, he couldn't help but notice, midthigh. Its low round neckline dipped to the swell of her breasts.

Alex was surprised her brothers had allowed her to wear such a revealing outfit in public. Evidently they didn't think there was a need to worry about any males showing interest tonight with the three of them standing guard.

"Hello, Christy," he said, in a deep, resonant voice as he handed her the flowers. "Thanks for agreeing to come to my rescue," he whispered, smiling at her. "I'll be back later to claim my dance, after the auction is over." In addition to receiving a dozen roses from the brother she was awarded, the sister with the winning bid was also guaranteed the first dance with him.

Christy Madaris smiled back at him and something in the pit of Alex's stomach gave a sharp jolt. "It's good seeing you again, *Alexander the Great*."

A low chuckle rumbled deep in Alex's chest. Christy, at the age of eleven, had given him that nickname after studying about the fierce Macedonian king in school.

"You remember that?" she asked as a smile trembled over her lips.

"How can I forget it? You used to annoy the heck out of me when you used to follow me around calling me that."

Her smile widened. "Sorry, Alexander Julian."

An easy grin played at the corners of his mouth. "You're forgiven, Christina Marie."

For some reason conversing with Christy warmed him with astonishing intensity. Within a few brief seconds he had lowered his guard of indifference where women were concerned. His throat tightened and an invisible band of iron squeezed his chest.

Suddenly feeling panicky and out of his element with her, Alex gathered control of his thoughts as well as of his mind and took a step back. He nodded to everyone else at the table before turning to walk off.

Marilyn Madaris leaned back in her chair after observing the exchange between her daughter and Alex Maxwell. She then noted the smug smiles on the faces of her three sons, Justin, Dex and Clayton. Christy had shared with Marilyn what her brothers had asked her to do to help Alex out of a jam tonight.

Marilyn shook her head as a lazy smile touched her lips. She wondered what her sons would think if they knew that they might have helped their childhood friend out of a jam, but in doing so they had given Alex to their sister on a silver platter. She doubted her sons knew that Christy's teenage crush on Alex had never gone away. Marilyn still remembered when Christy, at thirteen, had announced to everyone at breakfast one morning that Alex had promised to wait for her to grow up to marry him and proudly showed off the ring he'd given her.

It seemed that everyone had forgotten about that promise—possibly including Alex. She wondered what they would think if they knew that Christy had not forgotten it and intended to hold Alex to it.

Marilyn took a sip of her coffee. She had a feeling that things were about to get real interesting.

Chapter 14

Two hours later all the brothers except for Ashton had been bid on and awarded to some happy sister. Excitement and anticipation rippled through the audience more so than ever before. Conversations broke off as the room became quiet, almost deathly still.

Netherland was seated at the head table next to Syneda. She glanced around the room noticing the expressions of anticipation on a number of women's faces, especially Angela Meadows. Rumor had it that Angela was willing to give up just about her last penny to spend a weekend with Ashton, and Netherland had no intentions of letting the woman do that.

"This is the moment I understand many of you sisters have been waiting for, our final brother,

Brother Number Ten, Marine Colonel Ashton Sinclair," Trask said as he looked out upon the audience and into all the eager feminine faces.

"From Colonel Sinclair's bio you can see that he is a thirty-five-year-old Oklahoman and a graduate of Georgetown University. Presently, he is a colonel in the United States Marine Corps and takes their motto, 'Always Faithful,' very seriously."

Trask glanced around the room. "I'm sure most of you are familiar with the marines' slogan of 'Looking for a few good men.' Well, Colonel Sinclair is definitely one of them. A former member of the Marine Corps' Force Recon Unit, he has been awarded numerous medals of bravery for his part in protecting our country and preserving peace. The lucky lady who makes the highest bid for Colonel Sinclair gets to spend a weekend with him in New Orleans."

Trask's smile widened. "I present to some, and introduce to others, the brother of the hour, Colonel Ashton Sinclair of the United States Marine Corps."

To Netherland's way of thinking the lights seemed to dim as all eyes focused on Ashton, who seemed to miraculously appear on stage, although she knew his entry was done by some sort of special effects to make it appear that way.

Her breath, like that of every woman present, caught in her throat. Standing before them was the most handsome spit-and-polished marine she had ever seen. With hair flowing past his shoulders underneath his military hat, he was dressed in an officer's evening dress uniform, which consisted of a dress blue waistcoat and pants with a scarlet cummerbund—complete with ceremonial sword. Moving with stiff-spine precision he walked toward the front of the stage. When he came to a stop, he reached across his body with his right hand and withdrew his sword from its scabbard. The lights seemed to hit the gleaming, polished metal and radiate off every individual in the place as he raised it high.

It was a powerful stance that brought tears to Netherland's eyes. Ashton was definitely making a statement. He was making it absolutely clear that whatever woman chose him tonight would not only be choosing Ashton Sinclair the man, but also Ashton Sinclair the marine. She wiped her eyes when he lowered the sword slowly to hold by his side.

The room erupted in an uproar, mass pandemonium, as the women started screaming, hollering and giving Ashton a standing ovation. Women loved men in uniform, and there was no doubt that he was the top prize for the evening and, judging from the buzzing and whispers going around the room, it was clear that women who hadn't thought to bid before were now seriously considering doing so.

Trask had to rap his gavel on the podium for several long minutes to regain order. Netherland nervously bit her lips. Coming up with the highest bid wouldn't be as easy as she thought.

"Let's come to order so the bidding can begin,"

Trask was finally able to say. "Who will open the bid for Colonel Sinclair at five thousand dollars?"

He got six easily and didn't have any problems getting seven, eight and nine. "Do I have ten?"

"Ten thousand dollars."

Everyone recognized the voice of Angela Meadows. She had finally entered the fray.

"Angela Meadows has offered ten thousand dollars," Trask said, trying to keep the smile from his voice. "Do I hear eleven?"

He got eleven and twelve without any sweat. Angela offered thirteen and Sandra countered with fourteen. Some woman in the back offered fifteen, then Angela countered with sixteen. The woman in the back then countered with seventeen. Deciding not to be undone, Angela raised her bid to twenty with a satisfied, smug grin on her lips.

Netherland glanced up at Ashton. His gaze was on her and what she saw in his eyes took her breath away. No matter what woman was bidding on him, he wanted her, and his gaze was saying it. Amazing. It was as if she were reading his very thought. A surge of wanting and desire sizzled through her bloodstream as he continued to hold her gaze, almost daring her to look away, deny the silent statement he was making. Memories of sharing a bed with him with her body pulled tight against him, his strong body pressed against hers, infiltrated her mind, consumed her thoughts. Only Trask's strong voice penetrated her daze when he said:

"Angela Meadows has offered twenty thousand. Do I have twenty-one?"

The room got quiet, and Angela remained standing with a smug look on her face. Netherland turned around to look at the woman before returning her gaze to Ashton. Her gaze locked on his strong jaw and slightly curved lips, and he was looking at her as if he could read her mind as she had read his earlier.

Trask's voice rang out loud. "Going once, going twice—"

Netherland quickly stood. "Twenty-five thousand dollars."

The audience erupted in cheers and applause. Evidently the majority of the women present didn't want Ashton to fall into Angela's hands.

It was quite obvious to everyone that Angela was upset with Netherland's bid and was not about to be undone. "Thirty!" she snapped, glaring across the room at Netherland.

Netherland stared at the woman in wide-eyed startlement. Was Angela that intent on having Ashton? From the smirk on the woman's face Netherland quickly concluded that she was. Netherland couldn't help but wonder just how much money the woman was willing to put out for Ashton. "Thirty-five," Netherland countered.

The room got quiet, and Netherland refused to even think about where she would get thirty-five thousand dollars. Oh, well, she might as well kiss good-bye the money she had put aside to renovate the entrance to Sisters.

"Thirty-five thousand dollars!" Trask's voice crowed. "Netherland Brooms has bid thirty-five thousand dollars for Colonel Sinclair. Will you make it thirty-six, Miss Meadows?"

Nervous tension filled the room as Angela stood glowering at Netherland. She looked up toward the stage at Ashton. "I want to bid fifty thousand dollars."

Everyone, including Trask, was stunned. The room erupted in mass pandemonium once again. On stage it appeared that Ashton was taking it rather well and for a moment Netherland wondered if perhaps he wanted Angela instead of her since he seemed so calm about it. But then she noticed there appeared to be an odd expression on his face. He looked at her, and it seemed he was again reading her thoughts and was bothered by the uncertainty he read in them. He moved his lips in an intimate smile that was meant to assure her. It did. Any doubt she had resolved as he continued to look at her, smiling at her and silently beckoning her to believe in him.

Trask rapped the gavel on the podium for a full three minutes before regaining order in the room. "Miss Meadows has bid fifty thousand dollars, and all of it is destined for the Children Home Society. Is there a higher bid than fifty?"

Netherland swallowed deeply and was about to open her mouth to place a higher bid when some-

where in the back of the room, a female voice said,
"I'm offering a bid of one hundred thousand dollars."

Simultaneous gasps spread throughout the room
as everyone stretched their necks toward the back to
see who had placed such a high bid.

"Close the bidding. Now," Ashton ordered as he
whispered for Trask's ears only. Trask quickly moved
to do just that before either Angela or Nettie could
gather her wits and attempt to outbid the woman
standing in the back.

"Going once, going twice," Trask called out.
"Awarded!" he proclaimed. "For one hundred thousand dollars to…" He frowned. "Sorry, ma'am, I
didn't get your name."

Everyone watched as the young woman came
forward. The males in the room, some of whom had
become slightly bored with the bidding between
Angela and Nettie, sat up straight in their chairs and
cleared their throats. The young woman whose age
appeared to be in her early twenties was utterly
gorgeous. When she reached the front of the room
everyone stared at her in expectant silence. Netherland felt her heart completely drop to the floor. She
had lost out on her opportunity to spend a weekend
with Ashton.

The woman turned around and faced the audience.
"My name is Mackenzie Standfield," she said, speaking clearly and loudly for all to hear. "I'm an attorney
with the Oklahoma law firm of Standfield, Di Meglio
and Mahoney. The bid of one hundred thousand was

made on behalf of my client, Ashton Sinclair. Mr. Sinclair supports the Children Home Society and wanted to make this bid on himself, which allows him to select the woman he wants to take to New Orleans."

"He can't do that!" Angela Meadows's voice rang out loud in the room. She was clearly upset with the outcome of events.

"Yes, he can," Mackenzie Standfield responded to Angela. "My firm reviewed the rules for this event carefully. This is not a contest. Anyone can make the winning bid—even a participant—since all the proceeds are going to charity." She then turned her attention to the stage. "Mr. Sinclair will now select the woman of his choice."

When his attorney stepped aside, Ashton slowly walked off the stage with a dozen roses in his hand.

Netherland's heart thudded in her chest as she watched Ashton walk over toward her. She inhaled sharply, deeply and almost to the point of not exhaling when she realized what he was about to do. The gaze in his eyes held hers with unspoken confirmation.

Ashton's long legs made the pace easy for him, and he closed the distance between him and Netherland in record time. When he reached her he kept his gaze locked with hers. He handed her the dozen roses as he said loud enough for everyone in the room to hear, "I choose you, Netherland."

Cheers, catcalls, whistles and applause ripped through the room. Then in a soft, intimate voice for

Netherland's ears only, he bent his head toward her and whispered, "I choose you, Netherland, for always."

"Ashton—" Netherland could barely squeeze the one word past the deep lump in her throat. A single tear escaped her eye. She pulled a single rose out of her bouquet and handed it to him and said softly, "And I choose you, too, for always."

The corner of Ashton's mouth tilted into a smile. He accepted the rose before pulling Netherland into his arms. Ignoring everyone and everything around them, he kissed her.

There wasn't a dry feminine eye left in the house. It seemed every woman was crying. Except for Angela Meadows, who angrily walked out.

"Well, folks," Trask was saying as he looked over the audience and saw how emotional they had become. Even his own wife, Felicia, was sobbing. He shook his head. "That ends the auction portion of tonight's affair. I must admit that this evening has been quite interesting. We appreciate what each and every one of you have done for the Children Home Society. Stick around for the dance that will follow immediately."

Corinthians Avery Grant wiped her eyes as she tapped her husband on the shoulder. He turned around and looked at her. "Yes, sweetheart, what is it?"

"I hate to be a party pooper, but I'm in labor."

Trevor sat up straight. So did everyone at the table. Ashton and Netherland, who were still kissing, hadn't heard a thing. "How far apart are the pains?"

"Five minutes."

Trevor was up out of his seat. "Five minutes! Why didn't you say something earlier?"

"I wanted to stick around to see who would get Ashton. I didn't want Angela to have him."

Trevor frowned. "Well, you better hope our baby holds tight until I get you to the hospital." He took in a deep breath, looked around and began barking out orders. "Syneda, call Dr. Morgan and let him know we're on our way to the hospital." He looked over at Dex and reached into his pocket and pulled out his car keys. "Make sure my car is out front immediately," he said, tossing the keys across the table to him. He glanced at Justin. "I need you, Doc, just in case this baby wants to be born on the side of the road." He turned to Clayton. "I need you just in case I'm stopped by the police for speeding and can't talk my way out of it." He looked at the elder Madarises. "Please call my parents and let them know what's going on. Corinthians's parents are in town, and Mom and Dad will know how to reach them."

He then noticed that Ashton still had Netherland in his arms kissing her. He jabbed his elbow in Ashton's side.

Ashton glanced up sharply. He frowned. "What the—"

"Your godchild decided to make an appearance tonight. Let's go."

Picking up his wife in his arms, Trevor made a move to exit the building while everyone jumped to follow his orders. Corinthians smiled at everyone. "What can I say? You can take the man out of the military but you can't take the military out of the man. He looks for any excuse to give orders."

When a hard labor pain struck her, she decided to be quiet and save her breath for later.

Chapter 15

"Did I tell you how good you look tonight, Netherland?" Ashton asked as his eyes shone with appreciation straight into hers. They were just two of the many people who were sitting in the waiting room of the hospital anxiously anticipating word of Trevor and Corinthian's firstborn.

Netherland shook her head as she chuckled softly. "No, you never got around to that."

Ashton folded his fingers around hers. "Then that's another thing I have to make up for when I get you alone later." His quiet tone carried more than a promise that he would deliver on and a lot more.

She tipped her head back to look up at him. "You make sure you do that." Her voice was soft, seductive, barely a whisper, and it had that same smoky desire in its intonation as was reflected from the look in her eyes. Her entire body thrummed with sexual tension just from being around him. At the moment, there was nothing that could douse the undeniable desire she felt for the man who was still wearing his marine uniform and who was looking intrinsically male. Deciding to try and concentrate on something else, she glanced across the room at the other occu-pants. The three Madaris brothers and their wives, their parents, along with Trevor and Corinthians's parents, and Trask and Felicia. There was a lot of eager anticipation on everyone's faces. It would be the first grandchild for both the Grants and the Averys, and it was obvious they were overjoyed at the thought of becoming grandparents.

"It's over, folks."

Everyone jumped at the sound of Trevor's deep voice. He stood in the waiting room's doorway, still dressed in his hospital scrubs; his eyes brimmed with unshed tears, and his face shone with a smile of pure wonder, as if some miracle had just taken place. All the people in the room raced toward him. He held up his hand to halt all the questions coming to him at once.

"We have a son," he said, grinning proudly. "A beautiful nine-pound-eight-ounce future marine who entered the world screaming orders at the top of his lungs. Corinthians and the baby are doing fine."

"What's his name?" Caitlin Madaris inquired as a play of happy emotions darted across her features.

She and Dex would be having another child in seven months and because they had two girls already she was hoping for a boy.

"Rio Maurice Nathan Grant," Trevor answered, beaming. "He was named Rio because it was in Rio de Janeiro that Corinthians and I started our South American adventure. That episode holds a lot of special memories for us," he said as his eyes glowed with fond recollections. "And of course Maurice and Nathan are in honor of our son's two grandfathers," he added, smiling at his father, Maurice Grant, and Corinthians's father, Nathan Avery. Both men beamed with delight. It was evident they were proud to have a grandson named after them.

"How soon can we see them?" Corinthians's mother asked with tears brimming in her eyes.

Trevor smiled. "Is now soon enough? Corinthians can't wait to see all of you. Even after all she's been through tonight, I don't think she'll be able to settle down until she does."

Rio Maurice Nathan Grant was indeed a beautiful baby, Netherland thought as she watched him being held in the crook of his mother's arms. It was a beautiful scene, mother and child. It was so beautiful that Netherland found herself wiping a lone tear away from her eyes with her fingertips.

"There's nothing quite like the miracle of life, is there?" Ashton asked, looking down at her smiling.

Netherland shook her head and looked away.

Ashton's words reminded her of the one thing she could not do. Create life. She wondered if he wanted children and if so, would he be satisfied adopting? His next words gave her an answer.

"I can't wait to see your stomach swollen with my sons one day, Netherland," he whispered.

A chill raced along her spine, and she shivered. She forced herself to look up at him. "You want a child?"

Ashton saw the play of emotions that darted across her features and wondered about the cause of them. "Yes, and you will be the mother of my child. I saw it in another vision I had," he said. He still was not ready to tell her about the triplets. That kind of news was meant for another time.

"And I'm supposed to give birth to this child?"

Ashton looked at her, confused by her question. "Yes, of course."

Netherland took a deep breath and lowered her head when she couldn't meet his gaze any longer. A sheen of tears suddenly filled her eyes, and her vision blurred. She rubbed one hand over her flat stomach, a stomach that would never expand with the weight of Ashton's child.

"Netherland? What's wrong?" Ashton asked, concerned when he saw her tears.

His question got the attention of everyone in the room. She looked up at him, and the tears that were shimmering in her eyes struck him. "Netherland, what is it?"

"That vision is wrong, Ashton," she whispered,

her words catching on a strangled sob. "We can never make a baby together, and if your vision showed you that, then it was wrong." Filled to the brim with emotions she couldn't handle, Netherland turned and ran from the room.

"Netherland!" Ashton was about to race out of the hospital room after her when a firm hand on his arm stopped him. He swiveled his head to look down into Syneda Madaris's questioning eyes.

"Don't you know?" she asked quietly.

He frowned. His nerves were taut, on edge. He had no idea what was going on and why Netherland had run out of the room upset. "Don't I know what?"

"That Nettie can't have children."

Ashton's frown deepened. "Where in the hell did she get an idea like that from?"

Syneda was taken back by the incredulity of his question. It was definitely not one she had expected and immediately was angered by it. Folding her arms across her chest she narrowed her eyes at Ashton. "From her doctor, I would imagine. I'm sure it's not something she would self-diagnose."

He ignored the sarcasm in Syneda's voice. "Well, he told her wrong. She *can* have babies." Ashton pulled in a long, deep breath. He had to go after Netherland. "Look, I have to go find Netherland. Trevor will explain things." He then turned and quickly left the room.

All eyes turned to Trevor.

"Is he crazy?" Syneda asked, clearly upset.

Trevor shook his head. "No, Ashton isn't crazy. In fact, he's far from it, and if he believes Nettie can have a baby, then there's a real good chance she can, especially if he saw it in one of those visions of his. I know for a fact they are credible."

Syneda was not convinced. "What is he supposed to be? Some miracle worker?"

Trevor smiled. "I guess you can say that."

Christy Madaris smiled as she leaned back in her chair. The auction was over, and all around the room couples were paired off, dancing or talking. It seemed everyone was having a good time, and she thought it had been most romantic how Ashton Sinclair had bid on himself and had chosen Nettie Brooms as the woman he wanted.

"Ready for our dance?" a deep voice asked from beside her.

Christy glanced up into dark eyes that were familiar. At the age of eleven she had fallen in love with the man who owned those eyes. And although over the past few years their paths had barely crossed, her feelings had not changed. In fact, that old saying about absence making the heart grow fonder was very true in her case. But then she was a Madaris, and Madarises loved forever. "Yes, I'm ready," she said and stood.

Alex glanced around the room. "Where're your brothers?"

"They left."

Alex lifted a brow. "They left?" At her nod, he said, "They left you here alone?"

"Yes. Corinthians went into labor, and they wanted to go to the hospital to give Trevor support. They told me to catch a ride home with you. I hope you don't mind."

He did mind. He had spent the last thirty minutes sitting at the bar sipping a beer and trying to get his mind and thoughts under control. Christy was the first woman to affect him in a long time, and the problem was that he shouldn't think of her as a woman. He should still see her as the sweet kid he'd known all his life. But for some reason he couldn't. Taking a deep breath, he tried like hell to dismiss the attraction that intrigued and enticed him way beyond his better judgment. But it wasn't easy with her looking so incredibly sexy in a dress that showed off more skin than he was used to seeing on her.

"Where's your uncle Jake? And your cousins? Aren't they still around?"

"No. Uncle Jake just left. And Blade, Slade and Lucas left right after their dances with the winning bidders were over." Christy saw his jaw tighten and knew the idea of taking her home didn't sit well with him. "Look, Alex, if taking me home will be a bother, then I can call a cab."

He started to tell her to do that very thing, then decided against it. After all, her brothers had entrusted her to his care. "I'm taking you home, Christy, and it won't be a bother." He took her hand in his. "Come on, let's get that dance over with so we can leave," he said, leading her to the dance floor when the orchestra struck up a new tune. He let out a resigned sigh when he realized it would be a slow number.

"I won't turn into a pumpkin if I'm not in by twelve," she muttered, none too happily, when it seemed he was eager to be rid of her.

In the midst of the others around them, Alex pulled her into his arms and began swaying to the slow beat of the music. "Are you certain of that?"

Christy inhaled sharply, feeling the hard strength of Alex's arm around her waist and the press of his body against hers. Closing her eyes, she breathed deeply, inhaling the robust scent of the fragrance of an ultrasexy cologne and male heat. She shivered, and instinctively leaned into him, absorbing his embrace and savoring the feel of being in his arms. She reopened her eyes. "Yes, I'm certain."

Christy wasn't the only one going through changes. The feel of her in his arms had Alex's entire body in a spin. He tried to get a grip on the sudden rush of emotions he felt holding her. His heart was beating erratically, and his breathing was irregular. He couldn't help but wonder how in the world a twenty-year-old college girl could stimulate him so.

Mentally convincing himself what he was experiencing tonight with her was a fluke and completely absurd, he forced his mind...as well as his body...to relax. He decided to initiate conversations with her since it seemed that any silence resulted in a slow building of awareness to settle between them.

"You weren't at Trask and Felicia's wedding on New Year's Day," he said.

"No, I was performing at a championship football game that day."

"That's right, you are a majorette at Howard University, aren't you?" She certainly had the legs for it, he thought to himself. They were great-looking legs.

"Yes. I can't believe Trask and Felicia got married. I was totally shocked."

Alex chuckled. "You weren't the only one." After a few moments of silence he asked, "So, how is school going?"

Christy smiled. "Wonderful, but I'm enjoying being home during spring break. I miss being around my family and friends. I'll be glad when the summer rolls around."

"Big plans?"

"Yes. I plan to work with the twins at Madaris Construction Company. They're supposed to start construction on the Madaris Building by then."

"I know. I plan to be one of their tenants when it's completed."

"You are? That's great." Christy had begun to relax until Alex tightened his hold around her waist. The heat of his fingers penetrated through the silky material that she wore.

"You smell good," he said. His breath felt warm against her ear, and the huskiness of his voice vibrated against her spine. "You no longer smell like peanut butter. I take it you grew out of that."

Christy chuckled. She used to eat peanut butter straight from the jar by the truckload as a kid. "I still like it but not as much as I used to."

Although the two of them were trying desperately to keep up a steady stream of conversation, they knew something was happening between them. Something that made Christy's stomach feel all warm and heated inside, and made Alex's body tingle just from the sound of her voice. Dancing together wasn't working, and he was glad when the music finally came to an end.

"Are you ready for me to take you home now?"

"Yes."

His hold on her hand tightened. "Then let's get your things so we can be on our way."

In another area of the crowded room Rome's gaze found Jada, and the muted sound of the music faded in the background. A smile eased across his lips, and he headed over in her direction.

Jada saw his approach, chewed on her bottom lip and wondered if things were moving too fast between her and Rome. She liked him. She really liked him a lot but she knew they could never be just friends. She was attracted to him too much for that. She couldn't look at his mouth without remembering the deep, slow kisses that he could so effectively give.

She let out a resigned sigh. Getting back into the

dating scene was almost overwhelming to her. She had married Tony when she was nineteen, inexperienced and innocent in the ways of men, and from him she had learned the hard way. She had endured lessons she never wanted to be taught again. But a part of her wanted to believe there was still a chance she could share a good, lasting relationship with a man—sometime in her future. However, in the meantime she wanted to spend as much time with Rome as she could, enjoy the moment while it lasted and not think about how lonely her life would be when he left.

"Hi, you're about finished here?" Rome asked her when he had reached her side.

The deep huskiness of his voice strummed down her spine like caressing fingers. "Yes."

"Need a ride home?"

"Yes."

"I'll be at the bar waiting for you."

"All right." Jada watched him walk away. Ignoring the heat flushing her skin, she went about completing her final chores before she could leave and go home.

"Thanks for bringing me home, Alex. You don't have to walk me to the door."

"Yes, I do. You don't know if your parents have returned from the hospital yet, and I have to see you safely inside." He got out of the car and walked around the vehicle to her side. He thought that once he got her tucked safely inside, he would have fulfilled her brothers' expectations, and he could be on his way. The sooner he got away from Christy the better. Hopefully it would be another year or so before he saw her again. By then he would have figured out a way to better control his attraction to her. He was still trying to recover from the rippling heat that had been generated in the short span of time they'd been confined in his car together.

A short while later he was walking her up the walkway to the front door. "I probably won't get the chance to see you again before you return to school so I hope you enjoy the rest of your spring break."

"Thanks, Alex," Christy said when they had reached the brightly lit porch. She fumbled a few minutes in her purse before pulling out the key. After opening the door she turned to him. "Do you want to check inside?"

"No, that won't be—"

At that moment the shrill sound of the phone interrupted what Alex was saying.

"Excuse me, that's probably my parents calling from the hospital," Christy said before racing off to the phone, leaving Alex standing in the doorway.

He stepped inside, closing the door behind him. As she crossed the room to answer the phone, he thought there was something very feminine and alluring about her walk that made his heart thunder deep in his chest. He tried not to notice the sexiness of her legs beneath her short silky-looking outfit or the way the dress caressed her body, emphasizing the curves beneath the soft material. And he could just imagine her wearing a majorette uniform marching across a football field at halftime. Sweet, hot desire gripped him at the thought of those long, slender legs kicking up, kicking out and lifting high.

"Hello? Mom! Yes, I just got in. Yes, Alex brought me home." A few seconds later Christy's face broke into a wide smile. "They did! That's wonderful." She turned to Alex. "Corinthians and Trevor had a boy!"

Christy then resumed her conversation with her mother. "Yes, I was talking to Alex. He's still here. Sure, I'll be okay if you and Dad decide to go and celebrate with the Grants and Averys tonight. All right. Goodbye, Mom." Christy hung up the phone and looked over at Alex, smiling. "Isn't that wonderful for Trevor and Corinthians?"

"Yes, if you're into the family thing."

Christy lifted a brow. "You're not?"

"No. That's something I don't plan on getting into anytime soon. At least for another ten years or so," he said smoothly. Inwardly he asked himself why he was having this conversation with her. Why was he even still there? He had done his duty and had made sure she was safely inside so now he could leave. He should quickly walk out the door before he was tempted to give in to this crazy impulse and cross the room and kiss Christy Madaris senseless.

"Ten years? You plan on waiting ten years before getting married? I'll be nearly thirty-one by then," Christy said annoyingly.

Alex raised a thick brow wondering what had gotten her all upset and why her age at the time he decided to marry meant anything. "Yes, I guess you will."

She crossed her arms over her chest. "I don't want to wait that long."

Alex wished he could logically follow her conversation but she was downright confusing him. "You don't want to wait that long for what?"

"To get married."

Alex shook his head and decided to try another approach. "Christy, I'm sure you'll be able to marry before your thirty-first birthday if that's what you want."

"Not if you plan to wait ten years."

Alex was even more confused. "What does the amount of time I plan on waiting to marry have to do with you?"

Christy looked at him, surprise gleaming in her eyes. She then slowly crossed the room to him. "Don't you know? Don't you even remember?" she asked softly.

Alex looked at her serious expression. What was he supposed to know? What was he supposed to remember? "No. How about you tell me? Remind me," he said quietly.

She nodded slowly, seriously. "Better yet, I can show you." She lifted her finger to him and he saw the ring she intended for him to see. He quickly remembered it was an inexpensive ring he'd worn as a teenager on his pinkie finger. He had given it to her years ago.

"Do you remember when you gave this ring to me, Alex?"

He frowned. "Yes. It was on your thirteenth birthday."

"Do you remember why you gave it to me?"

Alex shrugged. "Yes, you had been crying that day because of your brothers' overprotectiveness. You thought you would grow up to be an old maid because no one would ever want to marry you because of being afraid of your brothers."

Christy nodded, and she looked at him, held tight to his gaze. "That's right. Now do you remember what you told me that day? What you promised?"

Alex frowned when he remembered. "Yes, I gave you the ring and told you that you didn't have to worry about your brothers scaring any of the guys away because I would be the one to marry you when you got older, and that I would wait for you..." The words trailed off when what he'd actually said to her that day almost eight years ago hit him in the face.

"To grow up," Christy finished for him.

Alex leaned back against the door as he studied her intently. Surely she didn't expect for the two of them... He shook his head. "Christy, you know I was just kidding with you that day, don't you?"

An angry glint appeared in her eyes. "I don't know anything of the sort. I assumed you were telling me the truth."

Alex narrowed his eyes at her. It had been no secret to anyone who lived in their old neighborhood that

Christy Madaris had always had a crush on him that started when she turned eleven and had lasted until she'd gone off to college at seventeen. Although he'd been flattered by it, he'd been careful not to do anything to take advantage of, or encourage, her tender feelings. Except—maybe for that one time on the day she had turned thirteen and had been crying. But what he'd done had been perfectly innocent on his part. He had a weakness when it came to females and tears.

"And you want me to believe since all that time, from the time you were thirteen, you thought I would marry you?" he finally asked her.

"Yes! Why wouldn't I believe it? You said it."

"I just told you that to stop you from crying. How could you have believed what I said?"

"Because you said it, and I've been wearing this ring for eight years to prove it. That's why I've never let my brothers' attitude toward other guys bother me and why I never got serious about anyone. I was promised to you. Everyone in my family knows that I plan to marry you, Alex."

He thought about Justin, Dex and Clayton and found that hard to believe.

"Even your brothers?"

Christy glared at him. "Yes. I told everyone that day. They probably have forgotten about it just like you've forgotten about it."

Alex sighed deeply. He remembered the Madaris brothers teasing him about it years ago because they knew he hadn't meant anything by it other than a way to soothe Christy's tears. Over the years either he or one of her brothers would bring it up and joke about it occasionally. He was more than sure that, like him, they assumed Christy had grown out of that crush. However, from the look on Christy's face, it appeared she had not.

He knew a quick and easy way to resolve the matter before it led to trouble and a whole lot of unnecessary pain. "If you thought I actually promised myself to you eight years ago, then it should be easy enough to get unpromised."

Christy lifted a brow. "What are you saying?"

"I'm setting the record straight. Now. Tonight. What I said to you eight years ago should not have been taken seriously."

His words hit Christy like a ton of bricks. She shook her head, confusion evident in her gaze. "But I've made plans," she said quietly. The hurt was evident in her voice.

A part of Alex felt his insides get ripped in two with the hurt he saw in her features. He felt even worse knowing he'd put it there. "What sort of plans?"

Christy lowered her head. She didn't know if she could find the words to explain.

"Christy? What plans?"

She lifted her gaze to his. He took a sharp intake of breath when he saw the lone tear in her eye. "You were to be my husband, the man I was saving myself for, the man whose babies I would have, the man I would love for the rest of my life."

Alex's anger flared. She'd had no right to make those sorts of plans that involved him, especially since her feelings weren't the result of adult emotions but of an infatuation that had started when she'd been a kid—which she wasn't anymore. "And you decided all of that just because of those words I said to you eight years ago?" he asked incredulously.

Christy stiffened her spine and glared up at him. "Yes. It was a promise."

"It meant nothing!"

"It meant everything to me, Alex!"

"I'm eight years older than you!"

"So! I'll be twenty-one in a few months."

"Then I'll be seven years older than you. You need to date guys closer to your own age."

"I've never wanted anyone but you."

"I'm a man, Christy."

"And I'm a woman, Alex."

By now they were nose to nose. Anger and tempers flared. Then suddenly, so did passion. Alex's gaze dropped from the angry fire in Christy's eyes to her peeved, parted lips. They were lips he had an immediate need to taste.

And so he did.

He pulled her into his arms and seized her mouth like the hungriest of men. Because at the moment, he was. His tongue swept inside and only after hesitating a few seconds, she responded to him with a burst of passion that nearly staggered him, kissing him back with a fervor that made him forget anything and everything, except for her. She tasted like heaven, and a rush of desire he had never felt before tore into him. He wanted more of her.

He wrapped his arms around her waist and slowly lifted her off her feet, closer to him. Their tongues mated, and they were helpless to the hot, searing need they were building within each other.

Unable to help himself when the urge to touch all that skin had tortured him all night, he lowered his hand and dipped it beneath the hem of her short dress and curved his hand possessively over the curvaceous swell of her soft behind. Pulling her forward, closer to him, he pushed his pelvis against hers.

He heard her moan, some unintelligible sound from deep within her throat, and knew this kiss they were sharing was the most intimate he had shared with a woman in a long time. He intensified the kiss when Christy tightened her arms around his neck, and he gripped her behind more firmly, cradling the very essence of her heat to him.

Alex knew then that kissing her wasn't enough. He wanted to taste her all over. He wanted to join himself with her in the most primitive way. At the moment, he couldn't think straight. He couldn't think at all. His mind was in a state of frenzy. His body was about to explode, and he wanted to be inside of her when it did.

He was about to lower her to the floor when the sound of a car's horn brought him back to his senses. He lowered Christy back to her feet and breathed in deeply, trying to regain control. He released her from his hold because he was too confused not to do so. He rubbed his hand over his face and wondered what the hell had just happened. One minute he and Christy had been yelling at each other and the next they were trying to devour each other's mouths.

Alex glanced over at her. She seemed as shaken with the kiss as he did. Her chest was rising and falling as she tried to get her breathing back on track. "Christy? You okay?"

She nodded before taking a few steps and burying her face against his chest. Instinctively, he tightened his hold on her.

"I'm sorry, Christy. I don't know what I was thinking," he groaned, his voice muffled by the torment he felt. He couldn't believe he had just kissed her that way. He glanced down at her and when he did, she lifted her head and looked at him. She drew in a long, deep, shuddering breath and as he continued to watch her, her lips, he thought, curved into a delicious, satisfied smile. "Don't apologize, Alex. That kiss was worth the eight-year wait. It was real nice."

He inhaled deeply, thinking that if anything, it had been hard and greedy. His desire for her had come on him fast and furious. For some reason he now wanted to show her what a "nice kiss" was like. Feeling his willpower dwindling, being shot to hell, he cupped the back of Christy's head and lifted her face closer to his. He leaned down and gently parted her lips with the tip of his tongue. Slipping inside he kissed her tenderly, the way a nice kiss should be. His hand moved across her back, down her spine to the curve of her bottom. Then he pulled her against him as he slowly and gently savored the taste of her as their tongues continued to stroke and mate slowly, tenderly. It was nice. Real nice. He heard her moan, the sound vibrating against her lips, and he continued to kiss her, taste her—over and over.

Moments later, breathing deeply, he tore his mouth from hers and looked down into her desire-glazed eyes and knew they were a mirror of his own. Had they continued kissing, their "nice kiss" would have flared out of control like wildfire again.

"Alex," she whispered. "I want to make love with you."

Alex straightened abruptly, remembering what she'd said was one of her plans…that she had been saving herself for him. He then remembered his relationship with her family, especially her brothers. The Maxwell brothers and the Madaris brothers had always been close since they had grown up in the same neighborhood, lived on the same street, their houses only a few doors from each other. Although they'd been older than he, Justin, Dex and Clayton had always treated him like a younger brother and their father, Jonathan Madaris, had always treated the two fatherless Maxwell brothers as sons. He knew that everyone, including his own brother and mother, would expect him to treat Christy with the utmost respect.

He sighed as he took a step back, reaffirming the

decision he'd just reached. "No, Christy. Your virginity is a very special gift that should go to your husband."

"But you'll be my husband one day."

"No, I won't." He needed to make her understand. He didn't want her to think the kisses they'd shared had changed anything. There was no way, although he knew that he was attracted to her, that he could continue to let her think something would ever come of it. He had to convince her that there could never be anything between them other than friendship. "What happened a few minutes ago was nothing but a case of lust, nothing more. You understand that, don't you?"

She shook her head. "No, I understand love, Alex, not lust. I love you."

Overwhelming frustration gripped him when he immediately thought of the hell that would break loose if anyone knew she thought she felt that way about him. Drawing a deep breath, he slid his hands into the pockets of his tuxedo slacks. He knew he had to get firm, and bring to an end what could be happening between them…for both of their sakes.

"I love you, Alex," she repeated softly when moments passed and the silence between them had stretched.

He laughed, and the harsh sound was intentional, to mock what she'd just said. "Love? You don't know a thing about love, especially not the man-woman kind. It's time you grew up and let go of childhood dreams and fantasies, because that's all they are,

Christy. You're not promised to me, and I'm not promised to you. The sooner you accept that, the better off we'll both be."

Without giving her a chance to respond, he angrily opened the door and walked out.

Chapter 16

Netherland tossed the towel aside after drying the water from her body. A few moments later, she slipped into her nightgown. She glanced at herself in the bathroom's mirror and inhaled deeply at the sight of her puffy eyes. She had cried all the way home from the hospital and wanted to cry even now but was determined not to. At least she had found out how Ashton felt about wanting a child before things had gotten too serious between them.

She suddenly paused, thinking she'd heard something, then shrugged, figuring it was Rome returning from tonight's affair at Sisters. But then something in the air made her shiver and at the same time, something warm settled down inside of her, making her stomach spin, her body burn.

She slowly stepped out of the bathroom and glanced around her semidarkened bedroom and breathed in deeply. Although she couldn't see him she knew Ashton was there. Somehow he had gotten past her alarm system again. Why had he come? There was nothing left for them to say to each other. She could never give him the child he would want one day.

But still, knowing that didn't stop her breathing from slowing down. Nor did it stop the nipples of her breasts from hardening against the soft fabric of her gown with the knowledge that Ashton was somewhere in the house.

Then she saw him.

He was standing in the shadows across the room, watching her but not saying anything. An element of some type of sexual charge penetrated the atmosphere surrounding them, increasing and sharpening their awareness of each other. She took a deep breath as self-preservation instincts surged through her but they didn't stand a chance right now, not with her adrenaline pumping fast and furious through her veins and with her breathing becoming long and deep.

And especially not when he took a step forward into the light.

All she could do was to stand there and stare at him. His eyes were darker than usual. His hair was undone and flowed around his shoulders, held back by a headband. He had taken the time to stop by the hotel to change clothes. He was no longer wearing his marine uniform but was wearing a pair of jeans and a fringed cowhide vest that was open, exposing a bare muscular chest that glistened with a thin sheen of sweat.

He took another step. Then another. Stalking slowly and increasing her heart rate with every move he took. Parts of her...all of her throbbed with the electrical energy surging between them—stimulating, invigorating. Arousing.

He came to a stop in front of her. The look in his eyes quickened the sparks that were going off deep inside of her. Taking a deep breath she looked directly into his eyes. "Why did you come, Ashton? Why are you here?"

He gave her a slow, sensuous smile and said calmly, "I came to kidnap you, Netherland."

Before she could comprehend what he meant, he quickly reached up and touched an area on the side of her neck, directly underneath her ear. His hand felt warm and firm.

That was her last thought before everything went black.

Rome's fingers curled around Jada's as they walked from his car. There was a brisk wind in the air and when she shivered, he instinctively gathered her close as they went up the stairs to her apartment.

When they stood in front of her door she turned to him. "Would you like to come inside?"

He smiled. "I was hoping you would ask." Moments later he reached for her hand before she opened the door. "Thanks for asking."

After a minute or two of strained silence she smiled and said, "You're welcome."

Once they were inside Rome closed the door behind them and immediately pulled her gently into his arms. "Can I kiss you, Jada?" He always asked, never assuming anything.

She looked up at him with both of her hands resting on his firm chest. "Yes. Please."

And so he did. With amazing gentleness, he touched his lips to hers, tasting her and letting her taste him. Without breaking the kiss, he picked her up in his arms and carried her to the sofa and sat down with her in his lap.

He continued kissing her for a few moments before finally coming up for air.

"Rome!" Her breath came out deep, uneven and she tightened her arms around his neck. "Hold me. Please hold me," she whispered softly, tightening her hold around his neck.

He held her as she requested, loving the feel of her in his arms. He wanted to do more than just hold her, but knew she wasn't ready for such a big step in their relationship yet, and he didn't want to rush her. Tonight, like the other nights before, he would just sit and hold her and make her feel special, as special as he thought she was. He would be leaving next week for Camp Pendleton in California, but he intended to return to Houston to see her every chance he got.

The need to keep her a part of his life was monumental to him.

"I enjoyed myself here tonight, Miss Gilford."

Rainey looked up from what she was doing and met Howard Reeves's heated gaze. She smiled. "I'm glad. If you're ever in town again I hope that you drop by." She had found out from Nettie—who for a short while had sat at the head table—that he lived in Chicago and was head of security for Chenault Electronics, a nationally known company.

A slow smile touched his lips. "I intend to do just that. But I was hoping I could get you to dance with me before I left. Will you dance with me, Miss Gilford?"

Rainey glanced around the room. A number of people had left already and only a few couples remained on the dance floor. Since Nettie wasn't there it would be up to her to close up the restaurant, which meant she had a lot to do. But the thought of taking a few minutes of her time and dancing with Howard Reeves was tempting. Too tempting to turn down.

She gave him her hand. "I'd love to dance with you, Mr. Reeves."

He took her hand in his. "Call me Howard."

"And I'm Rainey."

The orchestra was playing a slow jazzy tune by Miles Davis when Rainey went into Howard's arms on the dance floor. Desire, the likes Rainey had never felt before, sizzled through her bloodstream the moment he pressed her body against his. The two of them stared at each other, and a strong sizzle of sexual awareness touched the both of them. It had been that way all night, whenever their gazes had met across a crowded room.

"What do you think is happening between us, Rainey?" Howard asked in a deep voice, close to her ear.

Rainey's breath caught in her throat. Heat traveled up her legs. She cleared her throat and swallowed hard. "I don't know. What do you think is happening?" She didn't want to act coy and not acknowledge what the both of them knew but she wanted to hear him say it.

"I think we're seducing each other. Maybe intentionally. Maybe unintentionally. Whichever one it is, it's working big time." He pulled her closer as his hand caressed the part of her back the gown she wore didn't cover. She shivered beneath his touch and leaned her head back to look up at him. She shivered some more when she saw the heated desire that was evident in his eyes.

"I don't believe in casual affairs, Howard," she said while she had a mind to do so.

"Good. Neither do I," he said on a soft exhale of breath. "A long-distance affair will be difficult but in our case, one I believe is crucial. I want to get to know you better."

She gave him a slow smile. "And I'd like to get to know you better, too."

"How about if I make plans to come back and see you next weekend, or is that rushing things?"

Rainey's smile widened at the thought of seeing him again in a week's time. "No, I'd love seeing you again next weekend."

"All right, then, it's a date."

She placed her head back on his shoulder after saying, "Yes, it's a date." She knew that it would be a date she would be looking forward to.

Later that night Rome found a note from Ashton taped to the refrigerator door. It read:

Rome, I've kidnapped your sister for a week and have taken her to my home in Oklahoma. Trust me, she's fine. Also, believe that I know what I'm doing and that it's for the best. There are issues she and I need to work out. I'll contact you before you leave for Camp Pendleton on Thursday. If you have any questions or concerns before I call, see Trevor. And let Rainey Gilford know that Netherland has left town unexpectedly for a week so that she can handle things at Sisters.
Ashton

Rome lifted a brow after reading Ashton's letter. Nettie had surprised even him when she had entered the bidding on Ashton. And he thought it had been a good strategic move when the colonel had bidden on himself, which had allowed him to select the woman he wanted. That woman had been Nettie. He had made that clear in front of everyone present. Rome couldn't help but wonder what had happened to make Ashton want to take Nettie away now.

He decided to trust Ashton and patiently wait for his call.

Chapter 17

Netherland woke up and lay perfectly still. Although her mind tried to assure her that everything was all right, she knew it wasn't. For starters, she was not in her bedroom, nor was she in her bed. But the strange thing about it was that she was wearing her own nightgown.

Turning her head on the pillow she slowly glanced around a room that was totally unfamiliar. She blinked, trying to figure out where she was. The last thing she remembered was…Ashton.

She quickly sat straight up in bed.

"I was beginning to think I'd applied too much pressure to that nerve."

Netherland traced Ashton's voice to the doorway.

He was standing there wearing the same clothes he'd worn when he had shown up at her place. She blinked. Her mind was kind of foggy as to when that had been. Last night? This morning? Yesterday? "Where am I?" she decided to ask.

Ashton came into the room and stood opposite the bed. "You're at my ranch on the Cherokee reservation in Oklahoma."

"Oklahoma!"

"Yes."

"But how did I get here?"

"I chartered a plane and brought you here."

Netherland shook her head, trying to remember. "You came to see me last night at my place. Right?"

"Yes." He walked over to a table and picked up a chilled bottle of water out of an ice bucket.

"And you touched me, here," she said, placing her hand beneath her ear as she remembered him doing.

He turned around to her as he poured water into a glass. "Yes."

"I don't remember anything after that."

He walked over to her. "You wouldn't. I placed you in a deep sleep." He handed her the glass of cold water. "You need to drink this. Your body will experience extreme thirst for a couple of hours or so."

She took the glass he offered. After taking a sip, she looked up at him and asked. "You put me in some sort of unconscious state?"

"Yes."

In a way, that really didn't surprise her. The man

was able to bypass alarm systems, for heaven's sake. "Why? Why did you bring me here, Ashton?"

He sat on the side of the bed. "There are some things you and I need to work out."

Netherland looked at the glass, then back at him. "Some things can't be worked out, Ashton."

He inclined his head slightly when he said, "There's nothing that can't be worked out between us."

A part of Netherland—a big part—wished that was true, but knew it wasn't. "How can I fight a vision, Ashton? Especially when it's a vision that isn't true but one you believe in. Maybe I should have told you earlier of my inability to have children but I—"

"You can have children."

Netherland raised a brow as she looked up at him. "Excuse me?"

"I said you can have children."

She released a deep, angry sigh. He was taking the news of her infertility worse than Erik had. At least her ex-husband had accepted what she'd told him. Ashton didn't want to do that. He was in a state of denial. "I believe I know my body a whole lot better than you do," she snapped. Netherland's anger increased when Ashton had the nerve to smile.

"Yes, Netherland, for now you do but that will change soon enough. By the end of the week I will know your body better than anyone. Even you. Trust me."

Netherland thought about that for a minute, then said in a soft voice, "It's not about trust, Ashton."

"Yes, it is."

"Would you force yourself on me?"

The expression on his face indicated he thought the question was ludicrous. "Of course not!"

Netherland released a satisfied sigh. Now they were getting somewhere. The only thing she could count on right now was his sense of honor and doing what was right. It was something a marine lived by. "And you would not keep me here against my will, would you?"

A rogue grin tilted the corners of Ashton's lips. "Now that I *would* do."

"Why?" she asked, taken aback when she saw determination stamped all over his features. She drew a deep breath and looked away, avoiding the irresistible and tantalizing look in his eyes.

"Because like I told you earlier, we need to work out some things."

She forced herself to look back at him. "Some things can't be worked out with words, Ashton."

"I don't plan on using words, Netherland."

The husky tone of Ashton's voice made Netherland feel hot inside when a mental image of what he'd just alluded to flashed in her mind. She quickly took another sip of the cool, refreshing water, appreciating the smooth liquid as it worked its way down past the knot in her throat. "You're not a doctor, Ashton."

His gaze lingered on her damp lips. They were lips he had a firsthand knowledge of. "I didn't say I was."

Netherland met his stare with a frustrated glare. "Then what are you claiming to be?"

He reached out and gently traced his finger along her cheek. "The man who loves you."

Netherland sucked in a gulp of air, and tears immediately came into her eyes. "Not if you can't accept my deficiencies."

"I could if there were any. If you couldn't have my child I would adopt in a heartbeat. Your inability, if there was one, to have children would not keep me from loving you or having you in my life forever."

"If that's true, then why can't you accept what I'm trying to tell you?" she asked, placing the glass of water on the nightstand next to the bed.

"And why can't you accept what I'm trying to tell you? What are you afraid of? That I may be right?"

"No," she said quietly. "That you might think you're right but in reality you're dead wrong. I had a severe case of the mumps at eight, Ashton. The doctors told my parents then that it had left me unable to conceive. I went to a doctor again myself at eighteen who, after examining me, verified what my parents had been told ten years before." She looked down at her hands that were folded in her lap before looking back at him. "Don't you think I want to be able to conceive a child? But I've accepted that it won't happen and have gotten on with my life. I'm not alone in this. About six million women in the United States can't conceive or have difficulty conceiving, so I don't feel like the isolated case Erik made me out to be."

"Erik?"

"Yes, my ex-husband. Since he'd always wanted a big family, he didn't take the news of my infertility too well. That's the reason he divorced me."

Ashton's gaze narrowed. "The man was a fool. There were other alternatives. The two of you could have adopted."

"Yes, but he didn't want that."

Ashton reached out and took her hand in his, feeling the need to touch her. "What exactly did the doctor claim was wrong with you?"

Netherland released a pent-up breath before saying, "The problem is with my fallopian tubes. There's some sort of an obstruction that can't be surgically corrected. My chances of ever conceiving are less than twenty-five percent. So what does that tell you?"

"That there is a twenty-five percent possibility."

Netherland shook her head, pained at the thought that he still didn't want to accept what she was telling him. "Perfect!" she snapped, almost at her wits' end. "I just told you I had less than a twenty-five percent chance of getting pregnant, and you still want to play the part of the optimist?"

"When we make love, I *will* get you pregnant, Netherland."

Despairing anguish touched Netherland's heart because all it took was a look in Ashton's eyes to know he believed that. He actually looked confident. "And what do you have, Ashton? Super sperm or something?"

He shrugged. "No. As far as I know, they're the regular kind," he said calmly.

Netherland's chest expanded as she inhaled a deep breath. Never had she encountered a man who was so stubborn. "Well, it wouldn't matter if they were super sperm; they couldn't get past my blocked tubes."

Ashton stood. "Want to bet?"

Netherland frowned at him in sheer frustration before rolling out of bed. "And just how are they going to do that?"

"There are ways. I can show you better than I can tell you, Netherland. And it's all about love, faith and the gift of fertility that will be given to us when the time comes. The Cherokee people strongly believe in the power of loving, faith and healing. As my intended mate you have to believe in your heart that things will work out. Since you believe you have a medical condition that's keeping you from conceiving, what do you have to lose for me to prove otherwise?"

"You can't prove otherwise, Ashton. There are too many factors involved that may not work, one of which is the timing."

"The time is right."

Wariness reflected in Netherland's face. "How do you know?"

"A man knows when his mate's body is ready to conceive. Let me prove to you that I know what I'm talking about."

The eyes looking down at Netherland were deep,

dark and compelling as they tried to rid her of any doubt she had. He reached out and took her hand in his.

"Trust me, Netherland. Trust me." Then his mouth slowly came down on hers, demanding a response, eliciting her trust, binding her to him—body to body, soul to soul, heart to heart.

Netherland told herself that she would not get caught up in Ashton's kiss, but found herself caught up in it anyway. The dappled sunlight that filtered through the window bathed her with heated rays while still another kind of heat consumed her.

Ashton's heat.

His fingers moved up and down her back as he held her to him while his tongue plundered her mouth, taking everything she had and still demanding more.

He wanted her trust. He was demanding it.

"Ashton," she moaned softly when he finally broke off the kiss.

"Seven days, Netherland. That's all I want. I'm asking that you place yourself in my care for seven days. I left Rome a note letting him know that you're with me. I also told him to let Rainey know to take care of Sisters while you were gone. And I packed you plenty of clothes. So there isn't any reason I can't have you to myself for the next seven days. Is there?"

At the moment, Netherland couldn't think of one. She shook her head.

"And is there any reason why you can't trust me?"

A warning sounded somewhere deep inside Netherland, and a part of her wanted to plead her case again, to make him understand. But she was tired of fighting him, trying to make him see that nothing, short of a miracle, would get her pregnant.

"Ashton…"

"Trust me, Netherland."

After a tense moment of silence between them, she finally said, "I trust you, Ashton."

"And you will give me seven days?"

"Yes."

He pulled her back into his arms and held her close as relief coursed through him. "You won't regret it. Now I suggest you get back in bed and get some rest. Later today I'd like to show you around."

Netherland nodded slowly. A riot of emotions clamored within her, but when she gazed into the warmth of Ashton's dark eyes, that held both assurance and confidence, she wanted to give him more than just seven days. The part of her that loved him with all her heart wanted to give him the rest of her life.

Chapter 18

The sun was setting low, barely skimming the treetops when Ashton and Netherland emerged from the thickets of the woods holding hands. He had shown her a portion of the land and had given her a history lesson while doing so. He had told her that the Cherokee Nation was the second-largest First Nations tribe in the United States and that its land was rich with woodland and pastures, hills and valleys, and rivers and lakes. The Cherokee People had lived in the southeastern United States until their removal during the Trail of Tears. He also told her that some members of the tribe now lived in Oklahoma while others lived on Cherokee land in the mountains of North Carolina.

He talked about his deceased father, who at the age of twenty-five and a member of the Cherokee Nation Tribal Government, had met and fallen in love with the daughter of a military general stationed not far away at Fort Smith. It had been a match doomed from the start with interference from the young woman's family. The two eloped and he'd been conceived. However, within a year his parents had gotten a divorce. Ashton's voice had become bitter when he'd said that, thanks to his maternal grandfather, it had been a rather nasty divorce that had torn him between two families and two cultures.

Netherland glanced up at him. Tall, dark and extremely handsome were words that didn't quite do him justice. Neither did they cover the strength and masculinity he exuded without even trying. The stark blending of both cultures into his features, Native and African-American, made him so arrantly attractive it literally took her breath away.

She remembered how she had awakened that evening to find him gone. Getting out of bed she had showered and dressed in a long floral skirt and a peach pullover top, and after giving herself a tour of his home, she had sat on the sofa and waited for him to return. And while she waited, she had come to terms with a number of emotions within her. She loved him, of that there was no doubt. She trusted him. She didn't doubt that, either. What she did doubt was her ability to come through for him—in what he believed, and in what he wanted.

But by the time he had returned, she had tossed all her fears and doubts aside and had walked into his arms the moment he opened the door. She had wanted him to pick her up and take her to the bedroom and make love to her. Instead he had taken her hand in his and told her they were going for a walk.

"You should be hungry by now," he said quietly, breaking into her thoughts, as well as the silence that had suddenly surrounded them. "I can make a mean beef stew. How about some?"

She smiled. "That sounds good."

It was better than good, Netherland thought as she spooned the last of the beef stew from her bowl. It had been delicious. Returning to the cabin, Ashton had taken a large stew pot out of the cabinet; then he had expertly moved around the kitchen selecting the key ingredients he needed to make the stew. She had sat at the table and watched him, offering to help, but he'd told her it was something he wanted to prepare alone...for her. So she had talked while he had cooked. She told him about how she had used the money she'd inherited from her maternal grand-mother to purchase Sisters with dreams of transform-ing what had been an empty warehouse into an upscale restaurant and hangout for women.

"It's a nice place. You should be proud of yourself and your accomplishments, Netherland."

She smiled. "Thanks, and I am."

They ate in silence, finishing the meal with a lot on their minds.

"You can help me clean up the kitchen if you'd like," Ashton said, smiling over at her.

She smiled back at him. "Oh, you like having me around for the heavy stuff," she said jokingly.

"I like having you around period."

Netherland's body reacted to Ashton's words and the steady gaze that held hers. She tried to inject a semblance of normality and lightheartedness into her voice when she responded, "And what if I refused to help you with the dishes?"

He leaned back in his chair, locked his hands behind his head and continued to gaze at her. "Then I have to think of another way to get you to show your appreciation for the food I prepared for you. I'm sure if I think long and hard about it, I'll come up with something. And I'll make sure it's something we'd both enjoy doing."

Netherland watched as the pure, unadulterated sensuous look in his eyes said it all. Parts of her body responded as it throbbed and hummed when his eyes darkened. She cleared her throat. "You wash and I dry."

An easy grin played at the corners of his mouth. "Okay, but later, when you take your bath, I'll wash *and* I'll dry."

Netherland's breath caught in her throat, and heat surged through her. The two of them stared silently at each other for a long moment before she finally nodded. Ashton intended to keep that promise, and a sizzle of excitement as well as anticipation raced through her bloodstream just thinking about it.

"Are you ready to help me tackle the dishes?" he asked in a throaty whisper that tingled along her spine and made goose bumps appear on her arms.

"Yes."

He stood and held his hand out to her. "Come on, then," he said gently. "The sooner we can finish the dishes, the sooner we can get into other things."

The cleaning up of the kitchen, like dinner, was done in amicable silence. By the time the last of the dishes had been put away Ashton took Netherland's hand in his and led her from the kitchen into the living room. He crossed the room to the fire in the fireplace, sat on the floor in front of the hearth and pulled her down across his lap with her legs on either side of his waist.

Netherland faced him and looked into his eyes.

"For starters," he said, brushing a butterfly kiss against the corner of her mouth. "We'll talk about our future and where we go from here."

To the bedroom I hope, Netherland thought as the strong sensations of his fingers stroking her back brought a smile of pleasure to her lips. They were lips he was determined to taste as he touched his mouth to the corners of hers for a second time. "Our future?" she asked in a voice that sounded nothing like her own.

"Yes. As soon as it can be arranged, we'll marry the Christian way."

Netherland lifted her brow. "Is there supposed to be another way?"

"Yes, the Indian way. The way we'll do tonight."

His fingers, she couldn't help but notice, left her back and slid beneath the hem of her skirt and softly stroked her bare thigh.

"Marry? The Indian way? Tonight?" she whispered thickly, not sure if her voice had emitted the words loud enough for him to hear them.

"Yes. The ritual calls for the joining of our two souls, our two spirits and our two hearts into one. It will be just you and me, speaking words committing our lives together and to each other. To the Cherokee Nation our union tonight will be just as binding as any other because it will come straight from the heart. Our hearts."

She nodded, not capable of speaking, especially when his fingers continued to stroke her thigh. She felt an immediate sense of loss when he pulled his hand from under her skirt and reached out to her.

"Give me your hand."

He placed a beautiful leather band with studded diamonds around her wrist, then took her hands in his. She felt the strength of his hand enveloping hers. Then he closed his eyes and began softly chanting some sort of Indian song. When he finished, he opened his eyes, and their gazes locked.

"Netherland," he began in a hoarse voice, a voice that she could tell was thick with emotion. "Since the moment I first laid eyes on you, I wanted you. You are my soul, the very essence of my being. You are my kindred spirit, my mate. Heaven and earth may one day pass away but my love for you will last forever. I will honor this vow I make to you, a promise and pledge on the graves of all Cherokee warriors before me. I will be a good father to the children we will have together, honoring you as their mother and as my wife, my woman. To love and to protect you. I commit myself to you and no matter where I go, you will always be here," he said, placing their joined hands over his heart. "For always."

"Ashton." Netherland's voice trembled as tears clouded her eyes. She felt the rapid beating of his heart beneath their joined hands. His words had touched her deeply as he pledged his life and his love to her. "I didn't want to love you," she said softly. "I didn't want to be a part of your life, and I didn't want you to be a part of mine but I discovered the more I fought against you, the more I wanted you and was drawn to you."

She leaned in closer to him. "I love you, Ashton, with all my heart and with all my soul. I want to share your dreams but more importantly, I want to be a part of them. I hope everything in your visions comes true, and because of you I believe that miracles are possible. Because of you I believe in love. And from this moment on I surrender. I surrender all to you— my heart, my body and my soul."

"Netherland," Ashton murmured as he released her hands, bent his head and pulled her closer into his

arms. Before she could take her next breath, he
captured her mouth with his in a kiss that was long,
slow and deep, seeping heat from her lips to his. Their
tongues mated, crazed with passion, driven with need.

Netherland suddenly broke off the kiss. Gripping
Ashton's shoulders and tilting her body sideways, she
tumbled them onto the floor. For a brief few moments
they lay side by side, gazing at each other as they
tried to get their rising passion under control. She
then shifted to her knees over him. "Make love to me,
Ashton. Make me yours completely," she whispered
sensuously and at the same time reaching down and
sliding the palms of her hands up his shoulders.

With lightning speed Ashton hooked his arms
around her waist and scooped her off the floor with
him. He held her tightly, enfolded in his arms as he
carried her into the bedroom. Once there he gently
placed her on the bed and stood back and looked at
her, inhaling her sensuous scent. Reaching down he
lifted her top over her head, unhooked her bra and
tugged it off. Intent on divesting her of all clothing,
he went to the buttons on her skirt and slowly undid
each one. Moments later he tossed her skirt aside and
then removed her shoes. That only left her panties.

With unerring precision he slowly pulled them
down her gorgeous, long legs, then let the silky,
skimpy garment fall from his hand to the floor. His
gaze then covered every inch of her naked flesh,
starting at the top of her head, pausing briefly at the
center of her, before moving down to her toes. The

room was quiet. The only sound that could be heard was their erratic breathing being forced through constricted lungs.

"Now it's your turn to undress me," he said, stretching his hand out to her.

Netherland's response to his request was a throaty, sensuous sigh as she placed her hand in the palm of his. He gently tugged her upright and brought her against the solid wall of his chest. Wanting to see as much of his bare skin as he was seeing of hers, she began unbuttoning his shirt while placing lingering kisses along the side of his neck and jaw. She pushed his shirt off his shoulders and dusted kisses on his chest.

Cupping her chin, Ashton lifted her face up to stare down into her eyes. Then he slowly pulled her to him and kissed her, parting her lips with his tongue, his breath invading her mouth to conquer her soul.

Netherland wound her arms around his neck and gloried in the feel of his mouth on hers, tasting, mating. And at the same time his hand gently caressed the bare flesh of her behind, bringing her closer to the fit of him, rubbing the essence of her against the hardness in the front of his jeans. Moments later she pulled away from their kiss and her fingers went to the zipper of his jeans and tugged it down.

"I'll take over from here, sweetheart," Ashton said silkily as he took a step away from the bed.

Netherland watched as he began removing his jeans, then his loincloth underwear, dropping the last piece of clothing that hid him from her view. A startled gasp escaped her lips. She had not imagined him being so big, so powerfully virile. She forced herself to breathe between ragged breaths.

"I—I don't think it's going to work," she said in a deep, shaky breath, not taking her eyes off that part of him.

He came back to the bed. "We'll fit."

She shook her head, then met her gaze. "I'm not so sure about that."

A smile fanned the corners of his dark eyes. "I am. A woman's body is made to adjust for her mate. I won't hurt you, sweetheart."

Before giving her a chance to respond, he reached out and filled his hands with her breasts, slowly caressing each nipple as he watched her eyelids flutter weakly and a groan escape her parted lips. He seized the opportunity and kissed her, locking her mouth to his. Getting on the bed he pulled her back with him. Then he was touching, stroking her everywhere.

"Do you know how beautiful you are?" he asked hoarsely as his hand slid slowly across her flat stomach. He gently began caressing her in the area where her fallopian tubes were. "The gift of fertility will be bestowed upon us from the Spirits of Mother Earth to commemorate our union."

"Umm," was all she could say as she closed her eyes. His thumbs were moving in a slow, sensuous, gentle message over her abdomen, making her moan softly, deep within her throat.

He bent over her and closed his lips over one

nipple of her breast, then another, lavishing it with the hot, wet attention of his tongue.

"Ashton, please…"

Netherland's breathless plea only made Ashton's mouth continue to work its magic over her. Moments later, he let two fingers slip inside of her, to test the hot, moist heat of her body. She was ready for him.

Ashton's breathing was harsh and deep when he moved in place over Netherland's body and kissed her again, opening her thighs wide for him. Lifting his head he gazed down into her eyes. "I love you, Netherland," he whispered as his hands went to her hips to hold her in place. He then entered her, slow. And just as he had told her, her body automatically stretched and expanded to accommodate him. It was a tight fit nonetheless. He sucked in deep when he couldn't go any farther within her. He was nested to the hilt.

"I didn't think it would work," Netherland whispered, feeling the fullness of him buried deep inside of her.

He smiled down at her. "I told you it would. Now I will give you my sons."

"Sons?"

His lips tilted into a smile. "Yes, three of them. You're going to have triplets, Netherland."

Not waiting for her reaction to his announcement, he took her mouth in his the moment his body began moving inside of her, slowly, carefully easing in and out. His nostrils flared as the musky scent of their mating began filling the air. A low, strangled groan caught in Ashton's throat when Netherland wrapped her legs around him, drawing him even deeper into her body. He picked up the pace of their mating, thrusting his tongue in and out of her mouth with the same rhythm as his body was pumping in and out of her. He swallowed her groan when he felt her body begin climaxing beneath him. A guttural groan was ripped from his chest as the pleasure that racked her body filtered to his, making his body explode with the violent force of his release that spilled forth like a tidal wave, a flash flood, deep within her womb, stripping the very essence of his soul. For him nothing had ever felt so complete, so right and so perfect.

The heaving beating of Ashton's heart matched Netherland's, and the sheer magic of what they had just shared made contentment settle over her as the last ripple of passion overtook them. Dazed, she looked up into his eyes and whispered the one Cherokee word he had taught her that day.

"Wa-Do." Which meant thank you.

Chapter 19

Over and over, all through the night and the morning after, Ashton made love to Netherland, releasing all the love and desire that had been building between them from the first time they met.

And still he wanted more.

It was as if once he had tasted the essence of her passion, he couldn't get enough. It was close to noon, and they still hadn't gotten out of bed. She lay pinned beneath him as he moved his body in and out of hers, increasing the tempo with each and every soft moan she made. Locking her hands over her head, he rode her to sweet oblivion with every ounce of energy he owned while animalistic growls of pleasure rose in his chest and were ripped from his throat.

Netherland wrapped her legs around Ashton, tight, sealing their bodies, binding them as one. Jagged streaks of pleasure washed over her as they mated over and over, nearly driving her to the brink of insanity as he continued to withdraw and plunge deeper and deeper inside of her.

And then it happened, for the umpteenth time, they climaxed together, spilling into each other. Instinctively she spread her legs wide in response, lifted her hips to receive all he was giving, drawing him farther into her body and the very essence of her being. She opened her eyes and looked up at him and saw the taut lines etched on his face as they both spun out of control while he flooded her womb with his seed.

Finally, without caring that they hadn't eaten a meal since the evening before, they fell into an exhausted sleep, warm, comfortable and satiated in each other's arms.

Netherland, whose body still hummed with the aftershocks of their marathon lovemaking, suddenly came awake when she remembered something. She rose up on her elbow to look down at Ashton. "Triplets? You were teasing last night, weren't you?"

Ashton slowly opened his eyes and gazed up at her. "No, I wasn't teasing. You will have triplets."

"But—but that's not possible."

Ashton smiled lazily. "Anything is possible, Netherland."

Pushing one hand through her hair, Netherland lay

back in bed as she absorbed Ashton's words. She then looked at the man lying beside her. "Sons? So they will be boys?"

"Yes."

"And you saw this in one of your visions?"

"Yes." Rolling to the side, Ashton grabbed a pillow and jammed it beneath his head. "Does giving birth to more than one baby at a time bother you?"

"Only a man could ask a question like that," she said with a quiet laugh. "But to be quite honest with you, no, it doesn't bother me. For so long I thought I couldn't give birth to any baby, so to know that I'll have three is like hitting the jackpot."

"You're happy about it then?" he asked quietly.

Netherland smiled up at him, filled with emotion as she fought back tears. "Yes, I'm happy about it. I feel truly blessed."

Ashton ran a hand up and down her arm in long, soothing strokes. "So do I. But I'm also feeling hungry. How about if we get up, get dressed and get something to eat?"

"All right. What's after that?"

A devastating grin touched his face. "After that I'm sure we'll think of something to keep us occupied."

"And you're sure everything is okay, Nettie?"

Netherland paused in her conversation with her brother to glance across the room at Ashton. He was looking out of the window. Silhouetted in the dazzling rays from the sun, he appeared more mystical than man. Dressed in a pair of faded jeans and Western-style boots, and with the top portion of him bare, he showed off a powerful set of shoulders, a broad and muscular back and coal-black hair that was sensually mussed and hung loosely about his shoulders. As if he felt her eyes on him, he turned and slid his gaze over her in one slow sweep, reminding her of what they had been doing for the past three days.

"Nettie?"

She sighed as Rome pulled her back into their phone conversation. "Yes, Rome, everything is okay. They couldn't be better. Ashton and I married each other a few nights ago the Indian way, but we plan to make things perfectly legal when I get back and can make the necessary arrangements."

She glanced back over at Ashton, the man she now considered her husband, her mate, in every sense of the word. Her pulse quickened. He was still looking at her with that *I want you again* look in his eyes.

"I hate that I won't get to see you before I leave tomorrow," her brother was saying.

"Me, too, but I'm sure you'll be back to Houston soon, right?" she asked, smiling.

"Yes. Jada and I have agreed to continue to see each other. I have more leave time coming up next month, and I plan on taking it. I've even invited her to come out and visit me at Camp Pendleton. She's never been to California before."

"Do you think she'll do it?"

"I'm hoping she will although she hasn't agreed one

way or the other. I won't rush her into anything. I've agreed for us to take things slow, Nettie. I want her to see that all men aren't like her ex-husband. He hurt her."

"I know. I'm glad you've been there for her these past two weeks. She's been the happiest I've seen her since coming to work for me."

"And I want her to stay happy. I love her, Nettie. I didn't think after losing Kimmy that I'd ever love anyone ever again, but I do love her. And I can't wait for the folks to meet her. I just know Mom is going to like her."

Netherland smiled. There was no doubt she would. Their mother was someone who saw goodness in everyone and had a soft spot for everybody. "I hope you can get back for my wedding. It won't be anything elaborate. Just a gathering of a few friends and family in another month or so."

"I'm going to try my damnedest to make it back for that. You can't marry a second time without your brothers present."

A few moments later Netherland ended the phone conversation with her brother.

"I take it everything is still running smoothly without you," Ashton said in reference to her conversation with Rome and her earlier conversation with Rainey. He walked over to her.

"If they weren't running smoothly, would you take me back?" she asked him, smiling.

"No. I have seven days with you, Netherland. I've only used three. I have four left."

Netherland sighed. "Who's counting?"

Ashton grinned. "I am. I want to spend every moment that I can with you, sweetheart."

"And I with you," she said, not imagining it any other way. But she knew when reality set in there would be another way. She must not forget she shared him with the United States Marine Corps. "So, what do we have planned for this evening?"

When he gave her a sensuous look that spoke volumes and guaranteed earth-shaking passion, she quickly said, "Besides that."

Ashton laughed. "Getting bored?"

Netherland reached out and wrapped her arms around his waist, pulling him closer to her. She smiled up at him. "No, just getting to the point where I can walk again."

Rome glanced across the table at Jada. "Thanks for dinner. You really didn't have to go to the trouble."

"It wasn't any trouble, Rome. It was something I wanted to do and with this being your last night in Houston I wanted to make it special."

"Just being able to spend time with you makes it special, Jada."

She smiled at his compliment. "Thanks, Rome."

Rome watched her struggle to eat and knew that, like him, she didn't have much of an appetite. He was really going to miss her. A part of him wanted to cross the room, pick her up in his arms and take her into the bedroom and make love to her just to show her how much he cared. But he knew he had to stick with his plan of moving slow with her. She needed sweetness and comfort. Friendship. She needed for them to share a relationship that wasn't just physical.

"I checked in with my superiors at Camp Pendleton today," he said when silence surrounded the table. "I can get another leave in two weeks. That's a whole week earlier than what I had figured on."

Her smile widened. "I'll look forward to seeing you again, Rome." She took another bite of her food before adding, "And I thought about your invitation to come visit you in California. I think I'd really like that."

A huge smile shone on Rome's face. "I'd like that, too."

Anthony Roberts's eyes grew cold as he looked at the man who faced him on the other side of the glass booth. "You're stalling, Billy. What news do you have for me? And I want to hear all of it."

Billy tried not to tremble with the look and the harsh words Tony was giving him. After all, there was a thick piece of glass separating them, and guards were posted all around. There was nothing Tony could do but stew at the news he was about to deliver. "Jada found somebody else, man. A soldier boy."

A hard, furious look came into Tony's eyes, making him appear very dangerous even while he sat behind prison walls. "Are you sure?"

Billy swallowed. Maybe he should not have said anything.

When tense moments passed and Billy didn't answer, Tony raised his voice and with a vicious curse, he rammed his fist on the counter in front of him. "Answer me, Billy. Are you sure?"

Before Billy could respond, one of the prison guards came over. "What's going on here?" he asked.

"Somebody in the family died," Tony said curtly to the guard in way of explanation so the man could move on and get out of his business. The guard glanced at Tony and then at Billy before moving on.

Tony lowered his voice but the anger was still there when he asked Billy for the third time, "Are you sure?"

Billy leaned back in his chair. "Yeah, I'm sure. In fact, I'm positive. I've been watching her for the past few weeks just like you told me to do. The guy's been hanging around a lot and has been staying at her place real late at night."

Billy crossed his arms over his chest. A part of him was glad Jada had found somebody else. Tony had never treated her with any type of dignity and respect anyhow. It served him right. But the look in Tony's eyes made him shiver. There was a crazed look in them.

"Jada made a mistake, Billy. A costly mistake. Nobody two-times Anthony Roberts and gets away with it. Nobody. And she's gonna pay. Boy, is she gonna pay."

The next day Tony had another visitor, one he had summoned. It was one of the guys he used to hang around with when he had his freedom. Lamar

Stokes was someone who would do just about anything for a price.

"Look, man, I want everything laid out just like I'm asking. I need to blow this place as soon as I can. I got personal business to take care of. You hook me up right, and I'll throw another thousand in for old times' sake."

Lamar looked hard at Tony. "Why should I trust you, man? What assurance do I have you gonna deliver, and that I'm gonna get my bread? Cash ain't easy for a man in your position to lay his hands on."

Tony smiled to hide his frown. "Yeah, but I ran into some dough right before I got put in this joint. I stashed it away so the feds couldn't touch it. I'm gonna pay up, man, you have my word on it."

"I don't take nobody's word on nothin'."

"Okay, man, that's cool. I'll just have my cousin Billy lay an advance on you. You'll get the rest as soon as I get out of here. Just make sure everything goes down the way I want. Deal?"

Lamar rubbed his chin. Word on the street had it that Tony had come into some cheese and before he'd had the chance to blow it all, he'd gotten busted for knocking around his old lady. So there was a good chance he did have some bread stashed away somewhere. "If you cross me, Tony, there ain't no place big enough in this city for you to hide. Remember that."

Tony leaned back in his chair, relaxed. "Hey, I'll remember."

Chapter 20

"Who taught you how to gamble so well, Ashton?"

Ashton's laugh, soft and sexy, rumbled low in his chest. "Becoming a sore loser, are we?" he asked as he lifted his gaze from the cards he held in his hand to look at Netherland. The two of them were sitting Indian-style across from each other on the floor in front of the fireplace as they played a game of spades.

Netherland shrugged, grinning. "No, that's not it. You're beating me at a game I thought I was good at. How about giving me some slack."

"Sorry, I play to win."

He had leaned forward and had unknowingly given Netherland a whiff of his manly scent. For a moment she was tempted to throw the cards down and have her way with him. Again. "I figured you did, and you still haven't answered my question."

He smiled. "My father taught me. The Cherokees, like a number of Native Americans, own several casinos. My family owns two."

"No wonder you're good at it then." She leaned back on her arms. "It's getting hot in here. You don't mind if I take off my blouse, do you?"

Ashton regarded her with a smooth grin. "Not at all. Help yourself."

Netherland hesitated a moment, but only a moment before unbuttoning her blouse and tossing it aside.

Ashton had watched her every move. "Feel better?"

She smiled at him as she reached up and pushed a strand of hair from her face. "Yes. Much better."

"Had I known you wouldn't mind getting out of your clothes, I would have suggested that we play strip poker."

Netherland laughed as she went back to studying her hand. "Why? You've seen me without clothes several times over the past few days."

"Yeah, but each time is better than the last, and I discover something new. Like yesterday for instance when I noticed that butterfly tattooed on your right inner thigh."

Netherland sighed as she remembered just how he had discovered her small secret. A sensation of simmering heat passed through her with the memory. She felt hot again. Without saying anything she removed her bra.

"Are you trying to mess with my concentration, Netherland?"

She smiled up at him. "Whatever gave you that idea?"

He slowly dragged his gaze away from the sight of her bare breasts back up to her face. "You should know by now that I'm a breast man."

"I thought you were a leg man."

"That, too. And as you discovered yesterday, I also enjoy thighs."

The passion in his voice sizzled through her. "Easy, Ashton, if I didn't know any better I'd think you were getting aroused."

"And if I didn't know any better I'd think you were deliberately trying to arouse me."

"Would I do that?"

"Yes."

"You're right. I would," she confessed, shivering at the intensity in the dark eyes looking at her. She wondered if there would ever come a time where she would get enough of this man. She doubted it. No matter how many times they made love, she always wanted more of him. And although she had very little experience on which to base a comparison she knew that he wasn't like most men. For one thing, he had the stamina of a bull.

"I don't want to play cards anymore," Ashton said, placing his cards aside.

Netherland's hand stilled on her own cards and

she looked up at Ashton, and into his dark, heated gaze. "Then what do you want to do?"

"Mate."

Netherland watched as Ashton closed the distance between them on all fours. He looked like a wolf stalking his prey, and the sound coming from deep within his throat was an actual growl. He came to a stop when he was directly in front of her. "I like mating with you, Netherland." He whispered the words seconds before dipping his head and claiming her mouth, tumbling them backward onto the floor.

Desperate need coiled within Netherland with every stroke of Ashton's tongue as he made love to her mouth. Little whimpering sounds came from deep in her throat when he intensified their kiss. And his hands, she couldn't help but notice, were busy doing other things. They were touching her everywhere, caressing her breasts and fumbling with her panties underneath her skirt.

"Ashton!" His name came out on a gasp when she felt the heat of his fingers come in contact with the essence of her womanly heat. Touching. Exploring. Stroking.

Ashton broke the kiss long enough to remove the rest of Netherland's clothing and all of his own. "I can't seem to get enough of you, sweetheart," he whispered as he went back to her and began attacking her lips again. And then he pressed her flat on her back onto the floor, parting her legs as he moved over her and positioning himself between her thighs.

Slipping his hand beneath her, he lifted her hips slightly and drove himself into her.

His mouth came down on hers the moment their bodies joined, and they began mating. She dug her fingernails into his shoulders and hung on as he made one powerful thrust after another into her body, over and over.

The sensation of Ashton moving in and out of her body as well as the feel of her breasts rubbing against his chest stimulated her entire body beyond belief. She was about to shatter into a million tiny pieces from the experience. But Ashton wouldn't let her. He was intent on claiming her body and reminding her that what they shared was priceless, special and exceptional.

"Ashton," she whispered, arching into him when she felt she could not hold on any longer. "Now!"

"Not yet!" was his response before burying his face in the curve of her neck and increasing the tempo of their mating. He was drowning in a sea of passionate ecstasy as much as she was, but he refused to ask for a life preserver. He wanted to keep himself, rock solid, in the warmth of her soft depths a while longer. Never before had he felt this way with any woman, this amazing connection that he and Netherland shared.

Netherland groaned when she looked up and saw raw need shimmering deep in Ashton's eyes. And then her body hammered with an urgency that demanded immediate satisfaction.

Ashton's body suddenly felt that same need. He

plunged into Netherland one final time, exploding inside of her, pushing himself deeper and deeper. He felt her shatter in his arms and knew that at that moment they both had surrendered—to each other, to their bodies, their minds, their spirits.

Even with the turbulence they had just experienced, they were at peace.

Anthony Roberts heard the sound; his cue that everything was in place. He had gotten his cell mate, a man doing ten years for armed robbery, to agree to keep the guards in the dark for as long as he could. It had been easy to swipe the guard uniform out of the laundry room two days before. It had been a perfect size and fit. No one paid him any particular attention when he had walked out the front gate a free man. Lamar had been right on time with the stolen car he'd left for him in the parking lot. No one would have thought to look for a stolen vehicle—in of all places—the parking lot of a prison.

A few minutes later he was driving toward his destination. There were two women who would pay for causing him so much grief. First he would take care of that hotshot attorney and then he would give his wife a taste of his own special brand of torture.

Ashton was having another vision.

He was standing in a forest under the bright blue sky, yet all around him a fire blazed out of control.

The smell of smoke was scorching his nostrils, the heat from the flames was parching the bottom of his feet. His body ached with the tiredness he felt but somehow he forced himself to move on. He had taken a few steps and realized he couldn't move another inch. He didn't have the strength to do so. Then from a distance he heard Netherland call his name, and he tried to gather all his strength to continue, to move forward, away from the fire, toward the sound of her voice, but it was too late. Flames surrounded him. He was trapped.

Ashton jumped and sat straight up in bed. His body was covered in sweat, and his heart was beating three times its normal rate. He took a deep breath. For the first time he had broken away from his vision before he determined the outcome. Had he made it out of the fiery hell he'd been trapped in? Had he made it back to Netherland?

He wiped a shaky hand across his face wondering what this particular vision had meant. He glanced over at Netherland. She was still sleeping soundly, peacefully. Needing to hold her, he lay back down and gently pulled her into his arms and held her cradled against his chest.

The sleep that overtook him a few minutes later was not a peaceful one.

Clayton Madaris slid the manila folder, thick with documents, across the table to his wife. "This is the last one we need to discuss tonight. We have a hearing in the judge's chamber Friday morning. What did you think after reviewing it?"

Syneda leaned back in her chair and met her husband's inquiring gaze. "That we don't have a snowball's chance in hell of winning. Harold Kingston is as guilty of embezzlement as Nixon was of Watergate. I suggest we convince him to plead guilty and go for a lesser sentence."

Clayton smiled. "I disagree. I suggest he plead not guilty and take his chances."

Syneda lifted a brow. "Why?"

"I enjoy a good fight with the prosecution every now and then."

Syneda shrugged as she rose to her feet. "Suit yourself. Since it seems that we aren't going to agree on anything tonight, I suggest we call it a day."

Clayton shook his head, grinning. "On that I do agree."

A few moments later they were walking out of the office building where their law practice was located. Since Clayton had made plans to drop by the barbershop after work, they had driven separate cars. "I'll see you at home in a couple of hours?" Syneda asked, turning to her husband.

"Maybe less if Mr. P's isn't crowded." Clayton leaned over and placed a kiss on her lips. "Think your tummy can handle Chinese food tonight?" Since her pregnancy certain foods didn't agree with her stomach.

"I prefer barbecue."

Clayton smiled. "Then barbecue it is."

"The thin end."

Clayton shook his head, grinning. "All right, sweetheart. Drive carefully."

He watched as Syneda began crossing the parking garage to her car. He heard the revving of a car's engine the same time Syneda did and saw the vehicle aiming straight toward her.

"Syneda! Look out!"

Reacting on instinct to protect both the woman and the unborn child he loved, Clayton moved with lightning speed toward Syneda, who seemed to have frozen in place, like a deer caught in headlights. In desperation Clayton pounced upward like a panther and jumped toward her, pushing her out of the way just seconds before the car collided with his body, knocking him backward.

"Good night, Rainey."

"Good night, Jada. Are you sure you don't need a ride home?"

"Yes. I'm sure. I called a cab earlier. I'll just wait for it out front."

Jada walked out of Sisters thinking it was such a pretty night. Rome had left for California earlier that day, and she missed him already. She smiled and stepped aside when a couple entered Sisters holding hands with the look of love sparkling in their eyes. She checked her watch once more. She had called for the cab ten minutes ago. Usually it didn't take this long for one to come.

She had turned to go back inside to call for another cab when she felt a hand grab her from behind. She began struggling and was about to let out a scream when something that felt like a sock was stuffed into her mouth. She continued to struggle as she felt herself being dragged over to a car whose motor was running. Fear clutched every part of her body when she was shoved inside. When she heard the sound of her attacker's voice she knew she was about to relive her worst nightmare. Anthony Roberts stared her dead in the face with a crazed look etched in his features.

"What's wrong, sweetheart? Aren't you glad to see your husband?"

Ashton knew something was wrong the moment he heard the telephone ring. A quick glance at the clock on the nightstand next to the bed indicated it was two in the morning.

"Colonel Sinclair," he answered as calmly as he could, pushing himself up in bed.

The phone had also awakened Netherland. She pulled up beside him in bed and looked intently at Ashton. He wasn't saying anything to the caller but was listening attentively. However, she could tell from the look on his face whatever the caller was saying wasn't good.

"I'll be there in a couple of hours," Ashton said before ending the call and hanging up the phone.

"Military business, Ashton?"

He turned to her. His features displayed no inner conflict whatsoever, but the woman in her, the one who had spent the last five days in his arms, sharing almost everything with him, could feel the internal warfare he was trying like hell to hide. "No, that was Trevor."

"The baby?" she asked anxiously as her heart skipped a beat.

"Corinthians and the baby are fine. It's Clayton."

Netherland's heart missed another beat. "What about Clayton?"

He reached out and took her hand in his. "He was hit by a car tonight, a car that was aiming straight for Syneda. He pushed her out of the way and took the blow."

"How is he?" The words rushed from Netherland's lips and when Ashton didn't answer quick enough she said frantically, "Tell me! How is he?"

Ashton heard the agitation in her voice and understood. She and Clayton Madaris had been friends for a long time. "He's been taken to surgery."

Netherland inhaled deeply, knowing Syneda was probably going out of her mind. She then remembered something else Ashton had said. "Someone actually tried to run over Syneda?"

"Yes."

"Do they have any idea who?"

"Yes."

Netherland studied Ashton's features and knew there was more. There was something he hadn't told her yet, and she had a feeling it wasn't good. "Who?"

"Anthony Roberts. He broke out of prison earlier today."

"Anthony Roberts? Jada's ex-husband?"

"Yes."

Netherland took another deep breath when she remembered something Jada had told her about—the threats her ex-husband had made against her and Syneda at his trial. Netherland was out of bed and on her feet in a flash. "Someone has to warn Jada that he's out there on the loose! She needs police protection! She—"

"Netherland," Ashton interrupted in a soft voice as he tried to calm her down. "You need to contact Rome."

She sucked in a huge gulp of air, almost too afraid to ask but she did so anyway. "Why?"

Ashton had her complete attention. He took a deep breath before saying. "Because Jada is missing, and there is a strong possibility that Roberts has grabbed her."

Chapter 21

The crowd of people inside the hospital's waiting room got eerily silent when they looked and saw Dr. Marvin Goldstein standing in the doorway. Dr. Goldstein had been a friend of the Madaris family for years.

The crowd parted, and Syneda rushed forward, flanked on both sides by Clayton's brothers, Justin and Dex. Clayton's parents and three sisters stood directly behind Syneda and his numerous friends brought up the rear. All were there to give Syneda their support.

One look at Syneda, and Dr. Goldstein knew that due to her delicate condition it would not be such a bad idea to check her into the hospital, as well. It was obvious what had happened to Clayton had taken a toll on her. The last thing he needed was for her to become overly distraught. He knew she'd been checked out when she first arrived but he could tell by looking at her that she was emotionally drained.

"How is he, Dr. Goldstein?" Syneda asked, frantically close to tears.

Dr. Goldstein placed a comforting hand on Syneda's shoulder. "We were able to stop the internal bleeding and that's good. He has a cracked rib and a concussion. I consider your young man very lucky. Things could have been a lot worse if he would have gotten hit at another angle. And although the next twenty-four to forty-eight hours are critical, there is no reason for me not to believe that he'll come through this with flying colors. I suspect he'll be back on the golf course in full swing after an adequate healing period of three to four months."

Syneda let out a relieved breath and found herself leaning against Justin, then Dex for much needed support. They placed both of their arms around her. "When can I see him?" she asked.

"I'll let you know as soon as they get him settled in the recovery room. He's still unconscious and will probably remain so for a while. That was some blow he took."

"And all because of me," Syneda said as tears began filling her eyes.

"Now you listen to me, young lady," the doctor said. "What he did was heroic, and something any man would do who loved someone. You can't blame yourself for his actions."

"But that car was meant for me. I was the intended victim, not him."

"And had it been you, then I would be standing here possibly telling Clayton that we had lost both you and his baby. He knew what he had to do to save you both, and he did it. Let's just thank God that it turned out this way and you'll have young Madaris back in your life in no time."

No sooner had the doctor left than Lieutenant Karl Barton from the Houston Police Department arrived. Netherland, who had arrived at the hospital with Ashton thirty minutes before, made her way over to him.

"Any word on Roberts and where he has taken Jada?"

The lieutenant sadly shook his head. "Not yet. We checked the prison's visitors log and as a result, have picked up his cousin Billy Roberts for questioning. Another visitor he had recently, a thug by the name of Lamar Stokes, can't be found but we're still looking."

Netherland nodded. "You have to find Jada. Roberts is dangerous and abusive and has kidnapped her before."

"Yes, ma'am, I know. I'm very familiar with the case. I was the one who made the last arrest. Trust me. I want Roberts back behind bars just as much as anyone. This time I hope we throw away the key."

"I'm available if you need my help, Lieutenant,"

Alex Maxwell said, coming forward. "I have a background with the FBI's Missing Persons Division."

"Thanks for the offer, but Houston's finest should be able to handle things. The car Roberts was driving was stolen. He's dumped that one and has stolen another right on the outskirts of the city."

"So you think he's left town?" Ashton asked, coming to stand next to Alex.

"Yes, but which way he's headed, we're not sure. We've alerted the police departments in all surrounding counties to be on the lookout for a new white Camry."

After Lieutenant Barton left, everyone remained in the waiting room for more news on Clayton.

"Thanks for being here, Nettie," Syneda said to her friend a short while later.

"You know that Ashton and I had to come. How are you holding up?"

"Better now that I know Clayton will be okay. I just wish he'd regain consciousness. I want to tell him how much I love him and how appreciative I am for what he did for me and our baby."

Netherland gave her an assuring smile. "I think he knows that already, but I can understand your wanting to tell him."

Syneda nodded. "I'm also worried about Jada in the clutches of that madman. I understand she's been seeing a lot of your brother. Have you notified him about her disappearance?"

Netherland nodded. "Yes, and with Ashton's

help he's on his way back. He should be arriving in a few hours."

"I hope we have some good news to tell him when he gets here," Syneda said softly.

"So do I."

At that moment Syntel Remington walked in. His gaze immediately found that of his daughter's.

"Daddy!" Without a moment's hesitation Syneda left Netherland's side and went straight into her father's outstretched arms. And there she cried the tears she had tried so hard to fight back, while he held her and gave her comfort as only a father could.

Dr. Goldstein returned half an hour later. "Mrs. Madaris?" When he saw about four ladies getting ready to respond, he clarified by saying, "Mrs. Clayton Madaris." He smiled at Syneda. "I've told the nurses to let you go on in to see Clayton for a few minutes. Right now I only want him to have visitors one at a time every two hours. Once he regains consciousness, then he can have more."

Moments later Syneda entered the small room where Clayton lay quiet, still. His face looked bruised, cut and swollen, and his body was attached to an assortment of machines. She spent the next half hour with her husband, talking to him, telling him how much she loved him and making promises she intended to keep if he regained consciousness.

"Put those promises in writing, will you?"

Syneda snatched her head up and looked at Clayton. He had spoken. And he was looking at her. Tears clouded her eyes when she took her husband's hand in hers after buzzing for the nurse. "You can have anything you want, Madaris," she said, smiling happily through her tears. "Anything." The only thing she could think about was that he was no longer unconscious.

"What about a new set of golf clubs?"

The corner of Syneda's lips tilted into a grin. "Maybe I should clarify by saying, anything within reason."

Clayton tried to smile but it was obvious the effort was painful. "I'm still holding you to that promise of cooking more."

Before Syneda could tell him that he must have been hearing things, the nurse arrived. "He's awake and talking," Syneda said, smiling to the older woman. "Please tell everyone that he's regained consciousness."

The woman nodded and quickly left the room.

"How about a kiss?" Clayton asked.

Syneda ran her fingertips lightly over her husband's bruised jaw. "How can you think about kissing at a time like this? You just regained consciousness."

"So? How can I not think about kissing? I nearly lost you and the baby."

More tears sprang into Syneda's eyes. She brought his hand to her lips and placed a tender kiss on his knuckles. "No, sweetheart, we nearly lost *you*. Don't you ever pull a stunt like that again, Madaris. Do you hear me?"

"I hear you but I ain't listening. I'll do it all over again if I thought it would keep you and my baby safe." He was silent for a moment, then said, "I need that kiss, Syneda."

On tiptoe she leaned over the bed and gave her husband the kiss he wanted.

And that was how his brothers, sisters and parents, as well as her father, found them. They were still kissing and from the way things looked, they had no intentions of stopping anytime soon, with or without an audience.

Dex Madaris shook his head, grinning. "Why doesn't it surprise me that the first thing Clayton wanted to do after nearly coming back from the dead was to suck face with somebody?"

"And why doesn't it surprise me," Justin Madaris decided to add, "that his wife was so eager to oblige him?"

Marilyn Madaris smiled happily. A weight had been lifted off her heart now that she saw her youngest son was all right. She leaned back against her husband's strong, solid chest. "Probably because those two are so evenly matched," she said in response to her sons' comments. "I think we can all agree that Clayton and Syneda were made for each other."

Jada nervously looked at the man sitting next to her in the car. It seemed that they had been driving for hours. He had taken the sock out of her mouth a hundred miles back after feeling fairly comfortable that it wouldn't matter if she took the notion to scream her head off. They were nowhere near civilization.

"Where are you taking me, Tony?"

Momentarily taking his eyes off the road, he looked over at her with a sardonic look on his face. "Someplace where no one will ever find you. You've been a bad girl, Jada, a very bad girl. You've dishonored our vows and brought me shame. Since it seems that beatings don't work with you, I'm going to have to deal with you in another way."

Fear ran down Jada's spine. She didn't want to even think what he had in mind. "You won't get away with this. The authorities will find you."

He looked over at her again. The look on his face made her skin crawl with panic, dread and terror. She had never seen such a look on his face before, even during his worst fits of anger.

"Yeah, they may find me but I'm going to make damn sure they never find you. Count on it."

Chapter 22

Rome checked his wristwatch again, then looked out the front windows. Lieutenant Barton had called more than an hour ago, indicating there had been some new development. He rubbed the back of his neck with one hand, almost at the end of his rope. It had been five days and still Jada and Roberts had not been found. It was as if they had disappeared off the face of the earth.

"Keep the faith, Rome."

He turned his head to look at his mother. Her dark eyes shone with compassion and understanding. Nettie had called in the Cavalry. Within an hour of his return to Houston, his parents had shown up and by the next day, so had his three brothers. All of them were there, giving him support for a woman they had not met but loved just the same because they knew he loved her.

"I'm trying, Mom, but it's hard."

"I know but you have to believe that she's coming back and this nightmare will be over soon. You have to stay strong. She's going to need you now more so than ever before."

Rome nodded, knowing he would be there for Jada at any cost. Even if he had to resign from military service. He would make whatever sacrifices were necessary. "Where's Dad?"

Nadine Kalloren threw a quick glance to the other room and smiled. "He's in there talking to your sister's young man. Your father likes him. We all do. Ashton seems to have made her happy."

Rome nodded. Just as Jada had made him happy during the short while they had spent together. At that moment he heard the sound of a car door opening. Glancing out the window he saw Lieutenant Barton get out of the car. Following close on his heels, arriving in another car, were Trevor Grant and a man who, when he'd been in the Marine Corps, had become a legend in his own right—Drake Warren. He had heard that Warren was in town for Trevor's son's christening.

His mother's gaze followed his. She recognized the lieutenant but not the other two men. "Who're those other men?"

Rome smiled faintly. "Friends of Ashton's.

Recon men who used to be the marines' finest." And for the first time in five days Rome felt a leap of hope within him.

"Is that it?" Rome was saying to the lieutenant with hard-edge steel in his raised voice. "You came to tell us that the police apprehended Roberts a few hours ago but Jada wasn't with him, and that he isn't being cooperative and telling where she is?"

Ernest Kalloren intervened after sensing his son was about to really lose it. "Rome, calm down and let the lieutenant finish talking."

Rome shot a glance at his father. "He doesn't have to, Dad. I have a feeling what he's going to say." Rome met Lieutenant Barton's eyes. "You don't think Jada is still alive and will be calling off the manhunt now that Roberts is back in custody."

Netherland was up off the sofa in a flash. "Is that true, Lieutenant Barton? Surely you won't call off the search based on that assumption. She could be anywhere out there, needing help. Isn't there a way someone can force Roberts to tell where she is?"

"Yeah, just give me less than an hour with him, and I'll have him spilling his guts all over the place, literally."

Everyone's attention turned to the man who had made the statement. He was Trevor and Ashton's friend, Drake Warren, whom they called Sir Drake. And just looking into his dark-brown eyes led everyone in the room to believe the man was dead serious.

The eyes that returned all of their stares were cold, dark and lethal. According to Ashton, Sir Drake worked for the CIA, and he looked the part, a modern-day Rambo. He was handsome as sin yet just as dangerous. There had been a deadly calm about him when he'd been introduced to everyone, and he hadn't spoken another word until now.

And when he spoke it seemed that everybody listened.

"Well, yeah, I'm sure you could, Mr. Warren," Lieutenant Barton cleared his throat and said after a few moments of tense silence. "I'm sure that with the CIA, anything goes that will work. But here we have to worry about lawsuits, charges of police brutality and things getting thrown out of court for failure to acknowledge a person's human rights."

"Men like Roberts shouldn't have any human rights," Sir Drake said slowly, banefully. "As far as I'm concerned he lost those rights the first time he raised a hand to hurt his wife."

Ashton stood, deciding to spare the occupants in the room a summation from Sir Drake about his own personal brand of punishment. He doubted the women, as well as a few of the men, had strong enough stomachs to take it. Most people couldn't handle his friend's ruthless attitude and intolerance when it came to criminals.

"Are you going to call off the search, Lieutenant?" He asked the man the same question Netherland had asked earlier but one Lieutenant Barton had smoothly avoided. He wouldn't give the officer the luxury of doing that to him.

Evidently the lieutenant caught his drift. He met his gaze and said, "Not completely. But we will pull back until we have more concrete information. Right now, until Roberts decides to talk, it'll be like searching for a needle in a haystack."

Ashton nodded. "Any ideas where she might be?" He was good at reading body language, and although the lieutenant was saying one thing, he had a feeling the man was thinking another. Evidently the policeman's decision to pull back had not been his own but had come from a higher source within the bureaucracy of the law. The city, embarrassed by the way Roberts had easily escaped, was trying like hell to bring closure to their screwup. And why not? The young woman didn't have an immediate family who would stay on their backs to keep the case open. Ashton glanced at the many faces in the room. Boy, was that a wrong assumption. She may not have an immediate family but she sure had an adopted one who wanted her found.

Lieutenant Barton met Ashton's gaze as he leaned back in his chair. "Yes, I have some ideas but it might be pulling at straws."

"Let's hear them," Ashton said calmly.

Lieutenant Barton shot a quick glance over at Rome, as if deciding whether or not the young man would be able to handle what he was about to say. Making a decision that he would be able to, he began after clearing his throat. "One of the reasons we think Jada Roberts may not be alive is that we found a shovel in the trunk of the car Roberts was driving. The dirt samples off the shovel have been sent to the lab, and we hope to determine just where that type of soil may be located."

He took a deep breath before continuing. "But the main reason that I personally don't think he's killed her is his attitude when he was apprehended. He acted as if he had expected to be caught and that he knew a secret that no one else did. I think killing her would have been too easy for him, and he may have wanted to teach her a lesson. I think he's left her someplace where he figures she won't ever be found by anyone. In my opinion, he's playing a sick game, one that will eventually cost Ms. Roberts her life if she isn't found within a reasonable time."

The room got deathly quiet as everyone absorbed what the lieutenant had said. Ashton was the first one to speak. "So, at the moment, everything hinges on that dirt sample?"

"Yes."

"How soon will we know anything?"

As if on cue the lieutenant's beeper went off. "I'm hoping that's our answer now." He took the beeper off his belt and after glancing at it, turned it off. "May I use the phone?"

"Certainly," Netherland responded. "It's over on that desk."

A few moments later the lieutenant had ended the

call he'd made. The expression on his face alerted everyone in the room that it wasn't good news. "I'm sorry, the analysis of that dirt sample indicates it's from some region in north-central Texas, but doesn't pinpoint where. In order to do that we'll have to ship it to the crime lab in Washington and that could take days, even weeks to have that sort of an in-depth breakdown of the soil particles. If Ms. Roberts is still alive, we don't have that much time."

"We won't have to send it to Washington," Trevor Grant said. "I'm foreman for Madaris Explorations and my boss, Dex Madaris, will be able to tell you anything you want to know about any kind of soil. Dirt is his business and has been for close to twenty years."

A relieved sigh broke forth from Lieutenant Barton's lips. Then those same lips eased into a faint smile. "Then what are we waiting for? Have Mr. Madaris meet me at police headquarters immediately."

It took Dex less than an hour to analyze the dirt particles and come up with his own conclusion. "You're right, Lieutenant, this type of soil can be anywhere within the north-central part of Texas. However, soil with this type of richness, mixed with the type of minerals and vegetation particles it has, can only be found in one place."

"Where?"

"Deadpan Hollow."

Lieutenant Barton raised a brow. "But that campground has been closed for three years, ever since that wildfire swept through there and destroyed almost everything. The state declared Deadpan off-limits to anyone because it's a torch bed waiting to happen. It's been so dry up there it's liable to go up in smoke and burn to a cinder at any time."

"And that's probably why Roberts would consider it if he never wanted Jada found," Ashton said, trembling in anger. It was evident to him, as it had been all along, that Roberts had a sick mind. "So what are you going to do now, Lieutenant?" he asked, studying the man.

"The only thing I can do, which is to ask my superiors to contact the police department in that area for the man power needed to locate Ms. Roberts. It might be a long shot but at the moment it's all we have to go on. Let's just hope they back us on this."

They didn't. The police department claimed they could not spare any extra men to go on a wild-goose chase for a missing person. Besides, sending men into Deadpan Hollow was putting lives at risk when a fire could break out at any time.

That bit of news didn't sit too well with anyone.

"So, what do we do now?" Trevor asked the group as they left the Houston police station moments later.

Ashton smiled. "As usual, if Plan A doesn't work we go to Plan B. And I'm it. I plan to leave out first thing in the morning."

Later that evening Netherland's office at Sisters turned into a battle zone as men and equipment were moved in, with plans to use it as a command center. She eagerly gave up the space, wanting to do her part to help find Jada as soon as possible. Roberts still wasn't talking, and it was taking everything for her family to keep Rome from storming the prison and forcing the information out of Roberts with his fists. Earlier today her brothers had to hold Rome down while their father tried talking some sense into him.

"I finally got you all to myself, sweetheart."

Netherland looked up when Ashton walked through her office door. For the first time in nearly three hours, her office was empty. The men had left to bring in more equipment and wouldn't be returning for another hour or so.

She stood and walked over to Ashton. He looked tired, and she wondered how he thought he could locate anyone when he was already exhausted. And she told him so.

"I'm fine." He stared at her for a moment, as though he wanted to say something else. But instead he shook his head and took her hand in his. "We need to talk."

She raised her brow. "What is it? What's wrong?"

He smiled faintly at her. "Nothing to worry about. I just want to take some necessary precautions."

Netherland nodded, understanding. She then glanced around her office. "It seems like you're getting a lot of help." She knew that Alex Maxwell had hooked up his state-of-the-art computer that had a direct link to FBI headquarters and that Howard

Reeves, who had arrived in town that morning to visit Rainey, and who happened to also have an extensive background with the FBI, had offered his assistance. After being introduced to everyone he was immediately put to work.

"Yes, but the precautions I'm talking about are with you."

"Me?"

"Yes, you."

Netherland saw the concern etched on Ashton's face. The last thing she wanted was for him to leave town worrying about her. "Ashton, I'll be fine. My brothers are here, my parents and friends are here. I should be worried about you. You shouldn't be worried about me."

He looked at her. He hadn't told her about the last vision he'd had. The only persons he had confided in were Trevor and Sir Drake. And although they didn't fully agree, they had understood his need to go into Deadpan Hollow alone. He'd explained that it was connected to an Indian legend involving a test of worthiness he had to go through. He had been shown a part of the vision and had to actually endure the rest. The result would depend upon his skill and stamina and his will to survive. Besides, going into the Hollow was risky enough for one man. He didn't want others to put their lives on the line. And for that, he had to go in alone.

"I've put some plans into motion regarding us, Netherland."

"What sort of plans?"

"We need to get married before I leave."

She frowned, not understanding. She lifted her arm and showed him the leather band around her wrist that symbolized their union. "But we are married."

"We need to get married legally so it can be recognized by the courts, sweetheart, just in case..."

She swallowed, not wanting to go there, where he was thinking, but knew she had to anyway. "Just in case what, Ashton?"

It took a while before he answered. "Just in case something happens and I don't come back."

Netherland looked up at him, her dark eyes filled with distress, denial. She shook her head. "No. I won't think about that. I won't even allow myself to imagine it, Ashton."

He reached out and took her hand in his. "Netherland, you have to be realistic about the possibility that—"

"No!" She snatched her hand from him. "Don't you dare go there with me, Ashton Sinclair. I won't let you!" She met his gaze head-on, daring him to challenge her.

He did.

"I have to do what I have to, Netherland, to protect you and my sons whom you're carrying even as we speak. I'm certain of that. But what I'm not certain of is the outcome of my trip to Deadpan Hollow. I'll do everything within my power to return to you and my sons, but I have to take whatever steps needed to be assured that you're taken care of *if* something was to happen to me."

He reached up and tenderly caressed her cheek with his fingertips. "When I leave in the morning, I need my mind clear. I need to know that everything with you is taken care of. I need that assurance, that peace of mind, Netherland. Will you let me have that?"

Netherland sank into the chair behind her desk. Her strength was suddenly gone. She knew she couldn't deny him that. The last thing he needed was to be worried about her. "Yes."

"Thank you, sweetheart. I've already spoken with your parents and your brothers. I've secured a special marriage license, and I want a very private wedding ceremony tonight here at Sisters." A smile touched his lips. "I want to go away in the morning a very happy man."

Netherland slowly nodded.

Ashton studied her for a few moments before turning to leave the room.

"Ashton?" Netherland stood when he turned back around. His eyes captured hers. She started to tell him how much she loved him, how much he meant to her, and just how much she wanted him to return to her. But she knew from the look in his eyes that he knew what she was feeling and that words between them weren't necessary. And without any further hesitation, she crossed the room and walked into his arms.

Chapter 23

"By the power vested in me, I now pronounce you man and wife. You may kiss your bride, Colonel."

Ashton did just that as he pulled Netherland into his arms, crushing her to him as his mouth captured hers, while numerous cheers sounded in the background. Finally tearing his mouth away, he smiled down at her and saw happiness shining in her eyes. The same happiness reflected in his.

"I love you so much," Netherland whispered, letting her head fall forward on his chest.

"And I love you," he whispered back, tightening his hold on her.

The small wedding Ashton had planned had turned into a lot more with both family and friends attending. Trevor's father-in-law, the Reverend Nathan Avery, had officiated. Smiling, the couple accepted congratulations and well wishes from everyone and looked forward to a night spent in each other's arms. However, Nadine Kalloren was not about to let the couple escape until pictures, and a lot of them, were taken. She had hired a photographer to guarantee that very thing.

It was close to midnight when Netherland and Ashton arrived at his hotel room. He closed the door and leaned back against the frame, looking at her. He thought she looked absolutely beautiful wearing the tea-length white dress she had purchased that very afternoon. Everything had been rushed, but now as he stood looking at her, he knew the haste had been well worth it.

She smiled at him and said, "We never did dance together, did we?"

He regarded her with a grin as he pushed away from the door. "No, but that can be arranged." He walked over to the nightstand and turned on the radio. He moved the dial from station to station until he heard a song he felt was appropriate. He then turned to her. "May I have this dance, Mrs. Sinclair?"

Netherland crossed the room and walked into his arms. Then they began swaying to the sound of the slow music. There was something about the way he held her that made a lump form in her throat. It was as if he didn't know when he would get the chance to hold her this way again. She blinked back tears, not wanting to think about that. She had to believe that he would find Jada and return to her as soon as he could.

She closed her eyes, wanting to free her mind of everything except being held by Ashton, and to concentrate on the feel of his hips moving against hers, and the tantalizing male scent of him. Moments later when the song ended and she opened her eyes, she met his gaze and saw flickers of heat shifting in his. She also saw love so profound it took her breath away. A feeling of heartache engulfed her, and she wondered if this was how her mother had felt the nights before her father had left on deployment. Knowing he had to go but wanting him to stay.

"I'm going to miss you so much, Ashton," she whispered softly, looking into his eyes.

"And I'm going to miss you. Just remember what I told you that first night in Oklahoma. No matter where I go, you will always be here," he said softly, taking her hand and placing it over his heart.

Reaching up, she laced her fingers behind his head and pulled him down to her, taking his mouth, determined to pleasure it with passion beyond anything they had shared together. She wanted to give him memories to sustain him until he returned to her. She hadn't known how dangerous going into Deadpan Hollow was until she'd overheard Lieutenant Barton discussing it with her father. He'd said that place was a fire hazard, liable to burn to a crisp at any time, and that Ashton was risking his life going there in his attempt to find Jada.

And now, although a semblance of fear clutched her insides, she knew there was no way she could ask him not to go. Doing what he considered an honorable thing and standing up for what he believed in was what he was all about. So, she did the only thing she could do and that was to put everything she had into her kiss.

As she did, he returned her kiss the same way, putting everything he had into it, as well. His tongue latched onto hers, stirring explosive sensations and feeding a hunger that demanded to be fed. His hand was on her bottom, pressing her close and letting her know just how much he wanted her, just how much he needed her.

She continued kissing him with wild fervor, wanting memories to keep, as well. And then she felt herself being lifted into his strong arms. Very gently he placed her on the bed and began taking off her clothes, then removing his own. Then he came back to her, took her into his arms and began placing kisses everywhere on her body, making her quiver beneath his lips, the caress of his hands and the sensuous sound of his voice.

Then he was above her, entering her, giving her the full length of him, going so deep she felt him touch the crest of her womb before pulling out and coming back into her again. She arched her body, loving all he was giving her, all he was making her feel, and still wanting more. She clung to him, wrapped her legs around him as he stroked sensation after sensation from her body.

"Look at me, Netherland," he whispered as the warmth of his breath touched her face. "Look at me."

And she did. She met his gaze and felt the beating of his heart on her breasts as he held her tighter to him.

"No matter what happens, always remember that I love you."

Before she could say anything he dipped his head and kissed her again. Her body hummed, then began spinning out of control as he made love to her mouth and her body. And then the coil within each of them exploded, slamming them into the throes of ecstasy as she felt her womb flood with the force of his release as well as her own.

But she wasn't ready to let go. Neither was he.

She held him tightly within her, rocking her hips against him as he continued to move against her in a rhythm that was more dynamic than any music she had ever heard. More powerful than any tempo. The beat Ashton was hammering out was electrifying and earthshaking. She felt it and knew he felt it, too.

"Come back to me, Ashton." She breathed that plea just seconds before another explosion, one more powerful than the last, overtook them.

When Netherland woke the next morning, daylight was shining through the windows, and she heard the busy sound of cars in traffic. She sat up straight in bed as soon as she realized she was alone.

Ashton was gone.

She glanced across the room and saw a stack of papers that he had left on the dresser. Getting out of bed she walked over and picked them up.

Her heart nearly stopped beating.

The first was a copy of a power of attorney in which Ashton had given her the right to act on his behalf while he was away. The second was a copy of the marriage license the two of them had signed the night before.

Netherland closed her eyes and took a deep breath before she forced herself to look at the final document, having an idea what it was. Tears clouded her eyes when she reopened them and looked at the remaining document Ashton had left for her.

It was a copy of his will.

The date indicated it had been updated the day before and from what she read, he had left everything he owned solely to her. But what filled her with gut-wrenching emotions, so intense she could almost not endure them, was the paragraph above his signature that said:

To Netherland and my sons, I bequeath all my worldly possessions as well as all of my love. I will always be with them in spirit, to watch over them, protect them, care for them as only a husband and a father would, and to love them forever. Death will not end my love. It will magnify it.

A choked sound escaped Netherland's lips at the same time an ache started to unfold within her chest, the pressure of which was unbearable. She felt herself crumbling to the floor, crying in tormented sobs while praying over and over to God to return Ashton to her and to give her the strength to endure until she saw him again.

Chapter 24

Netherland stared at the two men, unable to speak. The news they had just delivered had basically knocked the wind out of her body. She latched onto Trevor's arm in desperation, hoping she had heard him wrong.

"What do you mean you lost radio contact with Ashton? That's not possible. Rome and Sir Drake are with him. They were supposed—"

"Ashton went in alone, Nettie. Didn't you know that?" Trevor asked gently as he eased her down in the nearest chair. It was evident what she'd just been told by Lieutenant Barton had come as a shock.

"No, I didn't know," she whispered, feeling light-headed. "Why? Why would he go in there alone?"

"Because he knew the situation was a dangerous

one and didn't want anyone else at risk. Your brother and Sir Drake set up camp on the outskirts of the Hollow and were keeping close radio contact with him. Things have been going fine over the past several days...until this morning."

Netherland looked at Trevor when he hesitated. She then looked at Lieutenant Barton and saw the uneasiness in his manner, as well. She knew something was wrong that went deeper than their losing radio contact with Ashton. She swallowed against the fear lodged in her throat and asked in a low voice, "What happened this morning?"

The silence she encountered was stifling, almost unbearable. "Trevor?"

He cleared his throat before hunching down in front of her. "A fire got started, Nettie, and it's blazing out of control. And although the water bombers are hitting the area pretty heavily, so far the fire hasn't been contained. The park service has ordered everyone to evacuate the area but Sir Drake and Rome have refused to leave. In fact, Sir Drake used his position with the CIA to get special orders to not only remain, but for us to move our command center there first thing in the morning. We want to be there for Ashton."

Netherland clasped her hands tightly together and forced herself to speak. "So you think Ashton is safe?"

Trevor hesitated before speaking. "I think the word *safe* would be stretching it a little," he said, forcing a tight smile. "But fire or no fire, Ashton is in his element. He knows his way around that type of habitat in his sleep. He'll find a way to get out of there or find some kind of wetland where he can hole up until the fire is brought under control. I believe he will make it through this."

Netherland pursed her lips and shook her head. "And so do I, Trevor. I've got to believe he's going to make it through this. I've got to."

Trevor stood. "You're right. We have to keep the faith."

Netherland nodded. "I want to leave with you in the morning, Trevor. I want to be there when—"

"Mrs. Sinclair," Lieutenant Barton interrupted. "I can understand your wanting to be there but there's nothing you can do there," he said rather gruffly. "Besides, even where the command center is being set up is dangerous and too close for comfort. The best thing to do is to stay here and wait for us to contact you."

"No! I will not stay here," she said, holding the lieutenant's gaze with such fiery intensity he took a step back. "My husband is in the Hollow, Lieutenant, because your superiors decided Jada wasn't worth the effort of pulling together a team to find her. Either I go in the morning or I will go on national television and tell anyone why my husband is in there risking his life instead of the Houston Police Department or the Texas Rangers."

The lieutenant stared at her for a moment before shifting his gaze to Trevor as if to say, *Do something with her.* Instead of doing something with her, Trevor smiled with both admiration and respect shining on his face. Netherland was a true marine wife. "I think Nettie being there is a good idea, Barton. There's no one else Ashton would rather see when he gets out of that hellhole as much as he'd want to see his wife."

Lieutenant Barton nodded, his expression grim. "Okay, Mrs. Sinclair, you can go."

In consideration for Netherland's comfort, a trailer was brought in for her own personal use. Two days had passed since she had arrived on the outskirts of the Hollow and still the fire had not been contained. In fact, it was still spreading out of control. Everyone, including Trevor, had tried avoiding any questions she had about how long an individual could survive amid that much heat and smoke. She decided that today she would not be put off. She didn't want to approach Rome, because he was dealing with his own personal misery. Since no radio contact had been made with Ashton for the past four days, Rome had no way of knowing if Jada had been found yet or if Ashton's search had gotten delayed due to the fire.

Netherland was about to leave the trailer and go in search of Trevor when he suddenly appeared in the doorway. The look on his face made her pulse quicken. "Trevor? What is it? What's wrong?"

After taking a deep breath, he motioned to the sofa and sat down wearily beside her. "The park rangers just had a meeting. The fire is spreading too fast and all their efforts to keep it under control have failed. Because the smoke is reaching such high altitudes, they're calling off the air searches in the Hollow."

Netherland gasped as panic struck. "But they can't do that. Ashton and Jada are still in there somewhere."

He placed his hand on hers in a calming gesture. "I know, but they refuse to listen to what we have to say. It will almost take something akin to a presidential order to make them send another chopper in there."

"There has to be a way to make them cooperate," she said frantically, trying to keep hold of her sanity.

Trevor's hand on hers tightened. "There is, and Sir Drake and I are working out the details of it now. I've contacted Jake Madaris. He has a lot of pull in these parts, and with him on our side we're trying to get more time. Thanks to his personal friendship with Senator Nedwyn Lansing, I feel certain that we'll get it and are getting prepared. Sir Drake, Alex and Howard are going over some land maps of the area. Alex thinks he's identified some sort of a deep trench that's underneath a small canyon. We have a feeling that's where Ashton is holing up, to wait out the fire. It's also the area where the fire is now headed. It will be hard to get a chopper in there, risky as hell, but we believe it can be done."

Netherland nodded. "Have the park rangers agreed to do this?"

"Willingly, no. But it's hard to refuse someone like Sir Drake without thinking of possible repercussions."

Netherland nodded again. She could definitely

believe that. She leaned forward and rested her arms
across her legs. "So what's the plan, Trevor?"

Trevor couldn't help but smile. Again he thought
of how well suited Netherland was as a marine wife.
She was every bit as tough and dedicated to a cause
as any gallant marine. A marine spouse had to be
strong enough to deal with fear of the unknown and
to understand that a marine had to do whatever it took
to get the job done. Ashton's decision to go into the
Hollow and search for Jada was based on a marine's
mind-set of being the first one in a dangerous situation and being the last one out.

"The plan is for them to attempt one more air
search. Sir Drake and I are going with them to make
sure they target the right area, and hope we played
our hunch right and Ashton is there sitting tight."

Netherland didn't want to think about what
would happen next if he weren't. "What do you
need me to do?"

Trevor took a long, deep breath and said, "Pray."

Four hours. It had been four hours since the
chopper carrying Sir Drake and Trevor had left. For
the first couple of hours Netherland had remained
inside her trailer doing exactly what Trevor had suggested that she do—pray—which was what she'd
been doing anyway since Ashton had been gone.

But she couldn't stand being cooped up inside the
trailer any longer. When she stepped outside, the rays
of the sun were so bright they almost blinded her. For

once she didn't appreciate the sunshine but wished a storm would come through to help put out the fire. The last time she had checked with one of the park rangers, the fire was still going strong, and they hadn't had any radio contact with the chopper in more than two hours, citing interference from the intense smoke as the cause.

Shielding her eyes from the sun she looked across the way and saw Rome. He was sitting on the ground alone, looking up toward the sky as if expecting some sign of hope that the chopper was returning. She quickly crossed the yard and when she reached him, she sat down on the ground beside him. She placed her hand over his.

"You okay, Rome?"

He didn't say anything for the longest time, didn't acknowledge her presence until after he'd taken a long, deep breath, as if to bring his thoughts under control. "Yeah, as well as can be expected. What about you?"

"Same here." Netherland looked at him, her eyes becoming dark with worry. She remembered Ashton once saying that during a crisis, one had to always remain positive, hold out for the best even in a situation where the worst seemed inevitable.

"So, what do you plan to do when you get Jada back?" Out of the corner of her eye she saw him snatch his head around to her. She held her breath. He would either take her question as cruel or hopeful. She was gambling on the latter. She was close to all her brothers but with only a one-year difference in their ages, she and Rome were the closest. They'd always had a special relationship.

For the longest time Rome didn't answer her question but she felt the hand underneath hers tremble. "I don't think," he finally said slowly, quietly, "that I'll ever let her out of my sight again. When I leave to return to Camp Pendleton, she's coming with me as my wife."

Netherland smiled and slipped her arms around her brother and held him tight. "I think that's a good idea, Rome. A darn good idea."

She heard the sound of the chopper at the same moment Rome did. A lump grew thick, deep in Netherland's throat as she watched the aircraft appear in sight, skimming the treetops and hovering over a flat stretch of land before descending slowly to the ground. Rome was on his feet in a flash but she had to muster all the strength she had to stand.

Rome's hand reached out for hers, holding it tight as the two of them, brother and sister, watched, trying to fight off the deep cold dread that surrounded them. The waiting was over. The next few minutes would reveal the outcome.

The minute the chopper settled down on the ground, three, maybe four of the park rangers scurried over to the plane, with Alex Maxwell and Howard Reeves close on their heels. Ducking to miss the whirling rotor blades, Alex and Howard slid open the side door.

Netherland felt Rome let go of her hand and take a step forward, then two. She held her breath when first Trevor, then Sir Drake descended, and for a moment it appeared they had returned with no one. Panic seized her and for one agonizing moment, she thought the fear that was unfolding in her chest would choke out the very life of her. Then she saw Trevor and Sir Drake move aside as a man-made stretcher was lifted out of the helicopter.

Rome, she noted, had taken off running but she remained frozen in place. Her view became blocked as Rome and a few other rangers moved in. Her heart slammed in her chest as the need to find out who was on the stretcher propelled her to take a step forward. But she stopped when someone else, a lone, tall figure came through the chopper door.

"Ashton!"

Netherland began trembling from head to toe, but somehow found the strength to move when he looked over in her direction, then headed toward her. She didn't stop running until she felt herself securely held in his arms. She didn't care that he smelled completely of smoke and sweat; all she cared about was that he was alive, and he was holding her in his arms.

His hand pressed her head against his shoulder as he cradled her body to him. "I came back to you, Netherland," he whispered roughly, hoarsely.

Netherland could only nod, too filled with emotion to speak, but she did lift her head to see that the person on the stretcher was Jada...and she was conscious. Rome was crouched down beside the stretcher holding her hand, talking to her. All around them orders were being shouted, and Justin Madaris, who had volunteered to be a doctor on-site, was already assisting with Jada.

"Where was she?" Netherland asked, when she was able to find her voice.

"She was holed up in a cavern. Roberts had forced her down a deep well, thinking she wouldn't ever get out. He had left her there with no food or water. But somehow, with sheer determination and a will to survive, she did get out, and was lucky enough to stumble across a small water hole and a blackberry patch. That was her food and liquid most of the time. She was trying to find her way around the Hollow when I found her. She'd become dehydrated and overcome with smoke but other than that, she was okay. She's one brave woman to have endured the weather, wild animals and unfamiliar terrain for more than a week. She'll make a good marine wife."

"That's good, because Rome intends to marry her," Netherland said, seeing the relief, happiness and love on Rome's face. Aware but not caring that they were surrounded by a number of people, she placed her arms around Ashton's neck and gazed into his eyes. "Thanks for coming back to me, Ashton. I was so scared."

He tilted his mouth into a smile. "According to Trevor you were brave, a real marine wife. And just to think you thought you never wanted to have anything to do with someone in the military. Imagine that."

Netherland returned his smile. "Yes, Colonel, imagine that." She then placed pressure on his neck to bring his mouth down to hers and gave him one torrid kiss.

Ashton returned his wife's kiss, hugging her tightly to him as he took possession of her mouth. At one time he hadn't been certain he would be able to bring himself and Jada out of that fiery furnace, but just when he thought it was impossible, he had looked up and had seen the chopper flying overhead—and in an area where there was no place for a chopper to land. Of course, Sir Drake had other ideas about that and had literally hung out of the chopper to extend a rope down to lift them up. His friend's daring escapades never ceased to amaze him.

Like a drowning man who needed the nectar of his wife's mouth, Ashton intensified their kiss and pulled Netherland even closer to him. Suddenly, he felt someone tap him, and not too lightly, on the shoulder. Frowning, he broke off the kiss to look up into Trevor's smiling face.

"The two of you are in the way, Colonel," Trevor said as his smile widened. "Some of us have work to do."

Ashton couldn't help but laugh. Those had been the same words he'd barked at Trevor when they had rescued Corinthians from the clutches of a madman. "Don't you have baby diapers to go change or something?" Ashton asked his friend smartly.

"Yes, just as soon as I can get the hell out of here.

And don't forget the baby's christening is on Sunday. It's a good thing you made it back for that. Corinthians would have been upset if you hadn't. And how about cleaning yourself up before then? All that mud and soot make you look like a bogeyman, and I don't want you to frighten my son." Trevor then turned to walk off, chuckling.

Netherland couldn't help but laugh.

"Do you think I look like a bogeyman, sweetheart?" Ashton asked her when she had stopped laughing.

"No, I think you look like my husband. My hero. My marine." She then proceeded to kiss him again.

"Boy, aren't we squeaky clean," Netherland said to her husband when he had slid into bed beside her.

"That's not all I am," he responded huskily as he pulled her into his arms.

Netherland turned slowly and cupped his face in the palms of her hands. "Make love to me, Ashton. Help me forget what I went through this past week. Help me forget."

"I'll try, Netherland," he whispered as he pressed his naked flesh against hers, breast to breast, thigh to thigh, leg to leg. His tongue flicked out to taste, to tease, to torment. Her breath turned ragged at the provocative touch of his mouth on her, sending her into a mindless, quivering mass of sensations. She buried her hands in his hair, she dug her nails into his back and she moaned his name over and over.

He had come back to her.

When his fingers delved into the moist, wet heat of her, a deep sob racked her body. And when she felt the hardness of him at the entrance of her, she lifted her hips to receive him.

They moved together as one, joined together, pushing out of their minds the memory of the time they had spent apart, the agony of not knowing if they would ever see each other again, and if they would ever again share this. Now that they were back together they didn't intend to part again.

Then suddenly Ashton held still within her, looked down into her eyes. "Wa-Do," he whispered hoarsely before starting his rhythm again. This time the pace was faster and faster, deeper and deeper. He threw his head back for one final, earth-shattering thrust at the same moment she screamed out his name in her own powerful release.

He rubbed his cheek against hers, overflowing with all the love any man could possibly feel for one woman. He had seen the difficulties ahead and had prepared for them…or so he had thought. He didn't think anything would ever have fully prepared him for Netherland Kalloren Brooms and what she did to his heart and his soul. This woman was his dream, his vision and his reality. He had come out of the darkness into the light. Out of the fire and back into her arms.

And that's where he intended to stay.

Chapter 25

The church was packed for the christening of Rio Maurice Nathan Grant.

Being held in his father's arms, the infant slept through the entire ceremony, even when he was passed around to each of his three godfathers, Dex Madaris, Ashton Sinclair and Drake Warren. Everyone had done a double take when Sir Drake arrived at the church in a suit. And a couple of the young women made sure he knew of their interest, which was a wasted effort since he didn't pay them any attention.

After the service everyone was invited to dinner at Trevor and Corinthians's home. Thanks to Rio's two grandmothers, who had done all the cooking, there was plenty of food for all.

Rio, now wide-awake, was being held by godfather number three, Sir Drake, with Daddy Trevor and godfather number two, Ashton, looking on.

"So who do you think he looks like?" Trevor asked, beaming, knowing the answer would be that his son favored him since quite a number of people had mentioned that fact already.

Sir Drake studied the facial features of the child in his arms. He met Trevor's gaze and said, "I think he has a strong resemblance to Corinthians's brother Joshua." Drake couldn't help but laugh when he saw the deep frown that appeared on his friend's face. He knew that Trevor and his brother-in-law did not get along.

"Don't you dare think something like that," Trevor bit back angrily, threateningly.

Sir Drake shrugged. "Well, if you didn't want the truth, you shouldn't have asked me."

Ashton decided to intervene before there was bloodshed. He quickly took the baby out of Sir Drake's hands just in case Trevor felt like hitting somebody. "What you need, Sir Drake, is a woman to keep you out of trouble."

Sir Drake was quiet for a few moments before saying, "No, I don't."

Ashton shook his head. "Yes, you do. It's been four years now, Drake. It's time to let things go."

"I won't be able to do that, Ash, until I find Solomon Cross and make him pay for what he did to Sandy."

Across the room, Corinthians saw the tense expressions on the faces of the three men who were standing in a huddle and passing around her son. "I think we need to intervene with that bunch," she whispered to Netherland. "Those three are the best of friends who would kill someone in a heartbeat to protect one another, but I'm not putting anything past them possibly killing each other if they got mad enough."

Netherland nodded and followed Corinthians as she crossed the room to the three men. Corinthians slipped between Sir Drake and Trevor, and Netherland stood next to Ashton.

"So, guys, what's up?" Corinthians asked, smiling.

Sir Drake chuckled. "Trevor got teed off because I said Rio favored your brother."

Corinthians nodded. She could see her husband getting upset because of that.

"Speaking of your brother, where is he?" Ashton asked, glancing around the room.

"Wherever he is, he can stay there," Trevor muttered, taking his son out of Ashton's arms.

Corinthians gave her husband a scolding glance. "Joshua should be here in a little while. His plane was late."

"Is he still licking his wounds after being defeated as Texas's first black governor?" Sir Drake asked, smiling as though the thought was really amusing to him.

"No, I think he's handling the loss pretty well," Corinthians said, now glaring at Sir Drake. She took her son from her husband. "And I want the three of you to promise me that you'll be nice to Joshua when he gets here."

Instead of making a promise they didn't intend to keep, the three men walked off.

"Well, at least I tried," Corinthians said to Netherland, smiling.

Netherland couldn't help but chuckle. "They dislike your brother that much?"

"And then some." Corinthians glanced over at the new arrival. "Syneda is here. Let's go find out how Clayton's doing."

Alexander Maxwell glanced across the room at Christy. Anger lit his eyes as he watched her flirt with Netherland's twenty-three-year-old brother Dakota Kalloren. Alex couldn't understand why he was getting so upset since the young air force cadet was close to Christy's age. But still, it didn't sit well with him, and as far as he was concerned it shouldn't be sitting well with the Madaris brothers, either. He glanced across the room. Dex was talking to Trask but it was quite obvious his eyes were also on the pair. Justin, it seemed, was also keeping a close watch. Unfortunately, Clayton was home flat on his back but Alex was certain that, had he been here, he would be looking on, as well.

Alex relaxed. For some reason he felt a whole lot better.

An hour or so later, he didn't feel so hot.

Christy approached him while he was standing

alone. "Here's your certificate for dinner for two from that auction, Alex. Considering everything, I'm sure there's someone else that you'd prefer taking. And here's your ring back," she said, handing him the ring he'd given her eight years ago. "You were right, it's time for me to grow up and put away childish dreams and fantasies. Especially those concerning you. One thing a Madaris has, Alex, is pride, and I will never let you trample mine again." She turned and walked away.

Alex watched her leave, suddenly feeling an enormous sense of loss although he knew he had done the right thing by being upfront with her that night. However, he would never have thought that doing the right thing would have him feeling so miserable. For a long moment he stared down at the ring before putting it into his pocket.

"And Clayton's doing all right?" Netherland asked Syneda.

"Better than he should or at least he thinks that way. He's trying to break all the rules Dr. Goldstein gave him." Syneda smiled. "The only way I can get him to behave is to threaten to tell his grandmother. You know Gramma Madaris. She'll have Justin and Dex hog-tie Clayton to the bed if he doesn't take orders."

Corinthians nodded. "Men. Why do they have to be so hardheaded?"

"I don't know about your hubbies but mine likes driving me bonkers. I can't wait until he's completely on his feet. He actually has me cooking. Can you imagine that?"

Netherland and Corinthians shook their heads. They definitely couldn't imagine such a thing.

"Well, tell Clayton I'm thinking about him," Corinthians said. "We all are."

"Thanks, and I appreciate the cards and fruit baskets. Next time he tells me he's hungry, I'm going to tell him to grab a banana."

Corinthians and Netherland couldn't help but laugh.

Rainey looked up at Howard Reeves, smiling. "I guess you won't ever volunteer to come visit me again after you were pulled into all that action that took place."

Howard shook his head, grinning, as he looked around the room. "Are you kidding? I felt right in my element, and I met a lot of good people this week. Some I now consider as friends. I'd definitely come back to visit again, if you'd let me."

Rainey's smile widened. "I'd like that."

"So would I. And I have some vacation time coming up and was thinking about taking a little cruise aboard one of Trent's ships. Would you like to join me?"

Rainey lifted a brow. "You want me to go on a cruise with you?"

"Yes. It won't be for another three months but I thought I'd ask early just in case you had other plans."

Rainey nodded. "I've never been on a cruise before."

"Neither have I."

"Should be interesting."

"To say the least. Will you think about it?"

"Yes, I'll definitely do that."

Across the room Jada stood with Rome's hand in hers. After a three-day hospital stay she was given a clean bill of health. She had been completely overwhelmed by all the love and attention Rome's family had lavished upon her, especially his mother. The older woman had made her feel special, and his brothers were super, too, welcoming her into the family although she hadn't given Rome her answer yet. She knew he wanted to marry her but she had to be sure he was doing it for love and not pity.

"You're not getting tired, are you?" Rome leaned down and asked her. He hadn't once left her side. If the truth were known, he hadn't left her side at all since she'd been rescued. During those rare times that he had, he had planted his mother right there to be with her. And at night he stayed at her place, sleeping on the sofa.

"No, I'm fine. You don't have to hang around me, Rome. You can go mingle if you'd like."

"I don't want to mingle. I want to stay right here with you."

She smiled up at him. "Thanks."

At that moment Netherland came up. "Rome, can I borrow Jada for a second?" Without giving him a chance to respond, Netherland locked Jada's arms with hers and pulled her away from her brother's side, ignoring his frown. When they were a safe distance away, she turned to Jada, smiling. "I thought I'd rescue you. Rome is determined to be your shadow."

Jada shook her head, grinning. "I don't mind."

"Well, you should," Netherland admonished her. "He shouldn't be suffocating you like that, you're among friends."

Jada glanced around the room. "Yes, I am, aren't I?" She had been told of everyone's involvement in her rescue, even people she had never met before. However, when they had been needed, these people had come through for her. And they were still coming through. Because of what he'd done to Clayton Madaris, as well as her own abduction, another twenty years had been added to Tony's sentence. And those who'd assisted in his escape were being dealt with.

"So what do you think of joining the Kalloren family? I know Rome has asked you to marry him."

"Yes, he has." She gave Netherland a quick glance. "Would you mind if I did?"

Netherland chuckled. "Heck no. I'd probably mind if you didn't. Almost losing you nearly destroyed him, Jada. He loves you very much."

Jada glanced across the room at Rome. He was staring at her, still trying to keep her within his sight. She was deeply touched to have someone care for her that much. "And I love him, too, Nettie. During the entire time I was in the Hollow I swore if I lived to see him again I would tell him how I felt."

"And have you?"

"No."

"Then I think he deserves to know, don't you?"

"I thought he had done everything out of pity, and I didn't want that."

"Everything Rome has done, he did out of love, Jada. He fell in love with you the moment he set eyes on you. Take it from someone who fought love for three years. Don't waste your time fighting it. It's a precious gift not to be taken lightly."

Jada nodded. "Thank you."

"No, thank you for making Rome happy again." She then watched as Jada walked back to Rome's side and took his hand in hers. Leaning on tiptoe, Jada whispered something to him. Whatever she said brought a huge smile to her brother's face. He gathered Jada into his arms and kissed her. Netherland couldn't help but smile at the couple's happiness.

"What are you smiling about?" Ashton asked, appearing at her side.

"Jada and Rome. I think she'll be accepting his marriage proposal after all."

Ashton nodded. "That's good. And by the way, Rainey told me to let you know she decided to leave early to spend a little more time with Howard before he returned to Chicago."

Netherland nodded. She suspected love was blooming between that couple, as well.

"I never got all seven of my days with you, Mrs. Sinclair. We only made it to five. We have two left. How 'bout we go home, pack and take off for Oklahoma?"

"Tonight?"

"Yes, tonight."

Netherland lifted a brow. She had given Rainey the coming week off but felt Millie Smith, her third in command, could handle things. "When do you have to report back to Washington?"

"I've extended my leave for another couple of weeks. Why?"

"Just curious. Do you have any idea where your next assignment will be?"

"Not yet. Does not knowing bother you?"

"No, not at all. Rainey has proven she can do a pretty good job of running Sisters without me. I think I'd like traveling around the country with you for a while."

A huge smile touched Ashton's lips. "I know I'd like that. So how about if we sneak away tonight? What do you think?"

Netherland placed her husband's hand in hers, feeling all the love she had for him flow freely from her heart to every part of her body. "I think it's a wonderful idea, Colonel. Let's go."

Rainey was pretty sure she had gotten her emotions under control by the time she and Howard arrived at the airport. After leaving Trevor and Corinthians's baby's christening party, they had stopped by her apartment long enough for Howard to kiss her with a thoroughness and expertise that had taken her breath away. The chemistry between them

was unbelievable. Even now she was having a problem breathing just thinking about it.

"Do you have time to walk me to the security
check-in point?"

Howard's question invaded Rainey's thoughts.
She looked into the darkness of his eyes and smiled.
"Yes, I'll make time."

He took her hand in his, and they began walking.
"I'll call you this week, all right?"

"Okay. I'll look forward to hearing from you."
Because of his help with Jada's rescue they'd spent
very little time together during the entire week he'd
been in town.

"When was the last time you visited Chicago?" he
asked, looking down at her as they continued walking.

"It's been quite a few years. Probably at least five."

"Would you come visit me if I were to send for
you?" he asked in a husky voice.

Without hesitation she said, "Yes."

"How soon?"

She smiled. A part of her wanted to think things
were moving too fast between them but she immediately dismissed the thought. "How soon do you want?"

"How about this coming weekend?"

She lifted her eyes to study his. "You sure?"

"Yes. I don't think I can wait any longer than that."

"Me, either." She could tell her response pleased
him.

His hand on hers tightened. "Knowing I'll see you

again this weekend won't make it so hard." He stopped walking and didn't say anything for a long moment as his dark gaze probed deep into hers. Finally, he spoke. "I know this sounds crazy, Rainey, but I've fallen in love with you."

Rainey blinked. They were standing in the middle of the airport terminal. People were coming and going all around them. But her complete attention was on the man standing in front of her who had just confessed to having feelings for her. She felt something for him as well, and had from the first. But she had convinced herself it was nothing more than a strong physical attraction, pure and simple. Now she knew that wasn't true because of the depth of her feelings for him. "No, it doesn't sound crazy, Howard, because I've fallen in love with you, too." She looked into his eyes, saw the smile that extended to his lips. Then he pulled her into his arms and kissed her. Long and thorough.

Afterward, out of breath, she stood before him smiling. "Saturday seems like a long time away."

"Then come with me now."

"What!" She pulled out of his arms.

"You're off work this week, aren't you?"

"Yes." Nettie had given her some extra time off because of all the extended hours she'd worked at Sisters when Nettie had been in Oklahoma with Ashton and then at Deadpan Hollow awaiting Jada's rescue. "But I don't have a ticket."

"That won't be a problem."

"I don't have luggage, which means I don't have clothes or toiletries."

"We'll buy anything you need when we get to Chicago."

Rainey looked up at him. "You're serious, aren't you?"

His gaze met hers. "Yes. I'm very serious."

The desire that flamed from the dark depths of his eyes touched every part of Rainey's body. She caught herself wringing her hands together understanding the implications of what he was asking her to do. While in Houston he had stayed at a hotel, but she knew he was asking that she come to Chicago and stay in his home...and sleep with him in his bed. She finally dropped her hands to her side. Hadn't she preached to Nettie the importance of not only finding love but holding on to it? And about surrendering your feelings to the man you loved? "All right, I'll go to Chicago with you, but I need to call Nettie."

Howard nodded. "I'll get your ticket while you're doing that."

Rainey again studied his features. "Are you sure about everything? Are you sure about us?"

Howard pulled her back into his arms. He rubbed his knuckles softly against her cheek. "Baby, I've never been so sure of anything in my entire life."

Rainey found the weather chilly in Chicago. After arriving in the city Howard had taken her shopping for the things she would need over the next few days. Then he had taken her to his apartment. He gathered her into his arms the moment the door closed behind them.

"I want you, Rainey." The tone of his voice was husky, deep and filled with desire.

It made her heart thud in her chest. She wrapped her arms around his neck. "And I want you, too."

Without wasting any time he picked her up into his arms and walked directly to his bedroom. She only took a quick glance around before Howard joined her on the bed. Seconds later, they were naked and in each other's arms after he protected them both.

After long moments of sensuous foreplay they were both shuddering and moaning with an intense need. Every muscle in Rainey's body felt alive, full of desire. Finally, Howard gripped her hips as he rose over her, ready to put a tantalizing finish to what they had started. Slowly he entered her body while both of them quivered in anticipation. She braced her arms on his shoulder, letting her manicured nails brand him as they dug into his skin.

He looked down at her. His eyes were covered in a fevered glaze of desire. "Ready?"

She looked up at him, loving the feel of him buried deep inside of her. Never had she felt this connected to any man before. Smiling, she answered breathlessly, "Yes."

His hands held her lips tight as he proceeded to make love to her, hard, fast and thorough, giving them both what they wanted and needed. His eyes locked on hers, and they knew that somehow they had found love in its purest form.

When their world exploded and they shuddered together in ecstasy, Rainey and Howard knew at that very moment the love they shared was too precious to lose and silently vowed to keep it always.

Back in Houston, Rome took Jada home to her apartment after leaving Trevor and Corinthians's baby's christening party. Just as he'd done the previous nights, he watched television while waiting for her to finish taking her shower so he could take his. His heart was overjoyed that she had finally agreed to marry him, and he intended to make her feel safe and well loved for the rest of her life.

After his shower he had taken all the things he needed out of the linen closet to sleep on the sofa when he heard her call his name. He turned and saw her standing in the doorway to her bedroom. Dressed in a long flowing blue nightgown, she looked too beautiful to be real, but then at the same time she looked unsure about something. He walked over to her and took her hand in his. "Yes, Jada? What is it?"

She met his gaze and smiled shyly. "I was wondering if…"

When she stopped in mid-sentence, he asked, "What were you wondering?"

She inhaled deeply. "I was wondering if you wanted to sleep with me tonight?"

Rome studied her features. Even before her abduction he'd moved at a pace that she would find comfortable. "What do you want, Jada? Do you want me to share a bed with you tonight?" He wanted her to be open with him and share her feelings with him.

"Yes. I want you to make love to me, Rome. When I was in the Hollow I thought about you making love to me. Thinking about it helped me make it through the days as well as the nights. I had to believe that no matter what, that you loved me and would always love me."

"I do love you, Jada. Don't ever doubt my love."

She smiled. "I don't anymore."

"But you did?"

"Yes. After I was rescued I convinced myself you couldn't possibly still love me after all the trouble I'd caused, and what you actually felt for me was nothing but pity. Now I know differently. I truly believe in my heart that you love me, Rome, and because I believe that, I want to show you how much I love you, as well."

"Jada, you don't have to show me anything."

"I want to. I have to." She stood on tiptoe and whispered, "Make love to me, Rome. Please make love to me the way a man is supposed to make love to a woman. His woman."

Jada's heartfelt plea touched Rome. "I will, Jada, and for the rest of your life you will be cherished and loved." He picked her up in his arms and crossed the room to her bed. After placing her in the center of it, he came down beside her and gathered her to him and kissed her. He wanted to remove her clothes, and his, but at the moment he continued kissing her over and over, again and again, while thanking God for returning her to him safely.

When they needed more than just kisses, he pulled away and removed his clothes, then hers. After putting on a condom he went back to her and kissed her again until he felt sensations burn through her right into him. It was only then that he let his body cover hers. She gripped his shoulder as he slowly entered the enveloping warmth of her body. He moaned at the intense pleasure being inside her brought him. Gradually he began moving in and out at a slow, easy rhythm, and her body moved with his, meeting each and every downstroke. His mouth continued to feed off hers in a kiss that was destined never to end.

But it did. He released her mouth when glorious, rapturous pleasure burst upon them, and they moaned out their fulfillment and sexual gratification. Jada gave a small whimper as tears slid down her cheeks. Rome kissed the tears off her face.

"I love you, Jada. For the rest of my life I shall love you."

Jada looked up at him with tears in her eyes. "And I love you, too, Rome. I thank God for you, your family and your friends. Tonight you showed me a beautiful side of making love. You've proven just how special things can be between a man and a woman. I've never known such tenderness, such fulfillment and such joy."

"Then let me show you those things some more, baby," he murmured, close to her ear and with all the love he had in his heart as he gathered her back into his arms.

Epilogue

Three months later.

Dr. Gilroy beamed radiantly at the couple sitting across from him in his office. "Congratulations, Colonel and Mrs. Sinclair. The tests have been confirmed. You're having triplets."

Ashton raised his eyes to the ceiling. "Tell us something we don't know, Dr. Gilroy, like how my wife is doing."

Dr. Gilroy frowned, clearly confused. "You knew before the tests were done that your wife was having triplets?"

"Yes."

"How did you know? Triplets run in your family?"

"No, just single births."

He glanced across his desk at Netherland. "What about yours?"

"No. In fact, I'm infertile."

Dr. Gilroy shook his head. "Whoever told you that must have been mistaken, Mrs. Sinclair. An infertile woman can't get pregnant, least of all with triplets."

Netherland shrugged. This had been her first appointment with a civilian doctor, and she decided not to argue with him. Her being pregnant had come as a big shock to everyone who had known about her medical condition. She'd had a hard time explaining to them that she'd been given the gift of fertility the night Ashton had married her the Indian way. "So how am I doing? And are the babies healthy?"

"Yes. From the sonogram it seems both you and the babies are fine. However, I'd like to do another sonogram in a few months. By then we'll be able to tell you the sex of the triplets if you want to know."

"We already know. They're all boys," Ashton said easily.

The doctor frowned at him. "Well, yes, er, we'll see."

"No, you'll see, doctor. I already know," Ashton said, looking at the man without cracking a smile.

A few minutes later Ashton and Netherland had left the doctor's office and were on their way home. Netherland glared over at her husband. "Did you have to scare the wits out of Dr. Gilroy, Ashton?"

He shrugged. "I couldn't help it. You know how I

feel about civilian doctors. The only reason I'm letting you get checked by one is that you wanted a second opinion. Now are you satisfied?"

"Yes. And the only reason I wanted a second opinion by a civilian doctor is that all my life I was treated by military doctors."

"Military doctors are the best, and Marine Corps doctors are exceptional."

Netherland shook her head. "Why doesn't it surprise me that you'd think that?"

"Because it's the truth. Just ask Sir Drake. They've pulled more bullets out of him than he can count."

Netherland knew she couldn't ask Sir Drake anything. Last they'd heard, he was working undercover for the CIA, somewhere in Russia. "I talked to Rome and Jada today."

Ashton smiled. "How are they doing?"

Netherland smiled, thinking of the couple who had gotten married before Rome had to return to California. "Fine. Jada loves California."

"Glad to hear it. And I understand Rainey is planning to get married and that Clayton is back at work," Ashton said as he brought the car to a stop at a traffic light. "The next thing on the agenda is names for the babies. Have you thought of any?"

"No, what about you?"

"No, but I have thought of something else."

"What?"

"That weekend in New Orleans we never did take. How about going away with me for the weekend?"

Netherland smiled. "If I don't go willingly, will you kidnap me and take me anyway?"

Ashton shook his head, grinning. "That night I was desperate. You can't blame me for taking such drastic measures. I had to get you off your turf and onto mine. It worked, didn't it?"

She glanced at her husband with love shining in her eyes. "Yes, it worked. In no time at all I had surrendered, which makes me wonder how the cowboys ever won a battle against the Indians."

Ashton grinned over at her. "They didn't. And the same holds true today. That's why the Washington Redskins usually whip the Dallas Cowboys' behind big time."

Netherland shook her head, grinning. "I can't win with you, can I?"

"No, but I can win with you. You're the best prize I could ever have, and for the rest of my life, I'm surrendering my heart to you gladly."

A love that's out of this world…

Cosmic Rendezvous

Favorite author
Robyn Amos

For aerospace engineer Shelly London, a top-secret
space project could be her big break—until she butts
heads with sexy hotshot astronaut Lincoln Ripley, who
launches her hormones right into orbit. Lincoln's got
a double mission: catch a saboteur…then take off with
Shelly for a rendezvous with love.

"Lilah's List is…a fun story that
holds one's interest from page one."
—*Romantic Times BOOKreviews*

*Coming the first week of April 2009
wherever books are sold.*

KIMANI™
ROMANCE

www.kimanipress.com
www.myspace.com/kimanipress

KPRA1080409

The "Triple Threat" Donovan brothers are back...
and last-man-standing Trent is about to roll the
dice on falling in love.

Defying
DESIRE

Book #3 in *The Donovan Brothers*

A.C. Arthur

When it comes to men, model Tia St. Claire wants no
strings, just flings. But navy SEAL Trent Donovan stirs
defiant longings she can't deny. Happily unattached,
Trent has dedicated his career to duty and danger, until
desire—and Tia—changes everything.

"If hero Adam Donovan was for sale, every woman in
the world would be lined up to buy him!"
—*Romantic Times BOOKreviews* on
A CINDERELLA AFFAIR

*Coming the first week of April 2009
wherever books are sold.*

KIMANI™
ROMANCE

www.kimanipress.com
www.myspace.com/kimanipress

Her family circle had always been broken...
until now.

Fan-favorite author

SHIRLEY HAILSTOCK

For Meghan Howard, Mother's Day has a whole new meaning! After she fulfills an extraordinary agreement with widower Thomas Worthington-Yates, Meghan's prepared to go her own way. But their undeniable attraction has Meghan dreaming of the unthinkable: a future—and a family—together.

Coming the first week of April 2009
wherever books are sold.

KIMANI™
ROMANCE

KPSH1100409

He's an irresistible recipe—for trouble!

Sugar RUSH

elaine overton

Life is sweet for bakery owner Sophie Mayfield.
She's saved her family business from a takeover, and
hired talented baker Eliot Wright to help sales. Eliot
is as appealing—and oh-so-chocolate-fine—as he is
hardworking. But when Sophie discovers Eliot is not
what he seems, Eliot must regain Sophie's trust—and
prove he's her permanent sweet spot.

*Coming the first week of April 2009
wherever books are sold.*

KIMANI™
ROMANCE

REQUEST YOUR FREE BOOKS!

2 FREE NOVELS
PLUS 2 FREE GIFTS!

KIMANI™ ROMANCE

Love's ultimate destination!

YES! Please send me 2 FREE Kimani™ Romance novels and my 2 FREE gifts (gifts are worth about $10). After receiving them, if I don't wish to receive any more books, I can return the shipping statement marked "cancel." If I don't cancel, I will receive 4 brand-new novels every month and be billed just $4.69 per book in the U.S. or $5.24 per book in Canada, plus 25¢ shipping and handling per book and applicable taxes, if any*. That's a savings of over 20% off the cover price! I understand that accepting the 2 free books and gifts places me under no obligation to buy anything. I can always return a shipment and cancel at any time. Even if I never buy another book from Kimani Press, the two free books and gifts are mine to keep forever.

168 XDN EF2D   368 XDN EF3T

Name _____ (PLEASE PRINT) _____

Address _____ Apt. # _____

City _____ State/Prov. _____ Zip/Postal Code _____

Signature (if under 18, a parent or guardian must sign) _____

Mail to The Reader Service:
IN U.S.A.: P.O. Box 1867, Buffalo, NY 14240-1867
IN CANADA: P.O. Box 609, Fort Erie, Ontario L2A 5X3

Not valid to current subscribers of Kimani Romance books.

Want to try two free books from another line?
Call 1-800-873-8635 or visit www.morefreebooks.com.

* Terms and prices subject to change without notice. N.Y. residents add applicable sales tax. Canadian residents will be charged applicable provincial taxes and GST. Offer not valid in Quebec. This offer is limited to one order per household. All orders subject to approval. Credit or debit balances in a customer's account(s) may be offset by any other outstanding balance owed by or to the customer. Please allow 4 to 6 weeks for delivery. Offer available while quantities last.

Your Privacy: Kimani Press is committed to protecting your privacy. Our Privacy Policy is available online at www.eHarlequin.com or upon request from the Reader Service. From time to time we make our lists of customers available to reputable third parties who may have a product or service of interest to you. If you would prefer we not share your name and address, please check here. ☐

KROM08R